Whiskey Tango Foxtrot

Someth[illegible] For

PHALANX PRESS

Whiskey Tango Foxtrot
Something to Fight For

* * *

Cover Art by
André Vazquez Jr.

CHAPTER 1

The South Carolina Dead Lands

The riverboat glided heavy on the currents of the muddy river. Shane stood with his back to the pilothouse and compulsively checked his rifle. Dropping the magazine and pushing his finger against the weak tension of the rounds, he knew he was down to his last twelve bullets. He sighed and reinserted the magazine before moving toward the stern of the craft. Close to the rail, he saw the girl sleeping with his worn wool army blanket still covering her. Shane dropped to the deck, slid closer to the girl, and nestled in beside her. He looked around to ensure no one was watching before he pulled back the blanket and lifted the girl's sleeve to check the bandage on her arm.

The swelling was gone, but the bite marks and scabbed over scratches were still visible. How the girl was still alive only God knew, but he had taken on the task of keeping her that way, and as long as she lived, Shane had a mission. With a mission, Shane had an excuse to push on rather than give in to the temptations of a peaceful death. If the other passengers saw the girl's wounds though, he knew they would throw her over the side… or worse. He pulled the bandage back over the wounds, wrapped her tightly in the blanket, and slid his pack in front of her to shield the girl from the others milling around nearby. Shane apprehensively put his trust in the band of survivors for the sake of the girl when normally he would be wary of strangers and keep his distance. So, although he knew they were not his friends, he had partnered with this motley group out of necessity; the girl deserved at least that much.

Shane looked to the bow of the old boat as they drifted slowly down the river toward the coast. He wasn't a nautical man, so he wasn't sure what type of craft it was. Wide and flat bottomed with a large open front deck, it had a small white pilothouse set in the center of its length. Sometimes he would see an armed man on the roof of the house. Most of the crew stayed inside when they weren't working though; he presumed they were avoiding the passengers that were gathered on the deck and scattered against the rails, or any open space they could lay claim to. Some of his fellow passengers were armed, but most weren't – or they were good at hiding their weapons. Either way, Shane avoided eye contact; he didn't want to look friendly or present himself as a victim to any of them.

He saw the captain – Shane still didn't know what to call the white-bearded old man in dingy yellow slickers – working an oar while another sailor was on the opposite side with a long pole, trying to control the direction of the craft. The boat had been without fuel since he'd boarded it with the girl. Finding this boat was the only thing that had gone well for him in a long time. Even before the fall, he'd never managed to catch a real break, even with the best of luck. "Unemployable" is what the VA called him – try finding a job, or a decent girlfriend, with *that* label. Outside of the army, Shane had never been good at anything; maybe that's why he went to the military installation at the edge of town when things began to fall apart.

He'd witnessed the violence from his fourth floor apartment, mostly on the TV, sometimes the radio, and after a few days, he just watched it from his window. It started overseas and had quickly spread to the Border States. They blamed it on terrorists using some new bio-weapon. Shane went through a month of PTSD pills in a week just trying to keep his anxiety in check as he watched the world fall apart around him. When the riots started and the city began to burn, he made a personal choice to die on the streets fighting, not hiding in his apartment like a coward. He dug through his hall closet until he found the small canvas bag.

Shane left most of his old uniforms in a dumpster when he was discharged from the Army, but he'd kept one. It was worn and battered but still bore all of his patches. It was definitely not the typical clean and pressed uniform that soldiers wore when on garrison duty state side. It was the uniform he'd worn on his last deployment, the one that sent him home with pins in his back and a headache that never went away. He put on the uniform and stood in front of his bathroom mirror, frowning. His hair was shoulder length; his beard long and unkempt. He barely looked the twenty-eight year old man that he knew he still was.

"Damn," he said, laughing and shaking his head as he undressed, "the Sergeant Major would have my ass."

Shane opened a drawer and removed a pair of clippers. He shaved his head and then his face. When enough of the matted hair had been removed, he lathered up and used a razor. When he was dressed again and looked in the mirror, he could almost see a bit of the soldier he had once been. He reached into a drawer, snatched up a bottle of pain pills, and dry swallowed several of them before he paused momentarily to look at the bottle in his hand. He grinned and then poured the remaining pills into the sink.

Still smiling to himself, he walked through his tiny apartment to stop in front of a small bookshelf that held a single framed image; he carried one just like it in his wallet. Even though he knew his old friends would laugh at him if they witnessed it, he put on his patrol cap and stood at attention. As the sound of gunfire and screaming began making its way into the hallways of his apartment, he looked at the photo of the confident young men in uniform gathered around an armored Humvee. He gave the framed photo a scolding face and saluted. "I'll be with you soon, brothers," he vowed. He then snapped his arm back to his side and walked out of his apartment into the smoke-filled hallway.

A violent thud rattled the boat, causing Shane to pull the rifle closer to his chest and snap out of his reverie. At the same time, his left arm instinctively dropped down to shield the sleeping girl. His sudden movement caught the eye of the captain, who shot him a sadistic grin. "Take it easy, soldier, just a submerged log hitting up against the bottom."

Shane pulled his arm back to his side and let the rifle rest in his lap. He looked off into the night over the rail and glanced at the far bank of the river. He saw a pack of them, their shadows cast long by the bright moon and stretching across the water toward him. The things walked slowly and followed the drifting boat, waiting for an opportunity to lunge at them and get on board. They were always hunting them, always ready to strike. He could raise his rifle and kill them until he was out of ammo, but more would come. It was useless—they were always there and he was always running from them.

Shane had been on the run with the girl since the fort fell. He was on tower watch when they breached the gate. They made him a team leader when he checked in and put him in charge of a number of junior soldiers.

Shane laughed to himself when he thought back to the moment he walked past the large crowd and to the small armory's gate. The other civilians barely noticed him, even with his uniform jacket coated in dried blood, the sleeves ripped. The civilians were too preoccupied with entering the small fort and escaping the terror that was moving toward them.

Not Shane though; he didn't care what was behind. He had already placed his fate in God's hands. What was behind him wasn't his concern. He moved stoically, like on a mission, and it was his job to be there. Not that he cared if the fort would accept him or not. He just knew if he didn't have a purpose, he would quit, and he didn't want to go out like that—with nothing to fight for. When the military police on duty saw him approach the gate, they pushed back the mass and dragged him forward through the crowds.

"Sergeant, what the hell are you doing out here?" one of them yelled as they grabbed his arms and pulled him through the barriers to behind the safety of the gates. Shane took a moment to look at the armed men around him but before he could speak, they looked suspiciously at the uniform he was wearing.

"Who are you with, sergeant? Why are you wearing that IR flag patch? Are you deployed? You on R&R leave?" one of them asked in rapid fire as he looked at the patches normally worn by soldiers on deployment.

Shane looked at the soldier with a dazed expression, still surprised to be taken in so easily. "Yeah... I was on leave. I'm just trying to make it back to my unit," he bluffed.

"Shit, sergeant, haven't you heard? All of the deployed units have been recalled. Your unit's probably on their way back to D.C. or Bragg. You better check in with the LT, maybe he can help you hook up with your command."

Shane nodded and looked back at the screaming civilians still fighting to get close to the gates.

"Sergeant!" the soldier in charge shouted, trying to regain his attention.

"Looks like you been through a lot," he said, indicating the blood on Shane's jacket.

"Yeah, it's bad out there; worse than anything I've ever seen."

"Where'd you come from?"

"Huh? Oh, down on 32nd street," Shane said barely above a whisper.

"What the… 32nd? That's out behind the roadblocks in the containment zone! How the hell'd you make it out of there?" the soldier said with disbelief in his voice.

"Walked mostly," Shane said.

The soldier laughed. "Well shit… we got us a Rambo, fellas. Private Nichols, get the truck and run the sergeant here back to the operations tent. I'm sure the LT will have work for him."

CHAPTER 2
Atlantic Coast Line

Brad watched men dressed in yellow and orange jackets walk the decks of the black submarine. Sailors appeared to be deploying an inflatable boat while more men stood atop the sail looking back at him with binoculars of their own. It'd been over two hours since they encountered the vessel. Two silent hours, with little to no contact other than a flashed Morse code message requesting they silence their radios, kill their engines, and cease the ping.

"They're prepping a boarding party," Gunner said casually as he watched the foreign team through his binoculars ready their craft. The men in orange lowered it into the water and attached it with lines and a flimsy netted ladder.

"What do we do?" Parker asked excitedly. "Who are they?"

"Doesn't matter who they are, let's get ready to meet our new friends," Gunner answered.

Joey Vilegas pushed his way toward the front of the group so he could see over the rail. Brad noticed that Vilegas had used the down time to put on his tactical vest and attach his weapon to the front with a clip. The rest of them were still casually dressed in their uniform trousers and t-shirts; only a few of them even carried side arms.

"How do we know they're friends?" Joey asked accusingly.

Sean put his hand on Vilegas' shoulder and gently directed him back to the wheel house. "Get that weapon inside and out of sight!"

Vilegas planted his feet and pushed back. "Why? Don't we want them to know we ain't defenseless, that we aren't a soft target?"

Sean grunted. "If they wanted us dead, we would be on the bottom already," he said as he walked back to look Vilegas face-to-face. He put his hand on his shoulder, with less aggression this time.

"So, let's just throttle back a notch and see what they have to say."

Vilegas looked down at the deck then glanced over his shoulder at the submarine. "Yeah, you're probably right; I'll be inside. If you need me, I'll be ready," he said as he turned and moved back to join Kelli on the bridge.

"They're in the water, Chief!" Brooks called out from the bow, causing all of them to turn their attention back to the visitors.

Sean moved back to the bow and watched the small boat pull away from the larger vessel. "Okay, fellas, they have the bigger bank and all the good cards, so let's just play this hand out before we go getting silly."

"Understood, Chief," Brad said as he stepped back and joined the rest of the crew near the wheelhouse. Gunner and Sean moved aft and descended the ladder toward the lower dive deck.

The ribbed inflatable moved in the direction of the Coast Guard vessel. There were six men on board; all appeared to be armed and in uniform. The boat made a straight line directly toward them, then cut an arc fifty feet off of their port side. The small boat moved past them, turned sharply, and came back up to within thirty feet of the Coast Guard vessel's dive deck before cutting their speed and stopping hard in the water. A man stood, looked at the ship, and then lifted a bull horn to his mouth. "Good evening, I am Chief Marcus Richardson. Request permission to come aboard," he shouted over the horn.

"Parker, Nelson, would you join us below and prepare to catch a line?" Gunner shouted in a voice loud enough to be heard by the approaching craft.

The small craft idled closer to the landing ladder. A line was tossed and caught by Corporal Parker who quickly pulled the small boat in and tied it to a cleat bolted to the deck. Extending a hand, Nelson reached over the rail and assisted with pulling the crew members aboard.

The sailors filed off the small boat and moved back to stand against the rail while holding their weapons casually. They wore plain blue utility uniforms and all were armed with SA80s that hung casually from their slings. The man that identified himself as the Chief stepped forward and again introduced himself. "Excuse me for the awkwardness of this introduction. As you are well aware, formalities have grown tiresome in recent days. As I said before, I am Chief Petty Officer Richardson of the HMS Attack and this is a portion of our crew."

Sean moved forward with his hand extended. "I am Chief Sean Rogers; you could say I am the current chief of the boat. Welcome aboard," Sean said, stepping ahead of Gunner. "Might I ask what brings you into our waters?"

Richardson smiled and returned Sean's handshake. He turned his head making an obvious display of looking over the ship and its crew. "You seem to be a bit out of place here. Your vessel has Canadian markings; Coast Guard even. Yet your uniforms— "

"Yes, we are a bit of a motley crew. It's a long story," Sean replied.

"One that my captain would love to hear. We were expecting Canadians, but I guess that explains the radio calls. My captain has asked that I extend an invitation to your captain and first officer… or perhaps your leadership element, as I seem to recognize an absence of officers on the deck."

Sean chuckled. "Yes, this is a bit of an ad hoc crew. Put together more out of necessity than by military protocol. Before I can accept an invitation, I need to know who we are dealing with."

Gunner, having held his tongue long enough, finally spoke. "Richardson, we have been out of contact with the States for quite some time. We really don't know what you are doing here. Or even where the United Kingdom stands as a nation."

"You really are unaware?" Richardson asked with a puzzled expression.

"Unaware of what?" Sean asked.

"There are no more nations, gentlemen; at least not in the sense that they existed months ago. And as to the question of us being in *your* waters… we haven't spotted a US flagged vessel in weeks. Most of your standing fleet has fled or is resting on the bottom."

Sean looked at Richardson with his best poker face. "I think you may be wrong about that; the fleet is out there—a carrier and her support vessels—I have seen it personally."

Richardson smiled. "Oh yes, the *fleet*. We know all about them. Anchored off the Horn of Africa is it? I assume from your current location, you know as much about the *fleet* as we do."

Gunner once again interjected, "Okay, okay, Chief Richardson, what is it we're all doing out here? What do you want from us?"

"Like I said before, sir, my captain would like to invite you aboard. He has much to discuss."

Gunner smiled back at the confident man. "Chief, I'll send three of my men, but I must insist that you and two of your own remain here and keep me company in their absence. I'm sure you understand."

Richardson looked at Gunner with a cold stare, slowly letting the corners of him mouth curl up into a grin. He turned and looked back at his own men before looking back at Gunner. "Sir, I don't understand... are you, or are you not, in charge?"

Gunner held his smile. "I would say we have ourselves a bit of leadership by committee. I may be the senior, or maybe not. You know how us Yanks tend to embrace our democracies. However, if I were in charge, I wouldn't abandon my ship."

Richardson shook his head and let out an exaggerated laugh. "I have no idea what in the hell you just said, mate, but I guess it all makes sense somehow. "

Richardson unclipped a radio handset that was attached just below his right collar. He turned away from Gunner, faced the rail, and spoke into the handset in a low voice. He nodded and clipped the handset back to his collar as he looked back at Gunner. "Select your party, it appears we will be spending some time together."

"Very well… Chief Rodgers, would you kindly pick two of your finest to join you for a friendly visit to our neighbors?" Gunner said without looking away from Richardson.

CHAPTER 3

The sun slowly rose, letting rays of light spill through the now leafless trees. Shane watched as the ship's crew steered the boat toward the center of the wide river. They tossed heavy weighted drag anchors over the side, and the ropes pulled tight, halting the forward motion of the riverboat. The crew refused to travel during the daylight, when the things ashore were least active. They picked those hours to sleep and lounge about in the hot sun.

It was the opposite on dry land but, out here, he had to trust the crew, or at least accept their decisions. He wasn't in charge and was relegated to being nothing more than cargo; a possible trigger finger if the need arose. The crew posted watches while the rest of them walked into the pilothouse and pulled dark shades over the windows. A door slammed and the girl startled awake. She struggled to sit up. Shane quickly moved to her side and calmly placed an open hand on her chest. She relaxed her tensed body and smiled at him. "Shane," she said calmly and grabbed his gloved hand, hugging it.

She was skinny and frail in Shane's eyes. Not that he had much experience with children; they all looked tiny and fragile to him. When he first found her in the aid station, he wanted nothing to do with her. He just wanted to keep moving, get on his way. But there was something different about her, maybe in the way she looked at him. Maybe because she didn't appear afraid. Something in her demeanor calmed him, but more importantly, she made him feel useful again.

He grabbed her below the arms and lifted her into a seated position on his rucksack. Then, he pulled a small bottle of water from his pack and used it to clean her face. He asked if she was hungry and she nodded. Shane pulled a small chunk of a granola bar from his pocket and handed it to the girl. She gave him a sour expression. "You need to eat, Ella," he said softly. She looked at him dreadfully, then took the bar and bit off a small piece. Shane placed the water bottle in her free hand and turned back to face the center of the riverboat.

The rest of the passengers were up and stirring about now. Families and loaners alike, with a few suspicious looking characters mixed in the group. None of them on a direct path and yet all of them just trying to stay ahead of the things on the shore. A quick movement in his peripheral caught his attention. A man dressed in rags had reached past Shane and snatched at Ella's wrist going for the morsel of granola. The girl winced in pain as Shane quickly turned and tackled the man to the ground. Shane had drawn his knife without realizing it and had the blade pressed against the man's neck.

Shane was prepared to pull the blade horizontally and open the man's throat. A fearful pleading scream behind him caused his grip to relax on the man. Shane rose up slowly, leaving the stranger lying flat on the deck of the ship. Ella was crying softly now. Shane moved back toward her, keeping his eyes on the man. A young woman ran forward and grabbed the ragged man. Forcing herself between Shane and the thief on the ground she pleaded, "Please don't kill him mister, he was just trying to get food for our boy."

Shane looked stone faced in the direction the woman was indicating and saw a child lying in a mess of blankets. His checks were shallow, obviously suffering from starvation. For many of them, the cost of this voyage was a significant store of food or fresh water; for some of the women, the cost was greater. Shane continued to move back, preparing to sit next to the girl when he heard a shout—this time from a male voice.

A man had stepped forward and was pointing to the girl. "She… she's bit!" the man yelled.

Shane turned looking at the girl. He could see that in the short struggle with the thief, the girl's sleeve had been torn, exposing the scabbed and bloodied wound on her arm. Losing his footing, Shane nearly tripped and fell into the corner where the girl was sitting. He raised his rifle and looked the shouting man in the face.

"It's not what you think, sir. Now go back about your business," Shane said calmly, as the girl curled tightly against his back to shield herself from the man's cold stares.

The young woman, who had come to the thief's aid, now stood and pointed as well. "No. It's true, I saw it, she been bit."

Others started to gather around, causing Shane to grow more concerned. He pushed back against the rail, keeping Ella between him and the ship's edge. "You all need to back up now, the girl isn't infected."

"She bit!" the young woman screamed again, causing Shane to focus on her.

The pilothouse door swung open and the old captain stormed out. The shouting man used the distraction to his advantage and dove at Shane to try to get to the girl. Shane dropped levels and spun, firing a single round that caught the lunging man in the chest. As the report of the rifle echoed off the river valley walls, the man dropped hard to the deck and rolled to his side. Blood spilled from his mouth as his eyes fluttered. The rest of the passengers pushed away in fear. Shane stood tall, still shielding the girl with his body. He looked back at the passengers. "I said she wasn't infected! You all know that, we've been with you two days! She would have been gone by now!" Shane yelled.

The captain walked calmly toward the shot man lying on the deck. He pushed the man with his boot then turned to look at Shane. "He's dead. You killed him."

The woman rushed to the captain's side. "She bit Captain, the girl got to go," the woman screamed.

The captain held up a hand, silencing the woman. "Well, soldier, is she bit?"

Still holding the rifle at the ready, Shane looked at the captain. He could see other members of the crew were walking out of the pilothouse, several of them armed. Shane lowered the muzzle of the rifle, hoping it would ease the tension, but as he did so, he saw the crew instead move more aggressively toward him. Shane let his free hand reach into a front pocket of his jacket. He pulled a M67 frag grenade. As he held the grenade forward, displaying it clearly to the armed men around him, he used his thumb to pop the already loosened pin and safety.

He watched the body language of the crew grow more fearful; they changed direction and moved away from him. The captain also moved back, raising his hands in the air. "Calm down now, soldier; no need for all of that."

"I already told you she ain't infected," Shane said, keeping the rifle on the captain with his right hand as he held the grenade with his left. "Her wound is nearly healed, the infected turn before they heal."

The captain frowned. "I reckon we're beyond that now, soldier. You know the rules on this riverboat. No infected, no killing. You broke both those rules. Even if she ain't infected, you still killed one of us. Now you know you got to go."

Shane looked at the captain and pointed to the man on the ground. "He came at the girl. It was self-defense."

"You knew the rules when we let you on. You got to go."

Shane pumped his hand on the grenade. "You put us out there, we're dead," he said softly trying to reason with the man.

The captain nodded and took a step closer. He spoke in a low voice so that the others couldn't hear him. "Son, I'm giving you a chance here. These people won't let you be after what you did. And the woman says your daughter is bit. I know it ain't possible with how long you been with us. But she ain't gonna let that rest."

"She's not my daughter," Shane said.

"Son, it don't matter to me who she is. If I walk away right now, my crew will shoot you dead—grenade or not—and those passengers will tear that girl apart out of fear of the virus." The captain looked back at the passengers and his crew, then back to Shane. Speaking louder for all to hear, "The water is fast here and it looks to be nice weather. You get moving now and you could make it pretty far, maybe even get to shore safely."

"We won't last out there," Shane said.

"I'm sure you'll get along all right. Now, I'm gonna give you a minute or two to get your shit together and get off my vessel. If you're still here, my men will shoot you down," the captain finished off quietly.

CHAPTER 4

Brad was in the center of the small inflatable with Sean and Brooks flanking him on either side. His hands were pressed flat on the bottom, trying to steady himself as the craft cut the wakes. As soon as Gunner gave Sean the choice of selecting his team, Brad knew that he would be on the short list. He would have preferred sitting this one out and watching it from the sidelines for once, but Sean had made it clear he thought of Brad as one of his team now. Brad was no longer a stranger to them and, truthfully, Brad knew he would have been disappointed if he *hadn't* been selected.

He hadn't picked up on much of Gunner's conversation with the British sailors. He could clearly feel the tension though. After their time with the fleet, he wasn't expecting rescue but he was still surprised at the attitude of the visiting sailors. Things happened fast once Gunner gave orders to board the foreign vessel. Sean called Brook's name, then Brad's, in quick order. Gunner told them they wouldn't need their weapons or armor. Brad had scrambled his way to the dive deck and was quickly ushered aboard the small boat. He didn't have time to talk to Chelsea or any of the others. When he looked back at her on the upper deck near the rail, he could see the worried and confused expression on her face.

As they drew closer to the submarine, he could see a group of armed men gathered on the front deck. Not a welcome party but more of a guard force. The sailors onboard the small craft hadn't spoken, other than to call out commands to each other while completely ignoring the Americans. Brad watched as one of them stood in the bow of the boat just as they bumped into the side of the submarine. Men aboard the sub tossed over a net and told them to climb.

Brad followed Sean's lead as he grabbed the netting and pulled himself up. When Brad reached the surface of the deck, he felt a strong grip around his wrists as he was pulled up and onto the deck. He swung his foot below him and slowly regained his balance. Brooks was similarly pulled up behind him, and then the rest of the sailors crowded them forward, toward the center of the deck.

He stepped forward and saw that he was surrounded by armed sailors. Just as Sean was about to speak, they quickly stepped back creating a hole. Two men stepped toward them and stopped when they were only a few paces from Sean. The taller of the two men examined their uniforms then looked at Sean. "And who is senior in this group?" he asked without introducing himself.

Sean smiled and looked over the tall, broad-shouldered older man. His hair was silver and cut short. Unlike the others wearing raincoats, this man was dressed in a pressed dark blue shirt with the sleeves rolled to just below the elbows. He had officer insignia on his collars and was wearing a holster on his hip, but his firearm was absent. His younger—and far more intense looking—sidekick was wearing the same uniform and an identical empty holster. The tall man caught Sean's obvious gaze at their lack of side arms.

"Ah yes, I was informed that you would be joining me unarmed. I thought it only fair to leave my weapon in my quarters," the man said, in a softer tone than before.

Sean chuckled. "Nice gesture. Forgive me if I don't celebrate. I see you still brought plenty of muscle," he said, looking left and right at the armed men surrounding them.

"Do the weapons bother you?" the officer said.

Sean smiled. "Nah, the sergeant behind me is a trained attack dog. I give the word and... well, you don't want to know," Sean said, laughing.

"Bloody Yanks," the officer said, letting out a small chuckle. He extended his hand to Sean. "I am Commander Stuart. This is my executive officer, Lieutenant Commander

Chatham, the ranking officers of this vessel. And you?"

Sean returned his handshake and made introductions. He then gave a brief description of their journey and how they had managed to come by the Canadian ship. Commander Stuart leaned in and listened with skepticism before walking them closer to the bow of the boat, creating a distance between them and the armed men. Once he was certain he was out of earshot of his guards, he turned to Sean. "You understand, Chief, we were expecting Canadians. If we had known you were Americans, we may not have surfaced."

"Do you have some aversion to Americans?" Sean asked.

Stuart smirked. "Yes, of course," Stuart said as if remembering a minute detail, "Richardson informed me that you are not up on current events."

"Please enlighten me, Sir," Sean answered, hiding his frustration.

"For starters, the last American flagged vessel we approached fired on us..."

Brad shook his head. "Impossible, why would they fire on you?" he said, stepping forward and making his disagreement obvious.

"Your government has broken into factions. My home government is, of course, loyal to your nation's capital and President—if he still lives. It seems that makes us an enemy to some, even though we are not a hostile force. We have to take precautions when approaching strangers," Stuart answered.

"Really… well, what are you doing out here, anyway?" Brad asked.

"Looking for answers; global communication lines have faltered. We were sent here to search for assistance. Our home is no better off than yours," Stuarts said.

"Assistance in this? What are you supposed to be bringing back?" Brad mumbled.

Sean raised a hand to silence Brad and then gave Stuart a concerned look. "What is it you could possibly need from us?"

"To be blunt, we are looking for help and stability. There are men within your borders who are not interested in that," Stuart said, the infliction in his voice building. He was clearly not used to being doubted.

Sean smirked. "That still doesn't explain who, or why, anyone would fire on you, specifically."

Stuart frowned and turned to his executive officer. They briefly exchanged hushed words before turning back to face Sean and the others. "Very well, please come below with me. I have something to show you that will help in your understanding."

Before Sean could respond, Stuart and his first officer turned and walked past them. The armed men quickly ushered them to follow.

They were escorted toward the sail of the vessel and through a hatch which led into a smaller space that revealed a ladder to descend below. Both officers quickly dropped in, followed by an armed guard, and then Sean was signaled to follow.

Brad watched Sean, then Brooks, drop into the armored hull of the submarine. Brad hesitated before stepping forward and placing his boot on the rung of the ladder. As he dropped into the body of the submarine, he could hear the humming of electronics and machinery. He ended up in a circular darkened space with grates on the floor. When he began to look around, more men came down the ladder behind him and forced him forward to follow the others. He moved through the awkwardly narrow passageway, trying to catch up with the others. Brad could see that the walls were lined with stacked containers of food and dry goods. He looked down at the containers curiously until a sailor pushed him ahead.

"Excuse our mess, we have to fit food wherever we can on board," the sailor said as he grinned and motioned him forward.

"Where do you find it all?" Brad asked him as he ducked to move though another hatch.

"All over. Mostly aboard dead vessels we find on the water. The ports are no longer safe."

"What about the infected on board?" Brad asked.

The sailor smiled. "We have become quite good at dealing with them. You would do well to get inside now, I expect the captain shall be looking for you," he said as he ushered Brad through another hatch and closed the door behind him.

The rather cramped room he entered was brightly lit. There were tables lined against the far end. Comfortable looking chairs, wood cabinets, and a large TV filled the rest of the space. Brad saw that Sean and Brooks had already been seated at the table, so he hurried to find a spot next to them. As he sat down, an enlisted man poured him a small cup of tea.

Stuart leaned against a wall while they were seated. "Welcome to the Officers Wardroom. I'm sure you would rather have coffee, but this will have to do," Stuart said and then took a seat across from Sean.

Sean sipped. "This will be fine. Now please, what is it you need to show us?" Sean asked, barely hiding his impatience.

A loud knock at the wardroom door grabbed everyone's attention. Chatham, who had not yet been seated, moved to the door and slowly opened it. Seeing who it was, he pulled the door the remainder of the way. In walked a confident young man dressed in dark camouflage with British insignia, followed by a tall older man in a worn United States flagged flight suit.

CHAPTER 5

He allowed the rifle to hang from its tactical sling as he used his right hand to stuff his meager belongings into the rucksack. As he worked, he held the grenade out with his left to keep the other passengers' attention. Ella was sitting against the rail watching him with wide eyes. He could see the onset of fear in her, and he wanted to calm her but knew he had to stay focused on the threats around him. Shane placed the last of the blankets into the bag and pulled the drawstring as tightly as he could.

Shane paused and looked back at the captain, considering arguing his case one more time. He could see by the look on the man's face that pleading would be pointless, though. He lifted the pack and moved it closer to the rail. "Ella, climb over," he said to the girl.

She looked up at him with frightened eyes but still slowly got to her feet. She placed a foot on the rail and he helped her to the outside. The riverboat only rode a couple feet out of the water and would make for a very short drop.

Keeping an eye on the passengers, he hoisted his rucksack over the rail with one arm and told the girl to grab onto it. "Ella, you don't let go of this, do you understand? No matter what, don't let go."

She grabbed the bag's straps and hugged it tight. She then looked up at him with fear and nodded her head, showing that she understood. Shane took the bag and swung it out from the side of the riverboat, the weight pulling at him, and let it drop. She hit the water hard and sunk below the surface before popping out and surging into the current. Shane could see the girl's head above the surface and her arms still tightly locked to the straps. Shane took a step onto the rail, still carefully holding the grenade over the deck. He saw the guards ready their weapons and slowly edge forward, as if preparing to shoot him the second he hit the water.

Shane stepped over the rail and looked back at the captain. He frowned then kicked off the railing, tossing the grenade onto the deck of the riverboat as he sailed back. He hit the water and turned himself before he broke the surface. He then swam hard with the current to catch up to his rucksack bobbing in the water nearly a hundred feet ahead. He saw impacts with the water as the crew fired at him and then heard the clap of the grenade, followed by shouts and screams. The explosion caused the chaos he was hoping for and the distraction he needed to create distance. Shane didn't want to kill any of them, but he couldn't allow harm to come to the girl.

He swam hard and lifted his head often to keep track of the floating pack. The water was colder than he thought it would be. It chilled his core and made his arms feel heavy. He hoped the girl would have the strength to hold on. He took long, deep strokes, slowly gaining on the bag. He watched it roll to the side and caught a glimpse of her pale skin break the surface of the water. The sight of Ella in the water energized him and he swam harder. When the bag was just within reach, he stretched and grabbed at the nylon fabric.

Shane pulled on the bag, rolling it so that the girl's upper body came out of the water and rested atop the buoyant pack. He forced himself into a sitting position with his boots pointed downstream before he looked up and saw the girl's face; her hair was wet and lying across her brow. Although she looked at him calmly, he could see in her eyes that she was terrified. He reached a hand up and, feeling her clammy skin, touched her wrist gingerly.

"It's okay Ella, I'm back," he whispered to her as he looked her in the eyes.

Shane then twisted in the water to look back at the small riverboat and saw the white and black smoke that now hung over it. He could see it was still anchored and knew they would not be pursuing them; the crew would be busy working to put the fire out. He also knew the shots and explosion would draw the infected closer. He and Ella would have to stay in the water long enough to get away. He shifted the sling around his torso so that the rifle hung across his back, then used his arms to push them to the center of the river and into the faster current.

The cold water numbed the pain of the always present ache in his back, but he could feel the cold take effect on his limbs as well. Shane looked at Ella. Her head was resting on the bag and he could see that she was shivering—her lips had turned a light purple. He would have to get her out of the water soon. He knew he could tolerate the cold temperature far longer than Ella could. She was frail, skin and bones, and with the little food they had eaten, the shivering would use up her calories. The shivering would stop and then she would die.

Shane wanted to get distance on the riverboat but he couldn't risk the girl; they needed to leave the water. He searched the shoreline for an opening in the trees—a place where they could quickly leave the riverbank, but still find concealment. He wasn't familiar with the area. He didn't know this valley where the river was fast-moving, wide, and mostly met with banks of sparse forest yet occasionally crossed by a large highway or rail bridge. A few dead towns, but not much that caught his attention. Now looking downstream, he saw one side of the river met with dark, tree-covered hills and the right bank lined with tall wetland grasses.

The forest would provide for better cover and concealment, but also a means for the infected to get close to him. The field was more open, but he could use the heat of the sun to warm the girl and the infected fled from the daylight for unknown reasons. Shane slid his hand to the girl and felt the cold, soaked jacket clinging to her back.

"Hold on, Ella, we're gonna get out of the water, okay?" he whispered to her.

She opened her eyes and looked at him blankly without lifting her head. "Are we… we... gonna find my Momma, Shane?" she barely said above the shivers.

Shane looked away toward the bank then back into her eyes. "Yeah, Ella, we're going to find your mommy, just hold on for me."

As the river turned right into a bend, Shane held the bag with his left hand and swam hard to the right shoreline. Trying to break out of the current, he was able to reach the shallows and plant a boot into the rocky bottom. The current was still too strong; the swift water made the pack feel hundreds of pounds heavier than it was, so Shane gave up on trying to pull the bag in. The river bend caused a bit of a shallow corner made up of stone and gravel, so he pulled the bag close to him, guided it forward, and kicked hard toward the bank until he felt the bottom close beneath him.

Shane pressed the toes of his boots into the gravel bottom and then pressed down to anchor the pack. Carefully, he lifted the girl to his chest so that her head was on his shoulder. She was unconscious now, but Shane could feel her breath against his neck. He hoisted the bag with his left hand and cautiously walked to the river bank. The grassy ledge over the river was above his shoulders. He dropped the bag next to his feet and lifted the girl to the high grass before he pushed the bag up beside her.

He crouched and then jumped into the bank, grabbing at the tall grass and digging with the toes of his boots, searching for purchase. His boots knocked away parts of the bank that tumbled and loudly splashed into the water below. Already committed to the noise, he continued the scramble. Pushing with his feet and pulling with his arms, he was finally able to roll onto the high ledge above. Shane fell to his side, belly crawled to the girl, and put his hand on the cold skin of her neck; she was still out. He needed to warm her quickly, but they had to move first. He couldn't stay in this place where he left the river; he had made too much noise. On his knees, Shane lifted his head above the high grass. The field stretched for at least a hundred yards away from the river before it met a blacktop road. To the left and right he saw nothing but open field for hundreds of yards.

Shane saw a small split in the grass, the makings of a game trail that ran parallel to the water's edge. Looking down the trail, he watched motionlessly. Searching far out, then closer in, he spotted a muddy human boot print on the path. He looked at it closely. A heavy work boot with a four-pronged heel, the edges of the imprint had begun to crumble and showed its age. He could see where objects had blown over it, possibly leaves. Farther up, the human trail had been crossed by a small animal track. He relaxed knowing the trail was old, but it was still a trail and could be used by others; it was time to move.

He swung his rifle back to his chest then pulled the pack over his shoulders. Carefully, he lifted Ella back into his arms and patrolled toward the center of the field as he moved forward to the blacktop road. He moved hastily, but still made an effort to be quiet. He would hide in plain sight today. The field grass was waist high and it would make for good concealment while the sun warmed them, but he would have to find a harder shelter before dark—before the things came out. He began to step forward then halted and looked down in surprise at another set of prints. It was the same boot, but headed in the opposite direction. He recognized the print from the four-pronged heel.

Whatever made these prints had wandered the field, hunted, and spent an unknown amount of time there. Shane kneeled down and examined it. Like the others, the edge had crumbled and begun to dry. It was old, but not days old. Only hours had passed since it was pressed into the soft mud of the field. Shane shook off the worry and went back to the task at hand. He continued moving in the direction of the road. When he found a natural low spot in the field, he pushed away the grass to form a nest and then dropped his pack. He removed his soaked uniform top and t-shirt before spreading them out on the tall grass. The air was still chilled, but the sun warmed his skin. He laid Ella on the jacket and opened his pack before untying the waterproof drawstring to remove the wool blanket. The heavy material had picked up some water but, for the most part, was still dry.

Shane folded the blanket in half and placed Ella on top of it. He then quickly removed her soaked clothing and draped it over his uniform to dry. When she was stripped down to her shorts he lifted her to his bare chest and then tightly wrapped the blanket around the both of them to trap in the body heat the girl desperately needed. Shane lay back against his pack and looked up at the sun. Feeling the heat of it on his face, he prayed that he had done enough to save the girl. As the adrenalin left his body, exhaustion took hold of him. When he felt the warmth returning to her cheek as it pressed against his shoulder, he relaxed but kept his arms wrapped snugly around the girl. He cupped the back of her head with his hand, breathed deeply, and closed his eyes. He just needed to rest... only for a minute.

CHAPTER 6

The man bedecked in dark camouflage walked across the wardroom, ignoring the seated strangers. He opened a cupboard, quickly scanned the contents, and retrieved a small tin of biscuits. He leaned back against a bulkhead and pried open the tin. A second man dressed in a flight suit timidly entered the room a few seconds later and, appearing unsure of himself, stepped to the table to stand looking at the Americans.

His flight suit was adorned with an American flag patch on the shoulder. Insignia that Brad didn't recognize was in gold over the name 'HOWARD' on a black badge pinned to the man's chest. Stuart looked up at the man nonchalantly and said, "Please have a seat, Doctor Howard."

Stuart paused to sip his tea before addressing Brad's team. "You'll have to excuse our friend. We just recently pulled him from the drink. He's still a bit soggy, I suppose."

The man in the flight suit gave Stuart an uneasy look and then took a seat at the far side of the table across from Brad and the others.

Sean looked Howard over. "Doctor Howard, is it? I assume you're an American by the flag on your shoulder."

Howard raised his head to look at Sean. "Well yes... of course I'm American. I am a doctor for Christ sakes... with the United States." Howard scowled. "I'm with the Public Health Services. I demand to know why these people are detaining me!" Howard shouted.

Howard's sudden outburst caused the camo man to set down his tin and walk closer to Howard's side. He spoke softly in a thick English accent. "Now, c'mon mate, what'd we discuss about yer temper?"

Howard looked over his shoulder at the camo man, then back at Sean. "Can you do anything to get me out of here? These men have been keeping me prisoner!"

Sean looked at the camo man in the face. "Special Boat Service?" he asked.

The man smiled and shook his head. "Close, mate; Lieutenant Meyers, Reconnaissance Regiment," he answered.

Sean returned the smile and nodded. "I see... so Meyers, why is it you're detaining my friend?" Sean asked, ignoring the others in the room.

Stuart laughed at the question. "We aren't detaining anyone. We responded to this gentleman's distress call. If we hadn't pulled him out of the water when we did, he'd most likely be dead by now. "

Howard leaned forward and slammed his closed fist on the table. "Listen to me, you fools, we are wasting time. You have to get me back!" Howard yelled.

The sudden movement caused Meyers to drop a heavy hand onto Howard's shoulder. He looked to Stuart for a sign. Stuart shook his head. "No, allow the doctor to stay. I'm sure he can behave himself."

Meyers smiled, squeezed the doctor's shoulder before slapping him on the back, then walked back to the tin of biscuits and pretended to ignore the conversation.

Stuart cleared his throat, causing the doctor to lift his head and look back at the men now staring at him. Chatham poured a glass of water from a pitcher on the table and then placed the glass in front of the Howard. Without speaking, Howard lifted the glass and gulped down the liquid. "We don't have a lot of time. The sample could already be lost, or degraded," he mumbled as he tapped the rim of the glass to signal Chatham to refill it.

Sean shot Howard a puzzled look. "The 'sample'?"

"Yes, the damn sample! Every minute we wait, we risk its degradation or loss. We shouldn't be here chatting, we should be headed back."

Stuart lifted a battered tan leather bag and removed a heavy folder which he slid across the table to Doctor Howard. "Maybe if you caught our friends up from the beginning, they would be more receptive?"

Howard shook his head. "I have already explained all of this!"

Sean looked at the folder. Stapled to the cover was a white sheet of 8x11 paper with 'CDC' printed on it in bold blue letters. "Please, Doctor, humor us. We are extremely interested."

Howard grunted. He opened the folder and flipped through sheathes of paper before removing a large color photograph. It was an image of a limb with an open wound. Howard looked at the picture intensely then slid it across the table to Sean. "What do you see?" he asked.

Sean took the photo and held it up to look at it before he showed it to both Brad and Brooks. Brooks reached for the photo and examined it closer. He slid the photo back to Howard. "Looks like a grade A Primal bite."

Howard nodded. "Primalis Rabia, yes, of course, a Primal. It cannot be confirmed, but we do believe the patient was bitten by an infected individual, a... Primal as you put it. Now, what else do you see?" Howard said as he slid the photo back.

"The wound is clean, probably a child – possibly a small female... wait... there are no signs of infection here, but this here," Brooks said, circling the wound with his finger, "superficial bruising around the injury. This can't be a Primal bite even though those are human teeth marks. How old was the injury?" Brooks asked, looking confused.

"Yes, finally! Are you a medical professional?" Howard asked, showing more enthusiasm.

Brooks shook his head. "Only in the 'field experience' sense, but I have treated... I mean, I have come in to contact with the... recently infected."

Howard began to look excited as he flipped another page and pulled another photo which he lifted and slid across to Brooks. "Now look at this; same patient, nearly forty-eight hours later."

Brooks lifted the photo. "Impossible, the wound. It's... it's healing! This couldn't have been a Primal bite."

"Yes, it is healing. It certainly should not be a Primal bite. The prognosis is six hours, ten at best, but there's more. Look at this," Howard said. His excitement was growing as he hastily searched and then pulled medical reports from the stacked papers. He laid them down in front of Brooks and pointed. "See? The patient's blood tested positive for the virus. Then later tests indicate that the patient is showing signs of effective antibodies, and then... see here? The virus is gone."

Brooks stared at the reports. "How?"

Howard smiled. "Exactly, *how*? That's what we need to decipher. Of course all of this is very simplified, but we hold three concise facts that need to be examined further. The patient was attacked, the patient's blood was positive for Primalis Rabia, and then the patient was clean."

Brooks pulled the lab results from Howard's hand and examined them closely. "I don't understand. The patient recovered from acute signs of the infection? This is impossible. What was the treatment?"

"There is no treatment; the patient was given minimal care for pain management. Most of the patient records are missing and all that is noted is that the patient's other family members failed to fight the infection. More likely, they didn't survive initial contact with the virus."

"Has this happened before?" Brooks asked.

Howard shook his head. "No, this is the first ever reported incident of a spontaneous recovery of the Primalis Rabia infection. Now, you must understand this could have been possible before but many patients, especially the weak such as the child in the photo, do not survive the initial attack. That's also what makes the vector so virulent. Only the strongest among us tend to survive the initial transmission of the virus. So it is the strongest among us who then become the carriers."

Brooks, looking more excited, said, "Who is it? The patient."

"She, the patient is a she. Her family was attacked near Atlanta—attacked very badly. The father was able to fight them off and break away. He was fortunate enough to get the child past the barriers and to a FEMA center, one of the few that still accepted walking wounded for treatment, but mostly for study. The mother... she was a loss. A shame, she may have shared the child's trait because the father certainly did not."

"What about the father?" Brooks asked.

"The FEMA camp allowed them in but put them under quarantine and took blood samples, of course. The father quickly succumbed to the infection and was put down. But the girl, she never turned."

Sean put up his hands. "Okay, enough. What does all of this mean?"

Howard looked, gleaming at Sean, but Brooks spoke first. "It means this girl could hold the cure."

Howard chuckled. "Not exactly, but it could at least be a treatment, or maybe the starting point for a vaccine!"

"Well, where is she then?" Brad asked, speaking for the first time.

Howard put his head down and looked at the papers in his hands. Stuart coughed, causing the others to look at him. "Well, Doctor, go ahead. Explain to the gentleman where your patient is currently residing."

"Fort Collins, a small base. Technically, it's a National Guard Armory on the Carolina coastline. It's of little importance to anyone —"

Stuart clapped his hands, interrupting Howard mid-sentence, and then extended his neck to emphasize his point. "And, Doctor, why is it you are not at Fort Collins with your precious *sample*?"

Howard sighed. "We did the best we could. One of our reaction teams had initially secured the patient from the FEMA camp, but no air transport was available. They attempted to reach Fort Bragg and had to divert to the coast after they encountered heavy buildups of infected populations. Our first contact with them was after they reached Fort Collins, one of the last remaining hard sites in the region. They were able to get a transmission through to us using the Armory's secured networks," Howard said, holding up the folder.

"We lost contact with Collins shortly after receiving the patient's file. My team was scrambled and, even using our longest range helicopter, by the time we reached Collins we were flying in on fumes. We could see from the air that the compound was lost. We circled and tried to find a safe landing zone, but the infected were heavily massed in all directions. There were signs of survivors and some sporadic vehicle traffic, so we tried to fly low and signal anyone alive on the ground... but it just drew in more infected.

"Our intent was to refuel at Collins for the return trip. With that scratched, we had no place to land that was clear of infected. They're drawn to helicopters, so every LZ we attempted was swarmed over before we got close. We ran to the sea—"

"We found your *friend,* here, bobbing in a life raft fifteen miles off the coast," Stuart said.

Sean pushed away from the table and stood. "This is a lost cause. If the Fort was overrun, then why did you bring us here? And Doctor, if this trip was so goddamned important, then why didn't they send another bird after you dropped off the radar?"

Howard stood with him. "I don't know why they didn't send another team. Maybe they did. Don't you understand? There could still be samples in the medical facility! We have to try!"

Stuart raised his hands. "Please sit," he said in a calm voice. "Chief, you asked earlier what we were doing out here. Communications between our nations went quiet nearly a month ago. Things at home are pretty grim, there is no cure in sight, and most of our population is held up behind walls the same as yours is.

"This is why we are here. We're looking for something—anything—that can help. Now, Chief, why are *you* here? What are you and your men willing to do to help end this?" Stuart finished.

CHAPTER 7

Shane opened his eyes and looked up at the sun still high above him. He put his head back against the pack. Keeping his eyes open, he strained his ears for any sounds of threats. If he stretched his neck, he could just see over the tips of the grass. A breeze was coming from the road and blowing toward him. It made the grass move in subtle waves and when the edges of the grass touched, it made a light whisking sound. Growing up hunting, he could pick up on the subtle differences in sounds between that of wild game and Mother Nature; the cracking of a twig or the rustle of dried leaves that could indicate a small deer or rabbit. Today the sound of a gentle breeze through the meadow was soothing. He allowed himself to lower his guard and settle back into the hide.

The girl was moving now; Shane could feel her squirm against his skin. He would allow her to sleep a bit longer since she needed her rest. Ella asked about her mom the last time he spoke to her. It'd been a while since she'd mentioned her mother. He could tell by the look in her eyes when she asked the question that she thought of her mother constantly. The toll the grief and travel took on the child was beginning to show. She was losing weight and rarely slept soundly at night. It'd been so long since he could provide her a secure place.

Shane watched the grass and thought about the night the fort fell; the night before he found her. He didn't know how the creatures had gotten inside. Maybe they just became too much for the iron gates to hold back. Maybe a wound had been overlooked on one of the guards. The firing came loud and rapidly, shattering the night. It could be heard over the screaming of the civilians and over the moans of the things pushing their way through the fences.

Shane was sleeping on the floor of the tower when it started. He was used to gunfire – it had become common in the fort over the last month – but what Shane heard from outside the tower that night was something different. The gunfire was sporadic and rapid. Panicked, the screaming of the soldiers jolted him awake. He was in the darkened center of the guard tower where his team had been living. He thought it was another bad dream, but the sounds of fighting came through the walls and the bright lights broke in through heavy tarps they'd hung over the windows.

He reached for his rifle and scrambled to the outer catwalk of the hastily erected tower in the corner of the fort. Flares were being launched, supplementing the bright generator-powered spotlights. Heavy machine guns and the crack of grenades joined the concert of noise.

He could see the things mixed in with the crowds, the bloodied and screaming men swarming the guards at the gate. Soldiers ran in all directions, firing into the massed mob. Shane saw his own two man team standing in shock, their backs pressed against the tower, rifles resting in their shaking hands. He ordered them to fire.

"What are we shooting at?" a private stuttered.

Shane looked at the chaos before he was able to comprehend the soldier's question. There were no clear targets. Screaming, raging people mixed in with panicked civilians were running through gaps in the fences, mauling and overpowering the guards. Some soldiers had taken up positions on the roofs of buildings. Others stood on top of vehicles while frantically trying to shoot into the crowds to stop the flood of infected. A Humvee was racing through the compound and bouncing the infected off of its heavy steel brush guards. A gunner in the Humvee's turret was firing rapidly to cut down paths of the crazed men that were fighting to get at the vehicle.

"If they aren't holding a rifle, kill them," Shane yelled.

Shane raised his own weapon and stepped to the rail. He fired steadily, trying to make every round count. He heard his men join the fight alongside him but when he observed the battle on the ground he knew the camp was lost. Too many had gotten inside. From his elevated position he could see the front gate that he himself had walked through weeks ago. It was open and the sand bag barriers tumbled over. The armory building was still secured but the things were pressed against the doors. Windows had been shattered and the things were trying to get inside. The compound's outer walls were still standing, but the grounds were covered with infected. It was hopeless.

He realized too late that he should have been thinking about escape and leading his men out of the tower. They were all around him – the tower was surrounded, his own team's gunfire had drawn them in. Shane looked down and saw the things trying to climb the tower walls. As more of them pressed against the tower, it began to shudder and shake under his feet. The gunfire from other parts of the camp had slowed. Shane saw the Humvee had finally been overwhelmed and was resting against a wall of the armory. Shane smiled; he knew there would be no retreat, no escape. This was it, his pain would end tonight. He looked to the privates standing with him. "If you want to make a break… now is the time, guys. I won't fault you for it. I'll cover you," he said to them.

The men had talked about what they would do in this situation, how they would escape. Sliding down to the far side of the wall had always been the least desirable choice. The tower stood in a corner of the compound; it was thirty feet up and a hell of a drop, but the privates had decided to risk the drop and attempt to jump to the far side of the fence. So far, the back corner of the compound's outside lawn was clear. They would have a long run if they made it to the ground, but with Shane providing cover fire, there was a chance they could make it to the tree line.

Every soldier at the fort was issued a grenade. It was an inside joke that the grenades were to be used on themselves to make sure they wouldn't turn, but now Shane would use them to help his men escape. They passed him their grenades and Shane wished them luck. A heavy rope was tied to the rail and they threw it over a portion of the catwalk that hung slightly beyond the perimeter wall. The first private quickly slid down the rope to the open ground on the far side of the fence. The things on the ground quickly caught onto what they were doing. The last soldier stepped over the rail and asked Shane to join them. He shook his head and told the man to go. Some of the infected ran directly at the fence trying to get to the private sliding down the rope to the far side. Others ran for the gate, trying to circle around, but the majority of the infected continued to push and heave against the tower.

The ones running to the gate became Shane's priority. He pulled the pin on the first grenade and threw it as hard as he could at the breach in the gate. The grenade landed in a mass of them and the explosion launched the bodies like a popped balloon while ripping body parts away to be scattered on the ground. The explosion had disoriented them, yet drew others to the loud blast. Shane pulled the pin on the second grenade and aimed for a new mass forming farther away. The grenade fell short but still rolled into the group. The blast had the same effect, knocking the things off their feet and tearing others apart. He saw them turn their hate filled eyes in his direction, suddenly forgetting about his men running across the open field.

Just below him, a tall male covered in blood and tattoos and naked to the waist, looked Shane in the eyes and screamed at him. Shane paused his firing as he saw what was happening; the other infected stopped, turned to look at the screaming man, then focused on the tower and ran at it. Shane stared back at the man in surprise. He was calling the others.

"They *are* fucking crazed!" Shane said out loud, still holding his fire.

Shane looked over his shoulder, saw that his men had made the tree line, then lifted his M4 and aimed at the screaming man. "Say good night!" he yelled as he pulled the trigger and put an aimed round into the tattoo-covered man's face, silencing him forever.

He shifted his point of aim, killing more of the screaming beasts until his rifle was dry. He reloaded, took his time, and placed carefully aimed shots into the tops of the heads of the creatures below him, regardless of how futile it seemed. Knowing each skillfully placed shot put one of them out of its misery, he continued firing until he was out of ammo and no more magazines hung from his vest. The tower again buckled hard under his feet and he fell toward the rail. He barely caught himself before nearly falling into the mass below. Another impact of the tower threw him away from the rail and back toward the enclosed space.

The door of the enclosure was swinging open. Shane ran for it, but a shudder of the tower caused him to lose his footing. He fell as he cleared the opening and rolled to the floor inside. He quickly got back to his feet and leaned against the far wall. Shane could hear the wood supports of the tower creaking as the heavy pine beams began to split. He pulled his own personal grenade from the pouch located on his belt, kissed it, and looked up at the ceiling of the small room.

"See you soon, Brothers," he said aloud as he reached to pull the pin.

A thunderous crack exploded in his ears, followed by the floor dropping from beneath his feet. The grenade slipped from his hand when he bounced off the ceiling of the enclosure. He saw white flashes of light and felt searing pain in his face while the tower toppled and he, again, smacked his face against a wall, then the floor. The tower crashed against the perimeter fence, halting the structure's fall. The sudden stop again tossing Shane into the now splintered and crumbling walls. The roof of the enclosure collapsed on top of him and trapped him in the wreckage. His head was spinning; his vision closing, blackness filling his sight. He struggled to free himself as the last of his strength left his body. The sounds of the screaming beasts softened and everything was suddenly quiet and peaceful. Shane allowed himself to relax giving into temptation to rest. It was over. He was done.

"Shane," he heard a voice call softly.

He heard more of them calling his name… calling him home. He squinted hard and struggled to open his eyes. He wanted to see the light.

****

The unmistakable sounds of a low flying helicopter woke him. He heard the screaming of the mob fade as they lost interest in the fort and chased after the sound of the aircraft. Pain seared through his injured back, his face had swollen, and his eyes were hard to open. Shane twisted and contorted his body, pushing against the wreckage until he was free. He pulled at the edge of a broken board and was suddenly sliding fast. He lost grip on the board, tumbled to the ground, and landed flat on his back, yelping in agony.

Shane rolled to his side and lay motionless, trying to breathe quietly, surprised he hadn't already been attacked. Bodies lay all around him on the ground. The sun was breaking the horizon and the orange glow of morning lit the camp. He squinted his eyes and focused on his surroundings. The armory doors were now broken and hung twisted on their hinges. As he slowly turned his head to look at the grounds, he found nothing still on its feet. Most of the active infected had already gone to shelter during the day, or were led away by the unknown helicopter.

Shane twisted and pushed himself into a seated position. He saw his rifle on the ground near him. He crawled towards the M4, picked it up, and used it as a crutch to push himself to his feet. He stood in a crouched position – standing upright caused more pain in his back. Shane thought of the open gate and about making a run for the tree line, where maybe he could find his men from last night. No, he reasoned, he wouldn't get far in his condition. His rifle was empty and he needed to treat his injuries. His eyes drifted to the armory. He knew there could be more infected hiding inside, but there was also a small arms room and an expansive aid station in the back office spaces. There would be pain meds and food.

He stood for a moment longer, listening, trying to slow his breathing to sharpen his senses. His head slowly rotated from left to right scanning everything. When he made a full movement, he started again, this time looking farther out. The fort had been destroyed. Wreckage and bodies were everywhere, but to his good fortune there were no signs of the standing infected; although he could still hear them in the distance.

Shane had picked up on their tones over the last few weeks in the tower. Like the beagles he used to hunt with as a boy growing up in Georgia, when these things were on the hunt for prey, their moan would change pitch and he could tell they were on a trail. The moan they used was to call others in the pack to join them. He shook his head as he recognized the animal instincts of the things were not unlike the stories of humans turning into werewolves. Things that had been office workers and store clerks were now mindless beasts on the hunt for meat.

They must be tracking other survivors from the fort, he thought. Shane had heard stories of the things moving into small towns, completely sacking it, and then tracking any of those lucky enough to escape on and into the next city. He knew he needed to move, get on the trail before they captured whatever they were after and began searching again. He needed to take advantage of the daylight when the packs tended to lay low and return to whatever dens the monsters called home.

He moved closer to the doorway of the armory and pressed his shoulder to the wall, letting it take some of the weight off of his aching back. Shane pondered going to his small living area at the back of the fort. He had a pack there and some meager belongings. But that would take him too far into the fort and he needed to move quickly and leave, to get away from this place before they returned. He leaned his body so that he could see down the long hallway to the open bay at the end. That was where the treatment areas were, as well as stores of food and ammunition. That immediately became his goal—to re-equip for the trail. Shane checked the watch on his wrist. He would give himself ten minutes to gather what he needed then get out.

Listening at the doorway, he heard nothing. Shane moved his hand to the back of his hip and felt the cold handle of his M9 Bayonet. He used his thumb to unsnap the small retainer strap and pulled the weapon from its sheath. As quietly as possible, he secured the blade to the small lug at the end of his rifle. Taking a deep breath, he let his body absorb the pain, stood upright, and pivoted into the hallway. No time for second guessing, he moved quickly and deliberately while sweeping the rifle in front of him, ready to lunge at any enemy.

He saw an armed man dead on the ground. Shane walked just past him then knelt down. With the expertise of a veteran soldier, he reached with his left hand and removed the magazine from the man's weapon. Without dropping his gaze from down the hall, he lifted the box magazine to his eye. It was empty. Shane knelt lower and let his left hand search the sticky uniform of the man until he found his magazine pouches, then he felt the man's chest and located his unused grenade. Shane lifted it and attached it to the front of his own vest. Without losing focus, he raised himself back up and continued down the hallway. Shane encountered more bodies but, knowing he had to move quickly and get out of the building, passed over them unless they were obviously armed. As he approached the open bay, he'd still failed to acquire any ammo.

Shane moved into the bay, pivoting as he moved toward the far corner where he knew the supplies were kept. The floor in the area had less bodies, but the space had still been turned over with obvious signs of battle. He inched between two pallets of food boxes and crept toward a hasty stack of ammo cans. Scattered all around them were the green cloth bandoleers and speed loaders normally packaged with military ammo. His heartbeat began to quicken as he realized all of the cans were empty. The defenders had expended all of it in their fight.

He dropped his head and exhaled, moving back toward the food pallets. He heard a metallic crunch under his boot and froze. Shane let his right arm drift to his boot and grinned when he felt the loose pile of rounds. He pulled off his patrol cap and set it on the floor next to him, then slowly swept his hand along the floor to gather the rounds. When he finished, he looked at his watch; he only had a few minutes before his deadline. He looked into the cap and saw he had gathered less than 20 rounds. It would have to do.

Shane shifted his focus onto the food stores. He used the end of his bayonet to cut away at the shrink wrap, and as he reached into the ripped plastic, he heard a muffled whimper and froze. Holding his breath and listening intently, he heard the whimper again. It was a child's voice. Shane rose up between the pallets and searched the walls. One of the medical doors was barricaded shut. A number of black-clad guards lay dead on the ground in front of the barrier.

The medical room had a large wooden door which someone had braced with boards and placed a heavy steel bar across. Bits of skin, fingernails, and claw marks covered the entrance. Shane focused on the door and edged closer. The whimper got louder as Shane's head was silhouetted over the single window in the door. A small, shattered wire-reinforced window covered with blood was embedded high in the door. Shane lifted his arm and used his sleeve to wipe away the sticky residue, then pressed his eye to the window. What he saw caused his knees to go weak and a pain grip his stomach. Inside the room, sitting on a hospital bed, was a young girl.

CHAPTER 8

"So why do you need us? You seem to have a boat full of able seaman," Shawn said grinning.

"Aye, that we do but we're just a bit shy of shooters on board," Meyers answered without allowing Stuart to speak.

Sean folded his hands together then let out a long sigh. "Okay, we've listened to your story. What's the plan?" Sean asked, looking over the printed pages in the folder.

Howard looked at Sean, confused. "The plan? What's the plan? Do you still not understand the importance of this? We need to get to the fort! There may be samples, something... anything we can use."

"Ugh, this again?" Meyers grunted. "You're awful confident about these samples. How do you know they exist? That this won't be a lost cause that gets all of us killed."

Howard reached across the table and pulled the folder back from Sean. He flipped through pages and laid them out in front of him. "These are lab reports. The men that risked their lives to get these wouldn't have destroyed them. And these things... these *Primals*, they would have no interest in samples. Even if they are lost, we have to recover the patient's body," Howard shouted, showing his frustration.

Brooks nodded and leaned forward in his seat. "I'm in."

Sean put his hand up. "Now hold on a minute, we don't know enough to commit to anything. Hell, we don't even know who this doctor works for."

"Doesn't matter, Chief, this is bigger than all of us. If there's a chance of a breakthrough, I'm going," Brooks said, pushing away from the table and getting to his feet. "I understand the rest of you having doubts, and I don't expect any of you to go along."

Brad looked down at the table but for the moment held his silence.

Meyers laughed. "Well, well, look at this; we got one brave Yank joining the team. How's about we get two? Three maybe."

Sean gave Meyers a smug look that quickly silenced him. "I tell you what, *left-tenant*," he said, exaggerating the accent reciting Meyers' rank. "You give me detailed plans and supplies, I'll pull a squad together for you. But… the doctor here is going to answer a few more questions about the people he works for."

"Easily done, Chief," Meyers said. "Time is of importance though; I suggest you begin readying your party as soon as possible."

"Nothing to worry about," Sean said, looking back at his men. "Brooks, partner up with the doctor here. I want to know everything about this place he comes from and this kid, and what it will take to recover these samples. Commander, could you please transport my sergeant back to our vessel so that he may prepare our team while your *left-ten-ant* briefs me in."

Stuart stood and walked to the door with Chatham close in tow. "I'll make arrangements for transport and we will send someone for your man when ready. I'll leave you alone with Mr. Meyers here to strategize." With that, he left the room and Chatham closed the door behind them.

"Okay, Meyers, let's cut the bullshit. What are we looking at here?" Sean said, walking around the table to stand next to Meyers.

"It's ugly, mate. I don't see how we can reach the fort from the near coast." Meyers stopped speaking, reached into a cargo pocket on his left leg, and unfolded a large military map. "Collins is here, inland between the coast and this large river. All these coastal areas are pockmarked with activity. But here," —he pointed to an area far south of the fort—"in this harbor, is an island base. We have picked up radio traffic, pings for help and that sort of thing, so it seems to be a friendly safe haven."

Brooks looked closely at the map and grinned. "You're joking. You do know what that is, don't you? You want us to go to Fort Sumter?"

"It's logical, mate. It's located in the harbor and clear of infected. From radio traffic, we know that it is occupied. If we get there, we can attempt to secure transport up river and get closer to Collins."

"You want to take a British submarine up Charleston Harbor?" Brooks asked.

"No, mate. The Skipper won't risk bringing the boat that close; that's why we stopped you, we need that little Canadian tug you been cruising on."

"Ahh… and the truth suddenly reveals itself," Sean said sarcastically.

Meyers shrugged and slapped Sean on the shoulder. "Of course, but my excitement of finding out there were Yankee *grunts* on board is quite authentic."

There was a loud knock at the door and a young sailor cracked it, sticking in his head. "Pardon me, the raft is ready," the young man said.

Sean turned to look at Brad who had been standing quietly with an uncommitted look on his face. "Brad, I need you to tell Gunner to ready the group to move ashore. For now, just give him the location. No need to reveal the mission yet, I'll do that later. I don't want shit going south before it starts."

"Anything else?" Brad asked nonchalantly, but showing obvious relief that he wouldn't have to tell the rest of the team they had been signed up to go into Primal territory.

"No, not yet. I'm going to try to squeeze some ammo and food out of our new friends here," Sean said, returning the slap to Meyers' shoulder. "I will see you tonight."

"Roger that," Brad said without emotion as he turned to join the sailor in the hallway. When Brad moved through the hatch, the sailor quickly closed it behind him.

"Just this way, Sir," the sailor said.

Brad nodded. "Lead the way, I'm ready to get the hell out of here," he grunted.

"Tense meeting that must be. The captain has been barking orders since he left the wardroom. You must have had some good things to talk about."

Brad picked up on the change of temperament with the escort from when they first boarded the submarine. He also noticed that this sailor wasn't armed as the others had been. "What happened to your rifle, *mate*?" Brad asked, being as direct as he could afford.

The sailor froze in his tracks and turned to look back at Brad. "Do I need it?" he asked with a frightened look.

"What? No, it was just that earlier, all the guards were armed and now I don't see any," Brad said.

"Oh, that, no... the captain stood us down. We were at general quarters till we figured out who you all were. You know pirates are operating out there." The sailor walked back to the spot on the passageway where the ladder led to the sail. "Just this way, sir, we'll be outside in a moment."

Brad stepped into the well and climbed the ladder up to another small space where he traveled through an open hatch and out onto the deck. There were noticeably less people outside now. Three sailors he recognized from earlier were positioned by the webbed ladder that led to the raft and a couple more were farther away, near the bow. Brad looked out and was surprised to see how late it had gotten; the sun was nearly setting over the water far to the west.

He heard his escort walk up behind him. "You ready to go, sir? We can board anytime."

"Please, call me Brad. Or Sergeant if you have to," Brad said.

"Oh, yes... of course, Brad, no offense intended. You can call me Ian."

"Nice to meet you, Ian," Brad said with a forced smile. "It's fine. I'm just ready to get back to my team."

The sailor yelled to the other men near the raft. They quickly scaled the net ladder and boarded the small boat, then turned to assist Brad and the other sailor. This time, Brad was offered a plank seat near the rear of the boat.

Brad looked out over the water and saw the Coast Guard ship. He could see some of his team standing against the rail and watching him with binoculars.

"How long you boys been out here?" Brad asked without taking his eyes off the distant Coast Guard boat.

Ian stepped across the raft and settled in across from Brad while the other men tossed lines and pushed away from the submarine. "Out here? We haven't been home since it started… if that was your meaning," Ian answered.

"That's a long time to be away from home. I've been on the run since my convoy was ambushed weeks... months… hell, I kinda lost track. Haven't had a break either."

"Yeah… time doesn't matter as much anymore does it?" Ian said thoughtfully.

Ian reached into his pocket and offered Brad a cigarette. Brad shook his head. Ian let out a small chuckle. "I know... these'll kill me, right? All the bastards out there that quit? Look at them now."

The raft's small outboard motor came to life. The pilot revved the engine and steered toward the surface ship. Ian took a long drag on the cigarette and looked at Brad. "My Mum enjoys a good smoke." He paused and shook his head, like he hadn't had the thought in a long time. Ian continued speaking while looking out over the side, toward the setting sun. "We was on combat patrol in the Barents Sea when it started. This thing—whatever it is—it had been burning for three weeks before we broke radio silence and was informed. The skipper raced us back to port against orders… the time we arrived it was gone. Nobody came to the pier to meet us; everything, just gone.

"We tried to reach others. There were a few surface ships about, most with infected aboard, but we found and paired with a Norwegian destroyer for a couple weeks. But this is a nuke boat. We can run for twenty-five years before refueling. Most things we run into don't have that capability. We helped the Nords anchor safely offshore then parted ways."

"You ever hear from them?" Brad asked.

"Not sure… radio traffic isn't shared with us peons," Ian said with a low laugh. "Likely they are still out there. I'd like to think so. Captain promised to return for them one day."

Brad looked down and out at the water. "I've made the same promises."

The engine's speed was cut and idled. Brad looked up and saw they were slowly drifting into the Coast Guard ship. He saw Parker run to the rail and throw a rope to one of the sailors sitting in the front of the raft. Working together, the raft was pulled in close to the dive deck. Brad got to his feet and was quickly pulled aboard by Parker.

"Good to have you back, Sergeant. Where are the others?" Parker asked as Joey and Chelsea climbed down the ladder to greet him.

Brad stopped and looked around without answering.

"Where's Gunner?" Brad asked.

Chelsea moved between Joey and Parker, stopping at Brad's side. "Everything okay, Brad?"

Ignoring her question, Brad looked over his shoulder at the other sailors. They were still on the raft. "You coming aboard, Ian?"

"Sorry, mate; got my orders. The others will be staying over with ya tonight. Nice meeting you, Brad," Ian said as the engine revved up and the raft raced back toward the submarine in the fading light.

CHAPTER 9

"Shane," Ella mumbled, pushing at the tight blanket. He woke with a start and almost knocked Ella to the ground as he reached for his rifle. He paused and looked up at the orange sky.

No, he thought. They had slept through the day. The exhaustion from the days of travel and the cold of the river had been hard on him, but they couldn't be in the open after dark.

The soldier shushed the girl with a finger to his lips then crossed his arms in front of him. Ella understood the signal, and she'd been a good student after spending days with him on the trail. She stopped and lowered herself to the ground to sit on her heels motionless. Shane reached out and felt her light tank top. It was nearly dry and still warm from the huddled body heat. He lifted her clothing that he had draped on top of his bag and quickly dressed her.

He hurriedly dressed himself and stuffed the blanket into his pack. He pushed a fist through a strap and tightly fastened the bag to his back. Shane stood high on his knees like a prairie dog and looked in all directions. They were losing the light and he cursed himself again for the mistake. They needed to find cover soon. The things would be moving—they may already be out and on the hunt. He knew sundown was when they had always arrived at the fort and by nightfall, their numbers were always at the max, howling and throwing themselves at the walls.

Shane looked left and right. He saw the blacktop of the road in the distance; it was paved so it would likely hold structures, but structures also attracted the infected. Beyond the road was a thick wooded area. It could provide shelter but, again, it was a likely hiding place for the beasts. There was no time to debate; *path of least resistance,* he thought. He swooped his right hand down toward the ground and to his side. Ella quietly got to her feet and moved next to him. As she stood, she grabbed the back of his belt. Shane turned back and ruffled the hair on the girl's head. He knew he was pushing her hard, but she didn't complain. She responded by hugging his hip and pulling at his belt, signaling she was ready. Shane stepped off; they needed to move.

It was important to balance his movements with the tactical situation. The sun was falling and he didn't know where he was, so he had to assume they were in the middle of an infested area. He couldn't move too quickly. They would make too much noise, and one thing he knew for certain was that the things were drawn to human sounds. Shane stepped quickly enough but not so fast that the girl had to struggle to keep up. Occasionally he stopped to allow her to rest as he dropped low in the grass and looked in all directions.

They reached a small trail that ran parallel to the road. Shane checked it for markings and, finding none, he turned and headed south. They moved quicker now; out of the grass he could step more swiftly and still remain silent. The sun was dropping fast and he would have to make a decision soon. There was a hill ahead. If he didn't find shelter after summiting the small rise, he would have to break for the forest and find a high tree to hide in. As if telling him to hurry, he heard a faint howl in the distance.

Shane froze, dropped to his knee instinctively, and brought up his rifle. They were awake. He had to get out of the open. He dropped low and brought out both arms without speaking. Again Ella understood the non-verbal instruction and pulled herself onto his pack. Lying across the top of his bag, she pushed her legs over his right shoulder and then lowered her arms grabbing at his left arm to put herself in a fireman's carry. Shane reached up and patted her leg, then got to his feet. He moved out with much greater speed now, trying to conceal the building panic he was feeling. His back burned as the pain of his old injury returned.

He heard the howl again. Shane ignored the pain and tried to jog. He knew it would make him less aware of his surroundings, but they were in the area and he had to move. As he cleared the top of the hill, he paused just long enough to look in all directions. To his right, he could see where the woods stretched toward the road and almost touched it. He scanned to the left and paused, near the river stood a small house. The girl squirmed, he knew she was uncomfortable but it couldn't be helped.

More howling, this time from the woods, made the decision easy; he turned and began jogging toward the house. He was back in the field, he knew he was making noise but the situation had changed. He would now trade speed of movement for the noise as more howling in the distance made him think that they weren't hunting, but rather calling to each other. His back began to spasm, the pain shooting bolts up his spine. He consciously took deep breaths and forced his eyes open, refusing to quit. The girl lifted her arm and touched the side of his head.

Shane squinted and reopened his eyes. The girl's touch gave him renewed strength. They had bonded on the road, even though they rarely spoke, and somehow he had connected with her. She seemed to sense his pain and would try to comfort him. In return, he held her hand when she called for her parents in the darkest parts of the night. Shane didn't know where she came from or why, but if not for her, he would have quit long ago. He lived only to save her. For her, he could face his pain a while longer.

Once he was close to the house, within a hundred feet, he stopped jogging and slowed to a walk. He wanted to have his breathing under control before he got within earshot of the building. With no time to stop, he scouted the structure while moving forward. It was a large two story house nearly a football field's length from the river bank. The sides were flanked with a tall covered porch. There were several sheds and wood piles in the immediate vicinity. To one side, a long gravel driveway worked its way through tall, uncut grass and overgrown bushes.

A sharp pain traveled from his lower back to his neck, causing him to jolt forward and nearly fall to his knees. Shane crouched to relieve the pressure and walked to an outcropping of overgrown shrubs near the home's porch. He got low to the ground and felt Ella slide down beside him. He reached for her arm and helped her maneuver under the brush and into a tight hiding spot. Then he slid his bag in front of her, completely concealing her position.

Shane backed away from the brush and quickly checked his surroundings. He could still hear the moans in the distance. They hadn't increased or changed from the casual calls to the more intense high pitched calls of the hunt that he'd heard during the attack on the base. For the moment, he was still undetected and he needed to keep it that way. He resisted the urge to check the action on his rifle; he knew there were 10 rounds left, but either way he couldn't risk a shot with so much activity in the area.

He reached back and attached the bayonet, then slowly crept toward the house. As Shane looked for a front door, he noticed that two of the house's windows under the covered porch were open. He could see light fabric moving slightly in the evening breeze. He got lower and approached under the cover of the porch rail to the home's steps. He was relieved to see that they were made up of fieldstone and poured concrete, no squeaky boards to contend with... yet.

He placed a boot on the first step and approached slowly, pausing to listen after every movement. In the fading light, he could see the front door was partially open but still covered by a flimsy screen door. Shane crept closer, cautiously applying his weight to the floorboards of the porch. They felt sturdy under his feet and the years of built up dirt and moss concealed any sound of his boots. He sidestepped and put his left shoulder against the structure to keep the door in front of him. He looked back in the direction of Ella and listened. The moaning was present but remained far off.

Shane placed his gloved right hand on the screen door and slowly pulled it open. It let out a slight squeak, but Shane was already committed so he opened the door completely and used a block of wood he found on the floor to prop it open. As soon as he stepped into the home, he could smell strong scents of mildew and decayed death. Whatever had lived here passed long ago. There wasn't even enough left to keep the flies interested. In a corner chair, he could just make out the badly decomposed form of an elderly woman. Her head was back and her mouth open, a red afghan blanket draped across her lap.

He quickly surveyed the room and moved on down a hallway, past a small bathroom, and on to a long galley style kitchen. The house was clean and well kept; pictures still hung on the walls and things were in their correct place. Shane swung into the kitchen door and looked beyond a tall countertop and saw that another body rested at a lunch counter—an old man dressed in denim coveralls and a stained white shirt. A John Deere ball cap sat hooked to the back of his chair. His right hand lay open on a scrap of paper, his left still clutching a small handgun. Shane raised the bayonet and approached the man tactically. As he neared, he could see the exit wound at the top of the man's head.

First floor clear, he thought to himself and looked at the stairway leading to the second floor. He debated moving on, but he wanted to get Ella inside. His fear of being separated from the girl won out so he rushed back down the hallway and into the yard. Again, he picked speed over caution and quickly snatched up the bag with his right hand and let Ella take his left. He nearly dragged the girl back across the long grass and up the porch. Once inside, he dropped his bag and placed Ella on top of it. Shane put a finger to his lips and the girl nodded with understanding.

Shane slid the block of wood away from the door and let it swing shut before he closed and bolted the heavy wooden door. He approached and attempted to close the windows. The first easily slid into place, but the second was stuck, probably from the weeks of being open to the southern humidity. Shane took a chance and pushed hard at the sash, the swollen wood broke free and the window slammed home with a slap. It sounded much louder in the dead silence of the house. From the corner of his eye he watched Ella jump.

"It's okay, it was just me," he whispered.

From above them, he heard the creak of a floorboard and saw the girl's eyes grow big as she looked up at the ceiling. Shane held his breath as he heard another noise: more creaking of boards, but confined to the same area. Walking on the balls of his feet, he quickly moved back to Ella. He hoisted the bag with her still on top and carried it to an empty corner of the room near a long sofa table. Shane pointed, and Ella dropped off the bag and quickly crawled under the table. They could hide here tonight and sneak out in the morning, leaving whatever lurked upstairs alone. No, that wasn't the way to stay alive. "I'll be right back," he whispered hesitantly. Shane raised his rifle and patrolled back toward the stairs, careful to remain silent.

When he passed through the kitchen, he stopped at the dead man. Shane reached out and pried the man's finger from the handgun's trigger, then released it from his grip. A small Walther P22; not much punch, but it would beat throwing rocks. Shane released the magazine and saw rounds stacked in the top, which was enough for now. He cleared the weapon and dropped it into his cargo pocket. He again saw the slip of paper, the man had written a note but his decomposing hand had all but obscured the text. Another creak from above brought him back into the moment. Shane turned and walked to the stairway. He cautiously placed his left boot on the step and slowly applied his weight. The old wood treads protested and filled the home with a sound that was quickly answered by the creaking upstairs. Shane continued moving. The higher he got up the stairs, the more the creaking turned to pounding and then stomping. But still no moans or screams… yet.

The stairway topped out at a long, open loft. Three doors stood against a far wall; two of which were hanging open. It was the door on the end where the pounding came from. Even without the moans, Shane began to fear that other infected outside would be drawn to the sounds of the pounding. His urgency to silence the thing increased. Shane stepped quickly to the door and tested the handle. It turned easily, so he pushed lightly and felt the door swing in. He let the door rest just inches open, preparing for an impact. Nothing happened, other than the pounding became frenzied.

Fearing the worst, he forced the door open hard and pivoted in with the rifle and bayonet extended, ready to attack. As he rotated into the room the stench hit him in the face. He reeled back and nearly vomited before he caught sight of the creature. The terror of the bloodied and soiled beast chained to a floor anchor was more than he bargained for. His back stiffened and he felt his muscles tighten as his system surged with adrenalin. Shane stepped back, fear moving his feet involuntarily. He fought the muscles in his arms to keep the rifle up. His hands shook as the creature lunged at him, the links of the chain clanking with every move of the infected man.

He felt the door behind him and stopped his backward movement. He crouched and quickly searched the room with his eyes. It was a boy's bedroom, a teenage boy. Rock posters hung from the walls, model cars on a shelf. But in the corner… that's where *it* was, chained near a soiled and bare mattress. The thing looked at Shane with hate while its arms maliciously reached for him. Shane could see where the thing had pulled at the chain so hard, it created wounds and had torn the skin on its neck. Its mouth was taped shut and its hands were balled, covered with fabric–old socks maybe—and taped into mitts.

The end of the chain had been anchored to the floor with a heavy bolt. Whoever did this knew the boy was dangerous, that he would turn.

"God in heaven, why would they keep it alive," he mumbled.

Shane looked at the young man with pity, seeing it for the thing it once was. He stepped forward with the rifle held firmly. He slashed with the bayonet and felt the resistance as it lacerated the boy's shoulder and neck. The thing stumbled back and then rushed again at Shane. The soldier was ready. He planted his left leg and lifted the blade to meet the thing. He caught it in the heart then, without pausing, yanked back on the rifle and stabbed forward to impale the thing's face.

Instantly, the creature went limp and dropped to the floor, taking the bayoneted rifle with it. Shane stepped in and planted his boot on the thing's neck, pulled back, and withdrew the blade from its skull. He stepped away from the dead creature, scanning the room as he backpedaled. Shane eased out of the doorway and pulled the door shut behind him, then leaned against the wall. He was breathing hard and sweat poured down his back. He rested there, catching his breath as the remaining light faded from the room.

His legs fell weak; he considered dropping to the floor and sitting against the wall, but moans from outside shocked him to his senses and reminded him of the girl. He should get back to her. Shane took a last deep breath through his mouth, trying to block the rancid air. He moved lightly through the room, reaching for the stair railing in the dark. He gripped the railing and cautiously walked to the bottom. The light was gone now, so Shane dug in his pocket for a small pen light. He covered the lens with the sleeve of his jacket and clicked it on.

Even with the lens covered, the surefire threw a soft glow over the floor in front of him. Shane only left the light on long enough to visually map the room then clicked it back off. He moved forward, making a wide path around the dead man. He padded through the kitchen and back into the doorway leading to the family room, where he had left the girl. Again, he clicked on the light, quickly searched the room, and clicked it off. He walked softly to the sofa table, reached down with his open hand, and touched the bag. He knelt down then dropped to his rear before he carefully scooted back until he felt the girl beside him.

Shane sat there and put his arm out. The girl grabbed his gloved finger and slid closer, then climbed onto his lap. They sat silently, Shane listening for every sound outside, every gust of wind, every howl, and every moan. The longer he sat, the more his eyes adjusted to the low light. Soon he could make out objects in the room and see the glow of moonlight coming in from under the doors and around the window's curtains. He knew the front door was locked and bolted, but in his haste, he had forgotten to check for a back entrance.

"Shane," Ella whispered.

"Yeah?"

"Can we leave? It stinks funny in here," she asked.

Shane looked around the room. She was right; the dead grandma in the corner, mixed with the mildew and rot, didn't make for a comfortable resting spot. He had only given the upstairs rooms a cursory glance, but at least there he could safely open a window. He heard more moaning coming from outside. They seemed closer now; he imagined them in the yard.

"Okay, let's go," he whispered to her.

Shane got to his feet and flung the heavy pack onto his shoulders. He grabbed his rifle and let it hang from its sling. He felt the girl reach for his leg, her hands slipped up until she had a solid handhold on his belt.

"It's gonna be really dark but just hold on, okay?" he whispered.

"Okay, Shane," Ella replied in low voice.

CHAPTER 10

Brad stood on the deck, suddenly tired. He looked through those crowded around him and watched the raft fade from view as it slipped into the darkness. Joey moved closer, a cigarette hanging from his lips.

"Sergeant, so what happened over there? Where are Sean and Brooks?" Joey asked.

"Huh, oh... we'll be going ashore soon. The Brits have located a survivor's camp. Chief's making arrangements," Brad answered, just giving away enough to feel honest. He turned and headed for the passageway to search for Gunner.

Chelsea moved in front of him. "Wait... aren't you going to tell us what happened over there?"

"That's all I have to say right now. I need to speak with Gunner; you're welcome to come with me if you'd like," Brad said moving around her. He walked to the port door and entered, turning to follow the ladder to the lower deck and galley. As he navigated the stairs, he heard the footfalls behind him and knew Chelsea had chosen to follow.

Brad stepped onto the landing and moved toward the galley door. The door's latch was down and secured. The fact that the door was latched shut confirmed his suspicions that this was where Gunner had taken the visitors. He held up and stood at the hatch, just as Chelsea moved up behind him. She reached out and grabbed his forearm as he was about to knock.

"Brad what's going on?" she asked.

He held his hand in the air, searching for the right words. "To be honest, I don't know what's happening and I don't know how to explain it all." As he finished he pounded on the door, then dropped his hand to open the hatch.

As he suspected, Gunner was inside with the visitors positioned around him at a table. Kelli had also moved from her position at the helm and joined them. They had all turned to look at Brad as he walked in with Chelsea following close behind.

"Ahh, great, you're back. Chief Richardson here had just gotten off the radio with his superiors," Gunner said.

Brad moved across the galley and touched the coffee maker. It was warm and heavy so he flipped a lever and filled his cup.

"So you know then?" he asked.

Richardson turned in his seat and stared at Brad with concerned eyes. "Yes, it has all been sorted out, Sergeant," he answered.

"Sorted?" Brad asked.

Gunner stood and walked over to fill his own cup. "Yes, Brad, Commander Stuart already sent us our destination. We'll be starting the engines and moving that way very soon. If we sail through the night, we should make Charleston by first light."

Kelli got up from her own seat. "On that note, I should be getting back upstairs. Nelson will have us at the North Pole if I leave him to navigate alone," she laughed, "If you gentleman will excuse me."

"Wait, Charleston? Why there?" Chelsea asked, taking everyone's attention.

Gunner spoke first. "The Brits here say they've made contact with a group of survivors holding out on an island—."

"They're at Fort Sumter," Brad finished.

"Fort Sumter… the one from the civil war?" Chelsea asked.

"One in the same," said Gunner, moving back to his seat at the table. "Makes sense, really— small, walled compound surrounded by water."

Chelsea moved across the room and sat in Kelli's now empty seat. "Is there anything else? Did you get word from the government? Do we know what's going on at home?"

Gunner waved a hand at Richardson, and then sat back in his chair. Richardson lifted his cup, sipped, and grimaced. "You really do not have any tea?" he asked. "I don't know how you drink this bitter crud."

He put the cup down and looked across the table. "Corporal Swanson, is it?"

Chelsea nodded. Before she could speak, Richardson continued, "From what Gunner has told me, you have all been out for some time. It's rather remarkable that you have made it all this way."

"Not all of us made it," Chelsea said.

"Yes, lots of death. We haven't had any official contact with your nation in over a month. Not since Washington fell," Richardson said.

"That doesn't make sense; they couldn't have all just gone."

"We know that as your government fell apart, some entities moved west into the mountains. Others broke apart and fell behind defensive lines—"

Brad rinsed his empty cup and returned it to a cupboard. "I know… we've already heard this story. Gunner was there as Washington fell. But still, how is it we haven't heard from anyone?"

Richardson laughed sarcastically. "What do you want me to say? That we've picked up reports day and night of communities being overrun, listened to them scream and beg for rescue? Families barricaded in their homes begging for help? Is that the news you are looking for? I have plenty of that. I have a radioman that can't sleep at night after the horrors he has listened to over the past month.

"I don't bloody know why the radios went silent in recent days. Maybe the generators finally died, maybe batteries have been expended. I can't afford to speculate; all we know is we have had consistent messages from Charleston. Have we reached out to them? No. But we still know they are there."

"Why haven't you talked to them?" Chelsea asked.

"Because there are others out there... others that want what we have," Richardson said.

"You mean the submarine?" Chelsea said.

"That among other things," Richardson said looking at Brad.

Chelsea saw Brad's expression change as Richardson looked in his direction. "Why do I feel like I am the only one in the room being left out of something?" she said.

The boat's engines started. Brad felt the vibration go through the ship's structure then, slowly, it edged forward as the throttles opened. Brad placed a hand against the counter to steady himself as the speed gradually increased. He looked at the drawn faces in the room. Chelsea's cheeks had turned red and he could tell she was upset but attempting to hide it.

"Why don't you just get this over with, Gunner? No point in hiding it until morning," Brad said, walking to a lone seat at a far table.

Gunner held his poker face and looked across the table to Richardson who nodded. Gunner sipped at the coffee then placed the cup on the table, holding it with both hands. "Okay, from what I understand there is an American doctor on board the submarine that just may hold the key to un-fucking the entire planet?"

Brad shook his head. "Really, is that how you interpreted this? The doctor doesn't have shit; he needs us for that."

"I don't understand," Chelsea said. "Who is this doctor?"

Richardson quickly relayed Howard's story, how he came to be on the submarine, and all about the patient. He told them about the mission they were planning to recover the sample and how the Americans and their vessel would now play a pivotal role.

Chelsea sat quietly absorbing Richardson's words. When he finished, she looked up at him. "You think this little girl could still be alive?"

Richardson looked at her thoughtfully. "If the doctor is right, we have to try."

"I'm going," Chelsea said.

Gunner put his hands up. "Okay, let's all slow down a bit. We don't have to make any decisions tonight."

Brad cleared his throat and stood. "Gunner's right. And to be honest, I'm tired of listening to these stories. I'm going to try to get some rest before I relieve the guys on deck. I suggest you all do the same, sounds like tomorrow is going to be a busy day."

Brad turned and, walking through the hatch, left the galley. He worked his way through the ship and into the small berthing compartment he shared with the other men. The lights were dimmed but he could see that Parker and Joey were still above on the deck. Nelson's rack was also empty—probably at the controls with Kelli. Brad found his bunk and sat on the bed as he removed his boots. There wasn't much he could do tonight and he really was tired of discussing the mission to find the girl… or her remains.

He knew he would go if asked, even though it was the last thing he wanted. Brad wasn't in the business of turning down the tough assignments. He was tired from his travels and just wanting to return home, but if Sean decided this was the right thing to do then he would get on board with it.

Having removed his boots, he lay back on the rack, planning to only take a time out before making his way above to check on the rest of the crew. The waters were calm here, the slow swells gently rocking the boat as it moved through the water. He imagined Brooks and Sean on the submarine hunched over maps, planning their next mission. The hum of the engine reverberated through the small berthing compartment. Brad rolled to his side and closed his eyes, just wanting to rest for a bit.

CHAPTER 11

Shane sat in a chair in the corner of the master bedroom. It was dark, but the moonlight lit the room in a shade of deep blue. The girl was sleeping soundly; he'd found blankets in a closet and spread them over the bed then wrapped her in them. Even though they'd slept the entire day, the girl drifted off quickly. Shane worried that it was from lack of food. He hadn't found much to eat and the barge captain had taken most of his supplies as a form of payment.

When he thought about the precious food he had turned over to the man and then basically being forced to walk the plank, Shane had no feelings of remorse about tossing the grenade. Besides, they surely would have killed them as soon as they hit the water and the grenade was the only diversion he had. The moaning grew louder and distracted him from his thoughts. He lowered himself to the floor and looked through the small crack at the bottom of the window.

In this back part of the house, he could just make out the river. The light from the moon reflected back at him. He recognized the small path that ran parallel to the bank. It was there that he spotted a small empty boat dock. The moan came again, closer this time. Shane got lower on his knees and intently looked into the distance. Concentrating, his eyes adjusted and he picked up on their subtle movements.

Three figures were on the path near the river but they appeared to be facing the house and studying it somehow. Shane wished for his night vision goggles. They were in his pack but the batteries were long dead. His rifle only had iron sites; it was an older model and had treated him well, but he wouldn't be able to see anything in the dark. He pushed the thoughts from his mind and focused on the figures near the path. He watched as the group separated; two continued on, while one turned and walked the small trail that led to the house.

Shane felt his heart rate quicken and sweat form on his back as the figure moved closer. He moved farther away from the window, concealing himself even more in the dark shadows of the room. He imagined the creature could see him, even though he knew it was paranoia, and he considered moving to the first floor to kill the thing before it could sound a warning to the others. Shane watched as it left the trail and disappeared close to the house. It was too close now for him to see, so he turned and moved back to the chair.

He lifted the rifle and let the handgrips give him comfort. Seated deeply in the chair, he listened. He heard the squeak of old boards as the thing stepped onto the covered front porch.

There was a banging and scratching of wood, then the rattle of glass. The girl sat up, frightened by the sounds. Shane moved to the bed, sat beside her, and put his hand on her back, whispering that it was okay.

"It's just checking the place out. Once it finds the doors locked, it'll move on, Ella," Shane whispered.

The noise stopped and Shane heard the creature once again plod across the wooden porch. He knew it was looking for a back door or an easy way in. Shane knew the things were lazy. They wouldn't force their way into a home, not unless they knew prey was inside. If a door was open, or they found an easy entrance, of course they would venture in. But Shane had never seen them risk injury to themselves to break into an empty room. *Maybe lazy isn't the right word for it,* Shane thought, *maybe it was a deep sense of self preservation. Breaking glass and wood for nothing wasn't a character trait of any animal.*

The squeaking suddenly stopped and was replaced by a more solid pounding. It must have found the back door. Shane prayed that it was locked. In his haste to secure a hiding place, he'd neglected to check it. He heard it pound again against the heavy door; the wood rattled as it tugged and pulled at the doorknob. Shane heard a moan from below, still not the rabid moans of them on the hunt but more of a frustrated whine. Ella took Shane's hand and pulled it to her cheek; he could feel her shaking. No longer hearing the thing at the door, he lowered himself onto the bed and lay next to the girl. He pulled the blanket over her and tucked her in tight.

He stared at the door, listening as the sounds caused his mind to drift. The house made tiny creaks and groans as most old houses would. Shane grew up on a rural farm where he was raised by his grandfather. His bedroom was not unlike this one, in the upper corner of a hundred-year-old farm house. In the days after his mother died, he'd spent many nights like this lying in bed listening to the house speak. He would imagine she was walking up the stairs, coming to get him to bring him home. But mother never came.

His grandfather was strict but not abusive. He raised him to respect hard work and to appreciate a job well done. He'd taught him how to hunt and fish, how to track an animal, and how to prepare it for the stove. He remembered going on long walks in the woods, his grandfather pointing out different plants and showing him how they could be eaten or used to treat a wound or an insect bite. If they had walked too far, sometimes they would bivouac in the open for fun and make their way back home at first light.

Later, when all of his friends were driving cars and chasing girls, Shane was home taking care of his grandfather as dementia slowly took hold of him. When his grandfather began to fall and could no longer stay home safely, the people from the state came and took him to a nursing home. Because Shane had just turned eighteen, he was allowed to stay alone until he finished school. Neighbors would check in on him from time to time, but those were still the loneliest days of his life. His grandfather passed away a day after he graduated from high school and a day after that, the tax man showed up to take the farm.

With nothing else to do, he enlisted in the Army, telling the recruiter he wanted to leave as soon as possible. The Army became his family; he suddenly had real brothers to call his own. Shane adapted to his new life and thrived. He never forgot the farm but the painful memories of the place faded from his mind. He was finally able to smile again and have hopeful thoughts about the future until one day, on a hot desert road, everything once again was taken from him—his new family, his health, and the Army.

Shane was lying in the same position as sunlight slowly filled the room. He pushed away from the bed, not really knowing if he'd slept or not. He felt as if his mind had never shut off. He was mentally and physically exhausted. His back was protesting, and when he stood, he felt the tightness in his muscles as he stretched. Shane moved to the window and looked into the yard. He stood motionless with an arm against the wall, silently watching, looking for any signs of them.

He heard the girl stir on the bed and turned.

"I'm hungry, Shane," he heard her say.

He looked at the watch on his wrist; it was nearly 8am, close to twenty four hours since their last meal. Shane lifted his heavy pack onto the bed and dug through a waterproof bag where he'd stored their rations. There wasn't much left: some crackers that had been crushed to dust, a small block of cheese, and more of the granola. He pushed the bag back into his ruck and zipped it shut.

"Okay, Ella, let's see what we can find downstairs," he said to her. Shane moved to the closet where he'd found the blankets the night before and pulled down a folded sheet. Shane looked back at her, helped her off the bed, and she smiled at him. "Okay, follow me."

He slowly walked down the open staircase, stopping every few steps to listen. He knew the room was clear. He'd secured it the night before, but it always paid double to err on the side of caution. He stepped onto the landing and looked into the kitchen. Bright light now filled the room and, scanning, he could see that it was empty. The old man still sat where he had left him. The body was slumped in a kitchen chair with its head melded into the countertop.

"Wait here," he told the girl as she came up behind him at the bottom of the steps.

Shane moved to the old man and covered him with the bed sheet. He then put on his gloves and grabbed the mummified corpse under the arms and dragged it away from the counter. The chair stuck to the body and made a scratching sound as it slid across the kitchen floor. Shane twisted, lifted the stiff body, and dragged it down the hall into the living room. He let the body sit in the middle of the now well-lit room.

Shane quickly assessed the space. There was nothing here for him. He looked at the old woman in the corner; she had been dead for a long time, same as the old man. The room held the stench of death and decay. He found an old blanket lying over a sofa arm which he quickly retrieved and draped it over the old woman. He heard Ella call for him so he retreated from the space and moved back into the kitchen.

The girl was waiting for him at the bottom of the stairs. She looked up at him. "What are you doing, Shane?"

"Oh, nothing for you to worry about. Now, let's see if we can get us something to eat," he said as he reached down and lifted her up. Shane carried her across the room and sat her at a round kitchen table. "You wait here and let me see what these people left for us."

Shane walked into the kitchen and opened a tall pantry that rested against a wall. It was nearly empty; a few mason jars filled with vegetables, a bag of flour, and a box of cornbread mix.

"Well, that's no good," he said as he moved toward a set of kitchen cabinets. Shane opened each door and drawer one at a time, finding dishes, glasses, and old cook books until finally, he moved across the room and opened a deep drawer next to the stove. He smiled when he looked inside then pulled out a nearly half-full box of corn flakes.

"Well, look at this, Ella," Shane said, holding the box up.

She smiled back at him and giggled. "Can we have it?"

"Sure can," he answered rooting through a cupboard for a couple bowls. He grabbed them in one hand and walked back to the table. He placed a bowl in front of the girl and filled it with the corn flakes. "Sorry there's no milk. If they had a cow, I'd go milk her for you," he said, causing Ella to giggle.

She reached into the bowl and grabbed at the cereal. "Mmm, it's good. Are you gonna eat, Shane?"

"Nahh, I'll let you have this. I'll eat some of them nasty canned vegetables. I figure I'd do better at tolerating them then you would."

The girl nodded in response as she ate. Shane walked to the old refrigerator, pulled a rag from his pocket, and used his left hand to hold the rag over his nose and mouth. He opened the door and looked inside. As he suspected, it was filled with rotting and molded food. But it also held several cans of soda and a few sealed bottles of water. He quickly reached in with his right hand and removed anything sealed then closed the door.

"Today is your lucky day, girl; you get a warm cola with your breakfast." He used the rag to wipe the top of the can clean and then popped the top. He took a sip of the warm liquid then placed the can in front of the girl. As he turned to walk back to the counter where he'd placed the other cans and bottles, a yellow box on top of the refrigerator caught his eye. He stopped, then walked over, reached up, and grabbed the box.

He already knew what it was: several hundred rounds of .22 long rifle for the pistol he'd found the night before. He sat the nearly-full box on the counter and moved to the stove. He stood staring at the knob. This was the most luck they'd had in days, but would it continue? He turned the knob and heard the gas hiss. Shane smiled as he turned it back off. He dug though his pocket for his small disposable lighter; it was low on fuel but this would be worth it. He turned the knob back on and held the lighter to the burner. It quickly lit and Shane adjusted the flame until it burnt a bright blue.

"Now maybe those canned veggies won't be so harsh after all. Heck, I can even make us up some pan fried cornbread," Shane said to the girl with an exaggerated grin.

CHAPTER 12

The slamming of the berthing hatch woke him. He looked around the dark space and watched Nelson stumbling around in the dark. "Turn on the light if you need to," Brad said, pulling himself up into a seated position.

"Thank you," Nelson said as he reached up and felt for a switch before flicking on the light. Nelson kicked off his boots, quickly fell to the bed, and stretched out across it. "Damn, I'm tired. Kelli doesn't ever give me a break. That woman is a hard charger to the core," he laughed.

Brad chuckled with him. "She doesn't mess around, that's for sure. Hey, what time you got?"

"Oh, it's nearly oh six hundred; we should be near the harbor in another few hours."

"Damn, I didn't plan to fall asleep like that," Brad said, reaching for his boots.

"Why not? Ain't shit else for you to do while we're out here," Nelson said.

"Yeah, I know, but I wanted to have a word with Gunner before we reached Charleston."

"About the girl?" Nelson asked.

"The girl?" Brad said, unable to hide the shock in his voice.

"The sick one or whatever she is. Gunner said we're going to go help –," Nelson paused and took in a deep yawn. "Find her or something."

"So everyone knows now, huh? What do the rest of the guys think about it?"

"Oh… I don't know; most of us just want to get off this damn boat. Sergeant, you mind if I cut that light?" Nelson asked as he rolled to his side.

"Don't worry about it, I'll get it on my way out," Brad said as he left the compartment.

Brad stepped into the P-way and looked back toward the galley; the hatch was dogged open and the light was off. He turned and moved to the ladder that went up to the deck. He found Joey lying back in a chair, sound asleep, with his rifle cradled in his hands. It had been Joey's habit to sleep up on deck when the weather was nice. The Marine didn't like being below decks if he didn't have to. Brad walked past him and climbed up to the bridge.

He got to the top deck and followed the rail to the wheelhouse, opened the hatch, and stepped inside. He saw that Gunner was sleeping in one of the leather captain's chairs. Parker was behind the wheel while Kelli sat in a far chair sipping coffee. She looked at him and nodded nonchalantly. Brad walked behind them and found the coffee pot. He poured a cup and sat at an empty navigation table. Brad saw that the GPS monitor screen was dark green, and in white letters it read *SAT NOT ACQUIRED*.

"So, you know where we're going?" Brad asked. "Would hate to get lost out here in the dark."

Kelli looked at him and pointed far ahead in the hazy fog. In the early morning light, he could just make out the red navigation beacon of the submarine.

"It isn't that difficult to follow a light; it's so easy a Parker could do it," she joked.

"Hey watch it," Parker said without taking his eyes off the view in front of him.

Brad tapped the screen. "How long has the GPS been out?"

"It comes and goes," Kelli said. "Satellites are still up there but with nobody to maintain them and the software, they're going to start dropping."

"How long for all of that to happen?" Brad asked.

"It's a loaded question. I'm no expert but I suspect the very low orbit ones are probably already failing. The higher up stuff might last ten years, a hundred years, or even longer. Doesn't matter though; with nothing on the ground to talk to them, they're just floating boat anchors."

Gunner snored loudly. His head leaned back then slumped forward without him waking up. Brad looked at Gunner and smiled. "So how long's that stubborn fool been up here? Anyone remind him there are racks below deck?"

Parker looked over at Gunner. "He's been up here most of the night. Said he wanted to be close—you know, as long as Chief and Brooks are over on the sub..." Parker said.

"Always on point," Brad half whispered to himself.

Brad heard heavy footfalls on the ladder. He looked over his shoulder and saw Joey walking toward the bridge with the British sailors following. Joey nodded to him through the window when they made eye contact. He pulled the hatch open and waved the sailors in ahead of him. He stepped through and closed the hatch behind them.

"Damn, it's getting chilly out there," Joey said.

"You're joking, right mate?" one of the British sailors quipped back.

Joey shook his head and marched towards the coffee pot. "No man, I'm from Cali; this is too damn cold for me."

"Fuck you, man!" Brad yelled jokingly. "You want to go back to Newfoundland? This is tropical compared to that rock."

"Yeah, yeah, yeah," Joey said as he finished pouring his coffee.

He moved across the room and leaned against a far console. "So anyway, Chief Richardson here was looking for Gunner," Joey said as he pointed to Richardson who had been standing quietly behind them.

Richardson grinned at being acknowledged and used the back of his hand to smack Gunner's chair. "This chap can sleep through a hurricane, can't he?"

Gunner jumped forward in the chair and looked around him. "What the hell is going on?" he yelled, reacting to the slap.

"Oh good, you're awake," Richardson laughed.

"I am now," Gunner growled.

"New orders, mate," Richardson said, holding up the radio. "Skipper says we are a couple hours out from Charleston. He wants us to hold in place while the others join us. Then we will reconnoiter ahead on our own."

"Why we going on alone?" Gunner asked as he yawned.

"Skipper doesn't want to risk the boat. Too many unknowns close to shore. Don't worry, Yank, he'll have us on radar and we can call for support if you get scared."

Parker looked back at Kelli. "They're stopping, ma'am," he said, pointing ahead at the submarine. Bright lights had been illuminated, casting a white hue through the fog and making the submarine appear to glow.

"Bring us up around their port side and keep us a hundred meters off... if that is acceptable Chief?" Kelli said, looking to Richardson for confirmation.

"Make it happen. Gunner can you join me on the dive deck? I'll let the team know we're ready for them to come aboard," Richardson said, moving back to the hatch. He un-dogged the latch and exited, followed by his men.

Gunner exhaled a long sigh while he got to his feet and followed. As he stepped through the hatch, he stopped and looked back at Brad. "Well… get off your asses, it's time to earn your pay."

"What fucking pay?" Joey asked.

Brad laughed. "It's a figure of speech, hero; come on let's go."

Brad moved out of the bridge, following the others down the ladder. When he reached the bottom, he saw that Nelson and Chelsea had already been called on and were standing with the others on the dive deck.

"Here they come!" Nelson shouted.

Brad jumped to the deck and moved around to the far rail. In the distance, he could see two inflatables cutting through the still water in their direction. It didn't take long for them to move up alongside. The first boat held Sean and the others. When the raft pulled up, they were quickly welcomed aboard. Then the second raft moved in and several large nylon bags were passed over the rail and stacked in the center of the deck.

Nelson carried one of the heavy bags across the deck and let it drop next to the others. "Shit's heavy, what's in them?" he asked.

"Food and ammo," Sean answered, moving across the deck to shake Gunner's hand.

Howard separated himself from the others and moved toward the bulkhead. He stood silently, holding a heavy leather satchel. Brad watched him as he nervously held the bag close to his chest. Meyers moved close to the doctor and stood next to him before speaking.

"Well, gentleman, it's up to us now. You will find gear and ammo in the bags. You are welcome to split up everything… except that black bag. That's my gear, so keep out of it. You can split that up when I'm dead," he shouted before turning to Richardson. "Chief, can you tell them we are ready to proceed to the harbor, and let's open this tub up a bit – I'm in a hurry to get this started."

"Aye, sir," Richardson sounded off, then turned and nodded to one of the British sailors who quickly turned to climb the ladder.

CHAPTER 13

Shane prepared all of the food he could. He filled his own stomach on the canned vegetables—eating cooked beans, tomatoes and carrots—while he encouraged the girl to eat all of the cereal. He knew it was important to get their calories when they could. Shane made pancakes with the cornbread and let them cook a little longer then they needed, trying to dry them out so that they would travel without spoiling. He found some Ziploc bags in the kitchen and packaged as much food as he could.

He retrieved their bags from upstairs and began rearranging and packing their gear. He removed all of their water bottles; most were empty but what water was left he poured into a tall glass that he told Ella to drink. The farmhouse had a well but would require electricity to run. He looked out of the back door to the river. He hated the thought of drinking the murky water, but here he could at least boil it on the stove.

Shane took all the empty bottles from his bag and lined them up on the counter. He found a small recyclable grocery bag in a cupboard and loaded all of the bottles in it. He pulled the small Walther pistol from his cargo pocket, then reached in and found the magazine. He pushed against the rounds and felt stiff resistance. The magazine only took two rounds from the box to top it off. He slid the magazine home and chambered a round.

The girl was still sitting at the kitchen table, babbling to herself and using a grease marker to draw on the wood surface. "Ella, I'm going to walk down to the dock and get water," he said.

"No, Shane, I don't want you to go," she pouted.

"It's okay; I'll only be gone a few minutes. You'll be okay in here." She agreed, but Shane saw the worry on her face as he took the bottle bag from the counter and slung his rifle.

He showed her how to work the lock on the kitchen door, and then he watched her work the lever with her tiny fingers several times to make sure she could. It was barely 10am, and he was confident he wouldn't see any of them this time of day, but he still wouldn't leave them an open door. He rubbed her head, brushed the hair from her eyes, and told her to just sit quietly. Shane turned the lever on the knob, then stepped onto the porch; closing the door behind him and feeling the latch catch. He heard the clunk of the bolt as Ella worked the lever. He checked to make sure it locked and then moved toward the steps.

Shane stepped onto the stone path that led to the river. The grass on both sides of the path was tall and overgrown. He knelt down and looked in both directions; he could just make out the muddy trail that ran parallel to the river. If they were out there, that's where they would come from. After sitting still for several minutes, he was confident he was alone and not being watched. Shane got back to his feet and hastily moved in the direction of the dock.

The dock was made up of aluminum planking and sat just above the level of the water. Branches and logs had piled up against it on one side, but the pylons still held it securely in place. Shane stepped onto the dock just far enough so that he could reach the water. He tied all of the bottles to a string and lowered them in one at a time, letting them fill and sink below the water's surface. He quickly pulled the rope and retrieved bottles after the bubbles stopped.

Shane turned and surveyed the area again to make sure nothing had moved in behind him. The way was clear, so he stepped off and started moving back to the house. He stopped when he crossed the trail—there were footprints in the mud. They were fresh, so they must have been from the things he observed the night before. Two of the infected were barefoot, but the third had a track Shane recognized. It was the boot with a four-pronged heel; the same track he'd spotted when he initially left the river.

Curious now, Shane followed the track a short distance before he saw that it separated from the others and moved toward the house before disappearing onto the stone path. *So, it* was *the one that went to the door,* he thought to himself. *Did the thing track us back to the house... all the way from the river bank? Or was it coincidence? We traveled from the road the night before, so it couldn't have tracked us from the trail, but why did it stop at the house? If it came back tonight, it may try to enter the place.* Shane was planning to hold up there for a few days while they rested, but now, with one this close and possibly tracking him, he couldn't risk it.

He looked around again in all directions, then rushed to the house. On the porch, he tapped at the door the way he'd discussed with Ella and the girl quickly opened it. Shane closed the door behind him and turned the lever to lock it. Not wasting time, he moved back to the counter and dumped the bag of bottles. He dug through a deep drawer and pulled out a large pot and placed it on the stove. Quickly, he poured the contents of all of the bottles into the pot and then put in the bottles themselves. After he turned on the heat, he quickly searched the rest of the house.

Shane didn't know where he was, or where he was going, and he needed to find out. He walked back into the living room and found a stack of old newspapers and mail. He unfolded the paper; it was a local county ledger of sorts. Dated late July, only a week or so into the fall, if he remembered correctly. This part of the country held up pretty well for the first few weeks. The southwest fell first as the infected crossed in from Mexico and up through California. Then it spread up and in through the heartland. Eventually, the Northeast was infected as the virus raged over the border from Canada and down the east coast. The paper was absent of any real news. There were only the warnings to remain indoors and some vague stories of rioting in Arizona.

The paper said *Charleston County*; the address on the mail read *Summerton*. The barge captain had said they were moving south to the sea and a survivor's camp near there. Shane found an old desk, dug through the drawers, and was rewarded with a worn state roadmap. He unfolded it and scanned its surface. On the back was a location guide. It wasn't precise enough to navigate, but he could use it to get his bearings. He tried comparing the address on the mail to the map. He couldn't pinpoint his location but could see the river on the map, and he traced it down to where it met the harbor. Moving his finger along the city outlines, he could see the greater limits of what was identified as Summerton, but it was on the wrong side of the river.

From the map, he guessed he was north of the international airport and somewhere on the west bank of the river. He knew they had traveled mostly through wooded areas, no big cities, and very few large bridges, so he must be just outside of the city. Still, where could he go? He couldn't travel the river south since the captain would surely be looking for him and would have put out the word about the girl. He couldn't go due west; Atlanta would be packed with infected. He knew from early reports at the armory that Fort Jackson was gone and abandoned, so the North was out. Then he remembered the stories about Hunter Army Airfield in Savannah.

After Washington D.C. was lost, many units broke up and fortified themselves in smaller bases. One of those units was the Ranger regiment headquartered at Savannah. Shane heard stories about the Rangers at Hunter Airfield having held off wave after wave of the infected. They even ran convoy operations out of the area, helping rescue survivors. Because the airfields were fortified and well-defended, the government was able to make relief flights to them.

That was at the beginning, though, when aviation fuel was still readily available. *Would the Rangers still be there?* Shane pondered to himself. *They should be; up until a few days ago even Fort Collins was still there, surely the Rangers would be.* He looked at the map and used a sheet of paper to guess the scale. It had to be at least a hundred miles over swamp and rough terrain if he traveled directly. *We don't have any other choice,* he thought.

"Yes, I'll get her to Savannah; it's her only chance," Shane whispered.

Shane folded the map and stuck it in a chest pocket of his uniform top. He surveyed the room one last time, looking for anything that would be useful. He checked his wristwatch; it was approaching noon so they would have to move soon. He rushed back to the kitchen where the water was boiling heavily. He turned off the stove and used kitchen tongs to remove the soft plastic bottles. The boiling deformed them, but they were now sterile and would still hold water.

Ella watched him curiously as he packed his rucksack with the bags of food while he allowed the water to cool.

"Are we leaving, Shane?" she asked, dropping the grease marker she'd been using to draw on the kitchen table.

"I'm afraid so, Ella. I don't think it's safe here."

"Where are we going?"

"I know a place; we can find friends there," Shane said, hoping is words were true.

"Will my momma be there?" she asked.

He frowned. Since the day Shane found the girl at the armory clinic, she'd occasionally asked about her mother. When he found her, Shane didn't waste time trying to recover information about her. His priority was getting her dressed and away from the area. He'd seen the bandaged wound on her arm and knew she would probably turn, but he didn't have it in him to leave her behind—besides maybe it *was* just a cut, he'd told himself. In that first day, she didn't speak. She had hung onto his neck and when he looked down at her she would stare back with hollow eyes. Shane figured she was heavily sedated or most likely in shock.

He'd managed to carry her away from the armory and down a long road, back into a neighborhood he was familiar with. They made it to an old auto shop and hid in it as the sun was setting, sleeping in the back of an old SUV that was up on a lift. The girl never spoke; all through the night she just stared at him with those sad, empty eyes. When morning came, he asked her if she was thirsty. In response, she asked him for her mother. Even now, he still didn't know what to tell her.

"Maybe, but we have a long way to go, so we need to hurry," he said as he moved back to the stove and prepared to fill the bottles.

"But I like it here," she whined.

"We'll find another place, Ella."

CHAPTER 14

As the Coast Guard ship navigated near Charleston, they spotted the island fort at the mouth of the harbor. There were no flags flying at the top of its pole, but there were obvious signs of life. White smoke billowed up over the walls from numerous fires. They could see a number of riverboats and other fishing type vessels moored together near the fort's ferry landing. Through binoculars, they could see people moving back and forth high on the walls and across the fort grounds.

Brad was standing on the bow with the others. Sean had his binoculars out, looking intently at the fort while Brooks was using a spotting scope to observe the far coast line.

"Beach looks empty," Brooks said, scanning left to right over the mainland shore.

"Aye, this time of day it'd be expected, but they'll show themselves in the evening. They always do," Meyers chirped back.

Sean lowered his binoculars and stepped away from the rail. "Your call, Meyers. They haven't answered the radio. You want us to roll up to the front door and pull into the driveway, or take the small boat and scout ahead?"

Meyers grinned. "Show of force, as you Yanks say; let's roll up in the big ship. Let them see our flags and weapons."

Sean forced a smile and stared at the fort's wall one more time. "Okay. Brad, get out front with Parker and Joey; have your rifles at the low ready. Chelsea, you're with me and Nelson on the dive deck. Brooks, find a hiding spot and get behind that rifle," Sean ordered.

Brad turned to face Sean. In a low voice, he asked, "Are we expecting trouble, Chief?"

"I don't know who's out there; we just need them to know that we aren't to be fucked with," Sean answered as he walked away, headed to the dive deck.

Brad unslung his rifle and checked the action; it was ready to go. He looked to his right and saw Joey and Parker making the same preparations. "Okay, fellas, let's soldier up. I expect there to be lots of armed men down there, so let's not go starting a gun fight on our first day back," Brad said.

"Roger that," Joey responded.

Kelli eased up on the throttle, slowing the boat to a crawl. People at the fort began to take notice. Men ran out to the dock and Brad saw them pointing excitedly. More people began crowding the tower walls as word spread of visitors. There was a long, T-shaped pier north of the fort and Kelli seemed to be maneuvering in that direction. Brad looked up and down the pier—every portion of it was occupied by some type of vessel.

They came around, steering a wide path and keeping their distance on the flotilla of boats. Kelli steered them around the pier, sticking to the deep water, then cut in slightly before cutting the engines and ordering that the anchors be dropped. With the engines silenced, they could hear the voices of shouting men being carried over the water. Brad looked intently at the dock that was only a couple hundred meters away now. He could see civilians and others dressed in bits of military uniforms.

He let his eyes drift west and to the south part of the fort. There looked to be a long sandbar connecting the fort to the mainland. Water ran over portions of it. In other spots, heavy rolls of razor wire and other barriers had been piled up to form a heavy perimeter through the shallows. Brad could identify bits of fabric in the wire and was sure that if he inspected them through his rifle's optics, he would find that they were Primal bodies.

"We got a boat approaching," Brad heard Nelson yell from the lower deck.

Brad turned to face back north and saw a small civilian--style cabin cruiser had started moving in their direction. Three men in uniform stood behind a small windshield. Brad ordered Joey to move to the other side of the boat and keep his eyes on the approaching craft. When it got to within a hundred feet, Gunner used the ship's horn to halt the boat. The man driving the smaller craft cut the engine and they slowly drifted in the water.

One of the men climbed up on the bow of the boat and waved a white flag. He was close enough that Brad could clearly see him now. Although he was dressed in Marine Corps digital camouflage, the man's face was heavily bearded. One of the two men behind the windscreen was also dressed as a Marine, while the third wore the digital blue camouflage of a Navy uniform.

The hatch of the bridge opened and Gunner walked out, stopping at the rail between Brad and Joey. He gripped the rail with both hands and yelled to the men in the boat. "Good morning, we are with the United States Military. Who is in command of the fort?"

The men on the small boat looked at each other, then the man on the bow tossed the white flag down. They seemed to be talking amongst themselves and laughing. Gunner yelled again, "Excuse me, did I say something that amuses you?"

An older man dressed as a marine, standing behind the windshield, stood on a seat and gripped the top bar of the glass. "So, what part of the military you with? 'Cause there sure as hell ain't no more United States."

Gunner ignored the question. "Are you armed?"

"No, sir, but I see you all are," the man yelled back.

"Good… go ahead and bring your boat in. We'll throw you a line, but let's keep your hands up," Gunner shouted.

The men on the craft seemed to be arguing with each other; one continually pointed back at the fort while the others shook their heads in disagreement. Finally, the older man moved back behind the controls and the engine started. As Gunner had requested, the others put their hands up and held the windshield so they could be seen. The boat pulled in close and drifted sideways. Nelson tossed a line that was caught by the man in the Navy uniform.

They quickly pulled the boat in and Nelson tied it off. Brad ordered Joey and Parker to keep their eyes on the water while he moved toward the ladder with Gunner. They climbed down to the lower deck, joining Sean and the others just as the older Marine was being helped aboard.

The Marine looked at all of them and then laughed again. "Hell, you all are Americans. What are you doing on this Canuk boat?" he asked.

Gunner stepped forward. "It's a long story. So, what's with you? Are the Marines in charge here?" Gunner asked, pointing to the globe and anchor on the man's hat.

"Shit... I wish; bunch of state troopers and damn park rangers run the fort. I'm Gunnery Sergeant Cordell, that's Corporal Rodrigo on the boat, and Seaman Anderson with him. We let the park rangers think they are in charge, but we're the ones holding this place together. Unfortunately, me, Rodrigo, and Anderson here make up nearly fifty percent of the service members at the fort," Cordell said, pointing to his two men still in the boat, "and I have a few more men up on guard duty."

Cordell paused and looked around the deck of the boat. "So... I showed you mine, now who are you?"

Gunner made introductions and gave the man a vague story of who they were and how they got there. He told him they were gathering information about survivors in the region and looking to move inland using the rivers.

"Hell, brother, why would you want to go out there? Most folks die trying to get here," Cordell said.

Sean moved in and pointed toward the main land. "You mean there is nothing else out there?"

Cordell scratched at his chin and turned so that he was looking at the far beach. "I heard there are some small pockets. Some National Guard guys holding up here and there. A state trooper barracks up north someplace is apparently doing well. There are some others buttoned up in an old cement quarry. But seriously, folks, even if you got to guys like that, they ain't looking to leave, or even share what they got. And hell, don't even get me started on the bandits and killers taking advantage of things.

"Now if you *really* are looking to travel up the river, we might be able to help you with that, but it won't be cheap. We make runs up the river a couple times a week and sometimes they find people looking to travel here, but it has gotten less frequent."

"You go over there?" Sean asked, pointing to the mainland.

"Nah… hell, no. We got guys that go for us; they travel in barges up the rivers. They clean out old warehouses and whatnot, bring the supplies back to us for trade. It's the new enterprise; folks pay them for passage, and we charge the boats to dock here and allow them to sell their goods to folks in the camp. You know," Cordell paused, scratching his chin, "come to speak of it, one of the boats came in yesterday afternoon and brought in a few stragglers. Would you be interested in speaking with them?"

Gunner looked to Meyers who nodded back. "I think I'll take you up on that offer. Could we see the captain of the boat that brought them in? We may have some business for him," Gunner said.

Cordell nodded his head. "Well, no time like the present," Cordell said, moving back to the rail and climbing aboard the smaller boat.

Gunner slapped Meyers' back. "You ever been to the States before?"

Meyers laughed in response then turned around, pointing at Howard. "Doc, you're up. Sergeant Thompson, is it?" he said, looking at Brad.

Brad stumbled, not expecting to be called on. "Yeah, that's me."

"Good. Doctor Howard, Sergeant Thompson is your bodyguard; do whatever he says. Stay by his side."

Gunner walked across the deck toward the rail. He stopped and spoke to Sean, "If we find what we're looking for, we'll be wanting to leave right away. Think you can keep this thing floating while we go ashore for a visit?"

"Only one way to find out," Sean said.

"Good. Alright, Gunny, we're ready."

CHAPTER 15

They left through the front door and worked their way back to the road. With the warmth of the day and walking into the wind, he was certain they could travel safely from the infected during the daylight hours. Even though confident, Shane had set a quick pace. The girl moved along playfully, pretending she was leading the way. Sometimes she would walk far ahead of him, stop in the road waiting for him to pass, and then she would run back up the road, giggling. Shane cautioned her not to get too far ahead, but she would just look back at him and smile. The large breakfast and sugary drinks had done wonders to raise her spirits.

The terrain was open here, with tall fields of grass standing on either side of the road. Beyond that, varying from twenty to sometimes ten feet, were tall, dark forests. Occasionally, they would pass a burnt home or a nearly destroyed house with broken windows. Shane would slow the girl and walk beside her until they cleared those danger areas. Habitable or not, houses were far and few between, so he hoped the infected population would be just as sparse. As they walked, he would often drift to the gravel shoulders of the road and check for tracks, bent blades of grass, or other signs of movement from the infected. He was always alert and kept a close eye on the girl, but he still allowed her to play her games.

Walking—or more closely resembling a skip—she stayed just feet ahead of him. He watched her suddenly stop. She froze in place then backed toward him and when she turned, he saw fear in her eyes. Shane hastened his steps and moved in beside her. He squatted down, and she pulled herself into his left arm.

"What did you see?" he whispered to her. Ella's hand dropped to his pant leg and she gripped the fabric. Her left hand rose and she pointed a finger at a far off bush.

Shane had grown to trust the girl's instincts over the past several days and raised his rifle in the direction she pointed as a voice called out, "Whoa, didn't mean to startle ya. You can relax there, soldier boy, no need for none of that."

A man's hands rose from the bush, followed by arms and a long, lanky body dressed in a hunter's camouflage pants and dark flannel shirt. His hair was unkempt, his chin a matted attempt at growing a beard. When he smiled, it revealed a mouth of blackened, broken teeth. The man, hands now raised over his head, continued stepping toward the road, speaking as he moved. "You ain't gots be ah'scared of me, nah, I'm nuttin' to worry 'bout."

Shane intensely observed the strange man as he approached, keeping the rifle aimed center mass. Ella crouched and pushed into him tightly. Shane was about to speak when he heard another voice from behind. "Now, I's the one you should be worried about," the voice called out.

Shane went to turn to look behind him when he heard the hammer of a firearm lock back. "Oh no, boy, you just stay right there. Damn, look at ya! You a big feller, ain't 'cha soldier?" he heard the new voice call out.

Shane froze, looking ahead as the first man continued walking toward him. "Stop where you are!" Shane yelled.

The first broken-toothed man stopped, but lowered his arms. "Now, I told ya, you ain't got nothing to worry about," the toothy man said, giggling as he lowered his hand to caress the handle of a large Bowie knife on his belt.

Shane lifted the rifle and tucked it tight into his shoulder. "Take another step, mister, and I will shoot you dead," he snarled, slowly rising to his feet. As he stood, Ella stayed with him, hugging his leg.

Shane could hear the man behind him move closer as his feet stepped onto the gravel behind him. Shane stepped right, to the center of the road, pivoting so he could see the second man. Short and fat with a stocking cap pulled down over his brow, he was carrying a short-barreled single shot shotgun with the hammer back. Shane kept his rifle in his shoulder and aimed at the toothy man in front while looking from the corner of his eye at the fat one behind and to the left.

"You stop or I'll kill your friend. I'm not giving you another warning," Shane called out.

The fat man stopped moving and squared up. Keeping the barrel in Shane's direction, the toothy man raised his right hand and showed a palm to his partner, signaling for him to stop.

"Now, is that any way for you to be talking to strangers? You's up on our land, walking our road, and you threatening to kill me?" the toothy man said, barely concealing a chuckle.

"What do you want?" Shane asked.

"We just looking to see what you got, you know, in exchange for traveling our road," the toothy man said.

Shane stepped again so that he could now completely see the fat man while still keeping the rifle on the first one. Ella followed him, holding his pant leg but not hindering his movement. "I don't have anything for you, now step aside and let us pass."

The toothy man let out another manic chuckle. "Ah hell, we'll take the girl then," he said as the fat man giggled.

Shane didn't reply, but he kept the rifle up. He could feel Ella's arms trembling. His finger caressed the trigger, he couldn't take the shot. The man behind him would be able to fire before he could turn and get a second round off.

"Now, why don't you be a good soldier boy and hand us that rifle whiles we talk about this," the first man said.

Shane saw the fat man begin to step. "I said don't move!" Shane yelled. He held the rifle tight on the toothy man, planted his feet, and prepared for a fight.

"Come on now, hand over yer rifle. If we wanted you dead, Earl woulda already kilt ya," Toothy said, causing the fat man to giggle again.

Shane knew the only reason the man hadn't shot was because he was worried about hitting Ella. That or the gun wasn't loaded. He could tell by their looks that they weren't hospitable to travelers. Shane knew if he fired on Toothy, Fat Boy would get off a shot that would no doubt hit him—and possibly Ella—from the distance they were standing apart.

"Come on now, we ain't asking again. Toss me the damn rifle, boy. You do it now and we'll let ya go," Toothy now yelled, losing his temper.

Shane relaxed his grip on the rifle. Focusing, he could feel the pressure near his belt where he'd placed the Walther pistol. He took a deep breath and squeezed the forward grip of the rifle with his left hand and slowly he lifted his right hand from the butt stock as he released the pistol grip.

"Okay, I'll toss the rifle if you promise you won't hurt us," Shane said, causing both men to giggle frantically.

Shane pulled the rifle out, holding it in one hand. Instead of tossing it to Toothy, he turned and threw it underhand to Fat Boy. The fat man smiled as the rifle sailed through the air. Assuming his victim was now unarmed, Fat Boy took his eyes off of Shane for just a split second. It was all Shane needed to use his right hand that was concealed from the Fat Boy's view. He reached under his jacket and pulled the pistol. Fat Boy saw Shane's quick movement, but by the time he recognized the handgun, it was too late for him to bring the shotgun back on target.

Shane drew the pistol and rotated. As he fully extended his arm he pulled the trigger twice; hitting Fat Boy in the right shoulder and face. Toothy yelped a high pitch scream and Shane swung his arm back in Toothy's direction. The man hadn't moved.

"Why'd you do that?" the man cried.

Shane ignored Toothy's question. As he slowly walked to Fat Boy, he kept the pistol aimed at Toothy. When he reached the body, he kicked the shotgun from its grip, reached down, and retrieved his own rifle. As he lifted it, Toothy lunged for him. Shane didn't hesitate and fired a single round, hitting the man low in the stomach. Toothy doubled over and let out a loud wail as he dropped to the ground and rolled into the fetal position.

"Why'd you do that?" the man howled again.

Shane slung his rifle and reached back for the shotgun. He opened the breach and saw it was loaded with a buckshot round. Shane removed the shell and tossed it to the street, then kept hold of the weapon. Keeping the pistol on Toothy, he searched Fat Boy's pockets and found more 12 gauge shells and a set of keys.

"Where is your vehicle?" Shane asked.

"What? We ain't got no car," Toothy whined.

Shane walked closer to the wounded man while dangling the keys in his hand. "Looks like you're gut shot. Unless you get some help quick you're gonna die very..."

Interrupted by the moans of the infected, Shane stopped and looked behind him. "Sounds like the gunfire woke them early."

"Okay, okay, if'in I tell ya, you'll take me with you?" Toothy pleaded.

Shane didn't answer but stepped closer. "Where's your vehicle?"

"Come on now, you can't leave me out here."

Another set of moans, this time closer, sounded in the distance. Shane could hear snapping trees as they moved from their hiding places deep in the woods.

"I'm leaving you here, but you have a choice, you can tell me where your vehicle is and I'll give you the shotgun. If you don't want to talk, then I really need to get going before your neighbors arrive."

The man lay on the ground wailing. Shane shook his head and stepped off at a quick pace with Ella holding his belt.

"Okay, okay," the man called out. "The truck's just over there, backed into that brush."

Shane stared into the area Toothy had indicated; he could just make out the metallic blue of a front fender.

"Alright," Shane said as he lifted the shotgun by the barrel and tossed it off to the side of the road. "There you are, go get it."

The man begged and pleaded, but it fell on deaf ears. Shane lifted Ella and jogged in the direction of the truck. The moans sounded like they were right on top of them by the time he reached the cab. Shane threw the door open and tossed Ella onto the bench seat. He stripped off his pack and threw it in beside her as he jumped into the truck, then closed and locked the door.

As Shane struggled to start the engine, he could see Toothy crawling across the pavement searching for the shotgun round. A loud bang jolted the truck forward. Looking in the rear view mirror, Shane could see one of the infected collide with the side of the vehicle. He turned the key, pumped the pedal, and the engine roared to life. He heard a scream, followed by a shotgun blast, over the sound of the vehicle and looked to the road just as the man was swarmed by infected. He pulled the gear lever, dropped the truck into drive, and floored the pedal. The bed bounced as the truck fought for traction, throwing dirt and gravel as it crawled to the shoulder, then squealed when the rubber grabbed pavement.

Shane raced forward, hitting several of the infected things. He cut the wheel hard and fishtailed into a slide as the truck's tires gripped the road. He straightened out and saw that several of them had made it to the bed of the truck. Shane accelerated until he felt the steering wheel vibrate in his hands. "Ella, get on the floor," he yelled and watched as the girl obeyed and dropped to the floor. She held her hands over her ears, trying to block out the infected screams.

Shane hit the brakes hard and turned the wheel to the left just enough to put the truck into a controlled skid and eject most of infected from the vehicle. He hit the gas pedal again and raced forward—all but one had been thrown clear. In his side mirror, he could see their broken and twisted bodies on the road struggling to get up. The remaining creature was still lying stunned in the back of the truck against the tailgate and trying to sit up; its arm looked broken. Shane hit the brakes again, causing the thing to fly forward and slam against the cab of the truck. He locked the vehicle into park and then stepped out onto the road. He pulled the pistol and methodically put two rounds in the thing's head, dropped the tailgate, and dumped the creature to the ground.

Shane walked away from the body and leaned against the tailgate, letting his heartbeat return to normal. As he stood there listening, he could hear the sounds of the engine gurgling a loud idle. He cautiously returned to the cab and closed the door behind him. He swallowed hard and looked down at Ella on the floor. "You can come up now," he said.

Shane watched as the girl climbed up onto the bench seat without emotion. She looked around the cab of the truck and buckled her seat belt. Shane grinned, then put the truck back into gear and started forward, now at a modest speed. He looked at the gas gauge and saw that he barely had a quarter of a tank of fuel. It wouldn't get him far, but he could at least find shelter before it ran out.

CHAPTER 16

The small shore team was led down a long dock where an assortment of boats were crowded in and tied off to both sides. Farther out, a larger flotilla of watercraft were anchored and tied together. Cordell noticed Brad looking at the cluster of boats and stopped.

"Salvagers mostly; some fisherman, hard types, but we put up with them because they bring in the supplies," he explained.

Gunner moved up next to Brad and stared at the ships, large flat-bottomed riverboats, and fishing trawlers. "If they are bringing in all of the supplies, then why do they need you?"

Cordell laughed. "Don't say that too loud, I don't think they have figured it out yet."

"So, what do you trade them, you know, in exchange for their *goods*?" Brad asked.

Cordell looked down, then away from Brad. "It doesn't work like that. The people living here… *they* make the trades. And, well, the rangers charge them a tax of sorts to stay at the fort. Most are required to pay in supplies, food, and fresh water in exchange to live inside the walls. Others provide services like security or maintenance."

Brad grabbed Cordell's jacket as he turned to walk away. "You charge the survivors a tax? And how in the hell do they have anything left to trade with them?" he said pointing to the clustered ships.

Cordell pulled away and answered over his shoulder as he walked on, "They find a way."

Brad pushed Howard ahead of him and followed the others to the gates of Fort Sumter. Standing at the head of the walkway, two guards were high above them on the walls. Looking right, Brad could see an open area outside the fort's walls, Crates and other bits of drift wood and garbage were piled recklessly. Farther on, a hastily built stone wall separated the fort from the sandbars. Men in civilian jackets patrolled the area with axes and rifles. As they approached the gate, Cordell yelled up at the guards and, after a brief exchange, a heavy wooden door slid open to allow them to pass. The interior of the camp was a former parade ground congested with shelters and had a narrow, muddy path leading down the center to a large, black painted building.

A heavy, musty smoke hung over the camp. The stench of open latrines and burning garbage was everywhere. The fort was ringed with high masonry walls and ancient gun positions, but was now filled with stacked and guarded supplies. Brad saw women feeding children with gaunt faces, plastic basins and pails positioned to catch rainwater, and men cooking small game over wood fires. As he looked at them, he thought back to the warehouse filled with survivors in Newfoundland. Their small refuge in the wilderness was paradise compared to the squalor he was seeing here.

Brad stopped and looked down an aisle between the roughly constructed shelters where a child was urinating into a bucket. Cordell stopped and yelled for him to keep moving. Brad looked at him.

"Excuse me, Gunnery Sergeant, what the hell is going on here? Who is in charge of this camp?" Brad said with obvious disgust, waiving his hands at the filth around him. "Why are these people living like this?"

Cordell's face turned red as he struggled for the right words. "Like I said *Sergeant*, the park ranger and the state troopers are in charge," he spit with a sarcastic tone. "Or at least they act like they are. I know what you're thinking, this place looks like a third world refugee camp. And dammit you're right, but the sorry piece of shit in there won't listen."

Gunner moved in next to Brad. "That's no excuse, Gunny. Why is a park ranger running a refugee camp?"

Cordell clenched his teeth and let out an exaggerated laugh. "Possession is nine-tenths of the law, brother. This camp was up and running when the boys and I got here. We try to help out as much as we can, but as long as the troopers are backing the rangers, we can't do shit to fix things. Not like I can walk on into his office and take over."

Meyers' cough interrupted them. "This is all very interesting business, but it's also not our mission, mate. How about we keep this moving along?"

Gunner nodded and waved Cordell forward. Cordell stepped off, walking up the litter-strewn path and then to a concrete walkway that eventually led to the black building. Cordell stopped at a set of stairs and briefly spoke to a guard clad in a partial police officer's uniform. The guard quickly stepped aside and allowed them to pass. Brad took a last look around and pushed Doctor Howard ahead of him as he took up the rear. They were led past a number of caged entrances and finally to a set of glass doors.

The room inside looked to have once been a museum. The walls were covered with broken display cases and old artifacts were piled in a corner. They walked through living areas filled with makeshift cots before coming to a closed office door. Cordell stepped forward and pounded on the door with his fist before opening it and walking in. He left the door open behind him so Gunner and the others followed him into the dimly lit office. Brad guided Howard in ahead of him then moved along the wall to the back of the office.

The room was rough and dusty. An old wooden desk with a worn leather swivel chair, some roughed in shelving, and a long leather sofa under a window greeted them. The sofa was occupied by a man wearing a state trooper's uniform leaning back at one end of it with his hat over his eyes. Another man in a green and tan uniform sat at the wooden desk and looked up as they filed into the room. Brad noticed a number of empty liquor bottles stacked against a far wall and more in a wastebasket near the door. The man in the tan uniform lifted a cup to his mouth, then turned to look at Cordell. "These the ones from the Canadian boat?"

Cordell nodded and said, "They are all with the military, looking for transport up the river."

The man with the hat pulled over his eyes grunted, "Why the hell would you want to go up there?"

Gunner took a deep breath and looked around the room ignoring the question. "Excuse me, who's in charge here?"

The man in tan gave Gunner a stern look. "Well, that would be me."

"And just who is *me*?" Gunner said using the most authoritative voice he could muster.

The man in tan sat confused for a moment before he pushed away from his desk, rose to his feet, and walked around the desk to face Gunner. He was a big man, but not in a fit way. He wore a simple park ranger's uniform, pockets undone, and the front open to reveal a yellowed T-shirt.

"Why… I'm Ranger Nevens! Head ranger here at Fort Sumter!"

The commotion caused the resting state trooper to lift his cap and survey the men in the room. The trooper, for the first time, seemed to realize that the office was filled with several frowning armed men and that the odds were not in his favor; his hand slowly drifted to his holster.

"Yeah, let's not do that," Gunner said as his own hand stroked the grip of his holstered 1911. "Ranger Nevens, you are relieved, this fort is now under military control and I thank you for your service."

"Now hold up, *gawd dammit*! You can't come in here and take over after *everything* we've done."

Gunner looked him in the eyes. "Yeah, we already had the walking tour and I've seen what you've done."

Nevens looked to the trooper, still seated, and said, "Well? Are you going to do something?"

The trooper pushed his hat down tight to his head, then yawned before getting to his feet. "Like the man said, they are in charge now." He stood and straightened his uniform then walked out of the office, leaving the ranger alone with the men.

Gunner continued to stare Nevens down. "So, are we going to have a problem?"

Nevens, now alone, backed away from Gunner and leaned against the desk. "I welcomed you here! I sent a team to meet you when we could have ignored you. You can't do this. Gunnery Sergeant Cordell, please escort this man back to his boat!"

Cordell smirked and ignored the ranger; he walked to the sofa and dropped into the trooper's previous spot. "Sorry, buddy, you ain't giving the orders anymore; time to make things right by the people out there."

Gunner exhaled and walked to the door. Pulling it open he said, "Nevens, you can leave now."

The ranger, red in the face, stopped to put on a heavy green jacket and tan ball cap. He gave Gunner a last angered look then walked to the door. Before stepping out, he stopped and looked back at Cordell. "I'll be in my quarters."

Gunner shook his head. "No, ranger, I need you to gather your things and move onto the parade field. Find a nice spot with the others.

While you're there maybe you can come up with some suggestions to make it more hospitable."

Brad pushed to the back of the room with Howard behind him as Nevens stood in the doorway scowling. Gunner looked him in the eye, "That's all, Ranger, move out."

Gunner brushed Nevens off with his hand, moved to the door, and closed it.

"Bloody hell, you strayed a bit off course there, didn't ya, mate?!" Meyers chimed in.

"I didn't see you standing up to voice your disagreement," Gunner laughed.

He moved around the desk and sat in the leather swivel chair, rummaged through the drawers, and stopped when he found a half pint of rum. He lifted a small glass and blew the dust out before filling it with the dark liquid.

"No reason we can't make things better for these people while we make our next move." Gunner paused and took a long swig of the rum, he grimaced and coughed, "That is some rot gut right there. Gunnery Sergeant Cordell, can you find this riverboat captain and have him brought to me?"

CHAPTER 17

The truck bounced and jerked as the front tire dropped into a deep pothole. Shane slowed his speed even more as he navigated the broken road. He looked down at the truck's gas gauge – the needle drifting just below the E. They'd passed several buildings, most burnt or with kicked-in doors and broken windows. Nothing inviting, but with the engine about to sputter to death, he was growing nervous that they would be walking again soon.

Shane slowed the truck to steer around a downed tree. As he moved past it, another tree from the opposite side of the road forced him into a serpentine pattern. Instantly, he felt the hairs on the back of his neck begin to buzz. He'd had the same feelings before as a turret gunner in Iraq moments before an ambush or a road side bomb. He had to make a split second decision to stop or go back. Trusting instinct, he put his foot hard to the pedal. The truck tires screeched in response as they fought the asphalt, coming out of the turn he was navigating through the downed trees. Shane heard the gunshots before he saw the shooter.

The windshield spider webbed. Ella screamed as Shane reached out with his right hand and forced her flat on the seat while he struggled to maintain control of the truck. He drove the vehicle hard through the remaining curve and into a straightway. Ahead, he could see the makeshift roadblock of old cars parked on the road at 45 degree angles. The attackers had formed the perfect bottle neck ambush. Two men stood behind the fender of the farthermost right car with weapons raised and muzzles flashing. Already committed, Shane kept his foot on the accelerator and sped for the small gap between the cars. Just before impact, he cut the wheel hard to the right and the truck collided with the car that the men were hiding behind. The crash almost bucked Shane from his seat, but the weight of the large truck and the momentum barreled them through the barricade as he regained control.

He heard the motor squeal from the fan being forced into the radiator and engine block. The truck pulled hard to the right. He could feel the resistance in the steering wheel, indicating a flat tire. More gunshots shattered the back window and a single round punctured a hole in the bench seat just above Ella's head. Shane let the right hand pull take him off the road, gunned the engine for all it had left, and raced to the tree line. The truck bounced hard as the rubber left the steel rim, causing it to gouge into the earth. Shane kept on the engine but was losing speed.

Desperately, he cut the wheel into the direction of the flat tire and hit the parking brake. The truck stopped abruptly, barely keeping the vehicle between him and the ambushers. The gunfire increased as rounds skipped overhead and pinged into the body of the truck. Shane forced the driver's door open with his boot. Keeping low, he grabbed Ella by her wrist, dragged her across the bench seat, and then positioned her behind the rear tire. The truck had sunk into the ground up to its floorboards. The soft earth and steel truck body now made for good cover.

Shane pulled his bag from the cab and left it on the ground. He crouched low and duck walked to Ella's side. After making sure she was okay, he readied his rifle, then dropped low to crawl near the back bumper. He could hear the men shouting panicked instructions to each other now. One appeared to be hurt—probably when the truck crashed through the barricade. Shane caught movement from the corner of his eye. A man ran bent at the waist and headed in Shane's direction. Shane lifted his rifle, aimed center mass, leading slightly and pulled the trigger a single time. The man took a final long step before falling face first into the mud.

Shane heard more shouting, but directed now. He held his breath and tried to listen. He could tell they were yelling to him, but he couldn't make out the words. Shane crawled under the edge of the exposed tailgate – careful to remain concealed – and stared intently in the direction of the roadblock. One man was in a sitting position against the crushed car he'd hit. Another was standing behind the far vehicle yelling in his direction. They were still too far away for Shane to understand him and he didn't care what they had to say; they'd shot at him, that made them his enemy. Shane turned back to Ella and told her to wait by the truck and he'd be back as soon as he could.

Shane knew he wouldn't have long before the infected showed up; he would have to work quickly. He put his head to the ground and crawled low through the high grass, letting the bandit's shouting guide him. As he drew closer, he could begin to make out the words. They were asking him to surrender, to come out and they wouldn't shoot him. Shane continued moving at a slight angle away from the voice, hoping to come out of the grass in a flanking position.

The shouting stopped, but Shane was now close enough to hear the muffled conversation between the two men. He focused on their words as he slowly worked his way closer to the roadside. The wounded man argued that the truck's occupants were dead. He wanted to leave and return to the camp before the infected showed up. The other wanted to know where his friends were, the owners of the truck. Shane lifted his head slightly; he was within fifty meters of the roadblock now. He'd come out of the grass and onto the pavement ahead of them. The seated man was mumbling now. The second asked for cover, then began slowly stalking in the direction of the truck and Ella.

Shane hid in the grass waiting for the man to walk beyond him. Once the man cleared Shane's position, he quickly popped up to a knee with the rifle aimed at the man's back. He called for the bandit to stop; instead, the man turned toward Shane. Two pulls of the trigger, and the bandit fell to the ground. Shane turned back to the wounded man and held his rifle on him as he patrolled forward. The man was whimpering incoherently now. Shane approached cautiously. As he neared, he could see the man's bloodied torso and an obvious broken leg judging from the angle of his boot.

The wounded man was young, mid-twenties maybe, but his condition and nappy beard made him look older. He was slender with a pale face and gray, bloodshot eyes. His flannel shirt was ripped and soiled, his denim pants covered in grime and dirt.

"Get your arms out and to your sides! Open your hands, show me your palms!" Shane yelled.

The man whimpered, but slowly stretched his arms. Shane moved closer and quickly searched him for a weapon. Finding a 9mm pistol with the slide locked back, Shane kicked the handgun away. He then grabbed the man by the shoulder and dragged him screaming farther onto the road. Keeping his weapon on the wounded man, Shane hastily searched the remaining vehicle. He found keys and a large red duffle bag of food on the back seat. Shane returned to the wounded man as he visually scanned the tree line for the infected.

Shane walked back to his prisoner and stood over him. "Where is your camp? How many there?"

The injured man grunted and attempted a roll to his side. Shane lifted his boot and stepped on the man's broken leg, producing a scream in agony.

"You need to stop with all of that noise. I'm surprised the infected aren't already on us."

The man stopped screaming. He held a blood-covered arm to his lips and breathed heavily into the sleeve.

"Now I'm going to ask again, where is your camp and how many?"

The wounded man grunted and rolled to his back, looking up at Shane with sunken eyes. "How many? You already killed us all man!" he cried. "David over there and Taylor, that was all of us."

"You brought this on yourselves when you shot at me."

The man's mouth frothed with bloody foam. He gritted his teeth and said, "We shot because you have Earl's truck."

"Oh, gotcha… I'd say Earl let me borrow it, but that'd be a lie; Earl's dead—and his buddy. Now last time, where's the camp?" Shane lifted his boot and pushed the toe of it against the man's outward bent leg. The man flinched and pulled away.

"Okay, okay, but you got to bring me with you. I'll show you," he gurgled.

Shane began to hear the faint moans of the infected in the distance. They were calling to each other with the baying sounds they used when they were on the hunt, probably tracking him from his last encounter with Earl. Shane walked to the still intact newer model Chevy sedan, pushed a button on the key fob, and the trunk popped open. Shane reached inside the trunk and used his knife to cut away the escape release wire. Quickly, he turned back and grabbed the wounded man. He rolled him to his belly and forced his arms behind his back. The man screamed and struggled with protests that Shane ignored. After being hogtied with the wire, he pulled off the man's belt and tightly tied it around his ankles. Shane dragged the man screaming across the pavement to the car and forced his body into the trunk.

He whistled a familiar call and saw Ella appear near the back of the disabled pickup. He circled his arm in the air and watched as she slowly moved in his direction. As Shane ran toward her, he told her to get into the car. Then he continued to the truck and retrieved his rucksack. On the return trip, he saw the first of the infected move out of the trees near the roadblock. Shane spotted the man he'd shot earlier; dead on the ground and still holding a SKS rifle. Shane slung his M4 and retrieved the dead man's rifle as he jogged back to the car. He raised the weapon and took aimed shots at the nearest infected.

He knocked the first of them to the ground with several hits to the chest. Shane continued firing into the approaching infected as he moved to the open door of the sedan. When he saw they were running directly at him now, Shane fired rapidly until the SKS was dry, then turned and tossed the empty weapon into the back seat. Shane dropped into the car and pulled the door shut just as one of them launched its body onto the hood. He put the key in the ignition and could hear the car respond with dinging that he could barely make out over the screaming of the infected and the terrified yelling of the man in the trunk.

The key turned and the engine started. Shane put the car in reverse and backed away from the roadblock as more infected impacted the car. He did a three point turn then gunned the engine, causing the infected to fall off of the vehicle. Shane had the car going straight down the center of the blacktop road. He looked over at Ella next to him; she was sitting with her seatbelt on staring straight ahead. Shane reached across the seat and patted her leg.

"You okay?" he asked her.

She looked up at him. She had dirt on her face that left a brown streak as she blinked away a tear. Her hair was matted and filled with leaves and bits of grass. She clenched her eyes again then opened them slowly. "Did they want to hurt us, Shane?"

Shane coughed, trying to hide his emotions. "Yeah, Ella, they wanted to hurt us."

"Were they bad men? Like on the boat?"

The man in the trunk screamed again and banged against the backseat from inside the trunk.

"Yeah, they were bad men, but this one is going to show us someplace safe to stay tonight."

Shane ignored the screaming and put his hand on Ella's head. She grabbed his wrist and held it to her face.

CHAPTER 18

Brad sat at an end of the sofa with Doctor Howard next to him. Meyers and Gunner leaned across the desk, obsessing over a map of the local rivers. The doctor fidgeted and ran his fingers through his pockets nervously. The unrelenting motion agitated Brad. A knock at the office door finally caused Howard to stop moving and sit upright as the knob turned and the door crept open. Cordell peeked in, announced he'd returned with the captain, and then motioned an older man dressed in canvas pants and a yellow jacket through the door ahead of him.

Cordell made introductions and showed the man a seat on a wobbly wooden chair. Gunner offered the captain a drink which he readily accepted. The captain pushed the tin cup through a heavy white beard and drank thirstily.

"Ahh, it's good," he bellowed.

Gunner laughed. "It's an acquired taste, I suppose."

The captain finished then held the cup up. Gunner walked around the desk with the bottle, sat on the desktop, and refilled the captain's glass. The captain grinned and sipped this time. "So, what is it you've brought me here for?

What is it you be wanting? Booze? Bullets? Women, maybe?"

Gunner looked at him. "Really, you can get all of those things?"

"Sure, and if I don't have it, I know where to find it."

Meyers chuckled from the corner of the room and rounded the desk, finding a place to sit next to Gunner. "I don't think we will be requiring such fine things from you. What we require is transportation."

The captain shot Meyers a puzzled looked. "Transportation? I assume that's your Coast Guard vessel anchored in the harbor. Why would you need me with that sort of horse power?"

Gunner answered, "Cap'n, we need to get up the river."

The captain took another long sip then shook his head. "Please, call me David." He took another sip, then took a deep breath. "No, nobody goes up the river except the salvagers. I bring folks back here on my return trip. I'll salvage supplies, get you what you want, but I don't take passengers up the river; too dangerous."

Gunner offered the bottle and refilled his cup. "Well, that's where we need to go, so we are asking you politely to take us."

David shook his head again and squinted. "Why would you want to go up river? Nothing up there but death."

"We're looking for a girl," Howard shouted, causing Meyers to scowl.

"Ahh, so it *is* women you're after?" David said, grinning,

"No. She's injured or maybe..." Howard paused, looking down at the leather satchel in his lap. "We have to find her, she has been missing since Fort Collins – "

"Collins?!" David exclaimed, interrupting Howard.

Meyers lifted the map and pushed it to the captain. "Yes, it's a distance up the –."

"I know where in the hell it's at. Tell me about this girl, why do you want her?" David asked, now looking agitated.

Howard swallowed hard. "She's a patient – "

Brad held up his hand, stopping Howard from continuing. He looked at David and could see the look of recognition in his face.

Brad leaned forward on the sofa and looked the captain in the eye. "What is it about Fort Collins?"

"Huh... It's nothing."

Brad stared him down. "Cut the bullshit. I saw the look you gave when you heard it mentioned."

David exhaled deeply. "I picked up a soldier on the river; he claimed to have come from there. He was traveling with a girl."

Cordell grunted. "Some coincidence. How do we know you're not lying?"

Brad held up his hand again. "No, he's telling the truth. Where are they now?"

David looked worried. He emptied the cup again and held it to Gunner, who shook his head and pointed to Brad, as if telling him to answer the question. David took a deep breath and sighed.

"There was a problem on the boat – a disagreement among the passengers – the soldier asked to be put ashore."

"Put ashore? Where?" Howard asked nearly shouting.

The captain shook his head avoiding eye contact. "It doesn't matter. The girl was infected."

"What makes you say that?" Howard asked.

"She was bitten; I saw it myself, on her arm," David explained.

Howard quickly opened the leather satchel and searched through the stack of papers until finding the photograph he was searching for, and then he held it up to the captain.

"The wound, did it look like this?" Howard asked.

David stared at the picture, then looked away and held the cup up to Gunner. "Please."

Gunner stared back at him. "The wound didn't look like that, did it?"

"No, it was healing," David gasped.

Howard jumped to his feet. "I knew it. She *is* here; we need to leave right away!"

Meyers looked at David. "You said they went ashore. Can you take us there?"

David became restless in his seat and looked as if he wanted to end the conversation. "I... I could take you to the general area. It's not far from here; less than a day under power. But I'm not sure that you would find anything. It's been some time and – "

"Wait," Brad interrupted. "Just why, exactly, would put a small girl ashore when you were a day out from the fort?"

David held his hands in his lap. Using his right hand to squeeze the fingers of his left, he avoided eye contact. "I'll take you, but we will need to leave soon. And my men won't be leaving the boat, and we won't be waiting for you."

"Aye, mate, why don't you answer the question; why did they leave your boat?" Meyers asked again.

"I said I would take you, do you want to travel up river or not?" David said, losing his temper. He got to his feet and looked to Cordell.

"I'll ready my crew; we leave as soon as it gets dark."

"At night? Why at night?" Brad asked.

David looked at him sternly. "We know what to expect from them at night. During the day they are unpredictable. I find it safer to have my entire crew up and alert while the infected are most active. We sleep when they sleep and we travel when they travel." David turned toward the door, then stopped and looked back. "My boat travels at dusk; if you're not aboard, we won't be waiting."

David left the room and closed the door hard behind him. Brad got to his feet and walked across the room, stopping near the door. "Cordell, can we trust him?"

Cordell laughed. "Hell no—don't trust anyone here."

Meyers got up from the desk and stretched. "Fair enough, can you arrange transport for us to the barge?"

"Of course, consider it done."

Gunner pointed to the door. "Okay then, the boat will stay in the harbor. We will leave a radio and some comms gear so we can keep in touch as long as we are within range. There's an officer on board and several men that will be staying behind. I'd recommend you bring her ashore and place her in charge of the camp."

Cordell smiled and stood. "We will make things right here. But first, let's get you moving."

CHAPTER 19

The road widened. Tall grass on both sides led up to hilly terrain and un-harvested fields before entering dark tree lines. They passed a cluster of small homes with broken windows and broken doors. Shane drove until they were in his rear view, then slowed the car and put it in park. He left the sedan in the middle of the road with the engine running. The man in the back had stopped his protests, but he could hear him moving around once the car had stopped.

Shane looked at Ella and told her to get into the back seat. He opened the door and reached down to press the trunk release button. He heard the click and pop of the trunk. Then the wounded man in the back began thrashing again. Shane stepped out of the car and grabbed the pistol from his belt, walked to the back of the car, and saw the man look up at him. The man opened his mouth to speak but before he could, Shane reached down and pulled the man from the trunk by his arm and let him fall hard to the ground.

He grabbed the man's shirt and dragged him to the passenger's side door, then stood him up on his one good leg. "I'm going to sit you in the car and you're going to lead me to the camp. You understand?"

The injured man clenched his teeth and nodded his head.

Shane pulled the wounded man away from the car and opened the door. He pushed him onto the seat, allowing the man to hit his head on the roof as he entered. He grabbed the man's shirt, pulled him upright, and then wrapped the seatbelt tightly around his waist. Shane pulled a length of cord from a cargo pocket, bound the man's hands to the lap belt, and used another length to tie the man's neck to the headrest support. "You all comfy?" he asked, not expecting an answer.

Shane closed the door and walked around, dropping into the driver's seat.

"Where to?"

The man grunted and turned his head to look at Shane. "Water."

Shane grinned. "You'll drink when we get there."

The man put his head down. Shane reached over, grabbed the back of his neck and forced him to look ahead. He demanded, "Now where to, or I'll dump you here."

"Just drive, you're going the right way."

Shane put the car in gear and accelerated, staying to the center of the blacktop road. The man mumbled and, again, asked for something to drink. Shane saw Ella looking at him in the rearview mirror, so he nodded to her. "Ella, there is a bottle in the bag. Would you get it for me please?"

After a moment of rustling, Ella stood on the backseat and handed Shane the bottle. He twisted off the cap and held it to the wounded man's lips, allowing him to drink. Shane pulled the bottle away and placed it in a cup holder. "So, where are we going?"

"It's not far," the man mumbled.

"Who were they? The others at the roadblock, they family?" Shane asked.

The man shook his head. "No, they were friends of my brother Earl. He was out huntin' with Gary. We was waiting for him to come back when we saw you driving his truck."

"Oh yeah, I remember Earl; short guy, fat, built like 250 pounds of chewed bubble gum? Yeah… good ol' Earl. So tell me, you always setup roadblocks and shoot at children when you go out *huntin'*?"

"He's dead, isn't he?"

"Very," Shane said, not taking his eyes of the road. "So what was the plan? Rob and murder; little bit of kiddie rape? I'd heard there were folks like you out here, but never ran into any."

"Honest, mister, it's nothing like that; they was just out hunting for deer and such."

"It's a good story, I'll give you that. So, how many times have you done this sort of thing? Send the inbred trash out ahead on the road to spook up unsuspecting travelers and you all hang back, jerking each other off, waiting to ambush anyone that makes it past them?"

The wounded man looked away, ignoring Shane's comments.

"Don't worry kid, I won't kill ya *today*. But if I catch you in a lie, or if I find more of your inbred cousins at this camp, I will make the last moments of your life very painful," Shane said in a calm voice.

"Why are you doing this?"

Shane feigned laughter and ignored the question. "What's your name kid?"

"Kyle," he answered.

"Kyle, everything I do, I do for her."

"You kill for her?"

"No, I protect her and I destroy anything that tries to harm her—"

"It's right up here, follow the white fence," Kyle interrupted using his neck to point out a quickly approaching high fence skinned in white sheet metal.

The fence was tall and set back off the road. Mounds of stacked cars and other junk could be seen piled high at points. Shane slowed the car and carefully eased over to the shoulder of the road. He put the car in park and killed the engine. Shane sat silently for a minute, hushing Kyle when he tried to speak. He opened the door and slowly walked to the front of the car while listening for sounds. He climbed onto the hood and moved to the roof of the sedan.

He could just barely see inside the compound. As it appeared from the outside, it was definitely a scrap yard. Piles of sorted metal were scattered around a central building while rows of smashed and stacked cars made up the far sides of the lot. From what Shane could tell, the high fence surrounded the entire compound. He stood waiting and listening; finally satisfied he was alone, he walked back down from the roof and reentered the car.

"How do we get in?"

"The gate's just ahead. There's a combo lock on the fence post."

Shane put the car in gear and continued up the road to where a small gravel drive veered off from the blacktop. He pulled the car off the road and wheeled up to the front gate. Kyle explained there was a small metallic box with a cipher lock welded to one of the gate's arms. Shane stopped just in front of it.

"No surprises, right, Kyle?"

"No, it's good. There used to be dogs, but we had to shoot 'em because they wouldn't stop barking at night," Kyle said.

"Maybe you should have shot your brother and his friends instead. What's the code?"

"Junior and senior's numbers," Kyle answered.

"What?"

"Eighty-eight, zero-three... ain't you into NASCAR?"

Shane ignored him and cautiously walked to the gate with his rifle at the ready. He moved as close to the vertical arm that held the cipher lock as he could, and carefully peered inside. No movement; a number of plastic drums and some boxes scattered around a gravel drive. Farther back, stood the structure. The windows were all shuttered and a steel door marked the end of the dirt walkway leading up to it. Shane stepped back and entered the numbers into the lock and turned the knob; he felt the lock click and the gate slid freely in his hand.

He pushed the gate open just enough so that he could get the sedan through. He quickly closed it afterwards, then drove the car up and past the single building before he backed the car in and cut the engine. He opened his door and stepped out, looked around briefly, then opened the back door and held Ella's hand as she jumped out and onto the gravel drive. Shane closed the door and walked to the metal door of the structure. As he walked toward the door, he could hear Kyle yelling to let him out of the car. Shane ignored him. There was a small chair next to the door. He told Ella to sit there and wait for him; if she needed anything, she should call for him.

Shane took a look back at the car and saw Kyle still securely strapped into the seat. He walked along the porch of the building and checked the knob. It turned freely in his hand. He let his M4 rifle hang from its sling while he drew the smaller Walther pistol. Shane turned the knob and pushed the door in. It swung open silently on well-oiled hinges. Light shone into the room from the open door, but when Shane leaned and peeked inside, he was surprised to see a low wattage light glowing dimly from the ceiling.

The room looked like a business space; a long counter was scattered with rusted car parts and bolts. Along a wall was a wooden bench, and on a table sat a mold-covered coffee pot. Shane stepped completely into the room, then shuffled to the right so that his back was against the wall. A green ledger book and cash register were on the far end of the counter, numerous automotive posters and calendars decorated a wall. A large steel sign on the counter read *Douglas Used Auto Parts*. There was a break at the right end of the counter that led to a doorway.

Shane followed it to hall. Its floor was made of smoothed concrete. Immediately to the right he found a small office furnished with a wooden desk covered with old Playboy magazines and crumpled food wrappers. The room was small, musty, and dimly lit by the same type of low-watt bulb hanging from the ceiling. Shane reached in and pulled the door shut before he continued down the hallway. He passed a filthy restroom with a propped open door and some type of cleaning closet with stiff mops and rusted buckets. The hallway ended at a heavy steel door with another dim light hanging above it. Again the knob turned freely, so Shane turned it and pushed the door open. A large automotive garage, smelling of oil and gasoline and at least sixty feet in length with five large overhead doors on the right wall, greeted him. The two nearest doors were closed and a sort of living arrangement was formed in front of them. As Shane walked past, he saw old couches and box spring mattresses. In a corner was a large pile of women's clothing articles as well as numerous pieces of luggage and duffle bags.

This was where they lived, he thought. Shane could see an old camp stove used for cooking, a large truck tire rim filled with wood embers from a recent campfire, stacked cardboard containers that held canned goods, and empty food boxes and wrappers. Shane patrolled through the space to the end where the last three doors were left open. There were oil drips on the floor inside where cars had been parked. *This must be where Earl kept his truck,* Shane thought to himself, looking at the muddy tire tracks and using the toe of his boot to scuff the fresh oil drips. Shane exited the building and followed it back around to the front where he found Ella still sitting in the chair.

She followed him back to the car and Shane drove it around the building, into the garage, and killed the engine. He got out and pulled a number of chains that quickly closed all of the open bay doors. He walked around to the backseat and opened Ella's door, then pointed to one of the old sofas in the living area. She quickly obeyed and exited the car. Shane moved to the passenger side and opened Kyle's door. He removed the cord from his neck and wrists but kept his hands and ankles bound.

"You sure there's nobody here?" Shane asked him.

"No, there's nobody else," he grunted.

"Okay, Kyle, here's how I see it. I can hang you by your wrists from one of these chains here," Shane said pointing to a number of chains and pulleys connected to the block and tackle hoists attached to the ceiling. "But I figure you'd be very uncomfortable and noisy, and that would prevent my girl from resting."

"Yeah, I don't like that idea either," Kyle said, looking at Shane fearfully.

Shane looked around the room. "I guess I could bring you over there and set you down on one of those mattresses." Shane looked towards Ella, then back at Kyle. "I don't know, Kyle, maybe I should just kill you now. Seems it would be a whole lot easier and save me a great deal of trouble."

"No. Honest, I ain't gonna be no trouble. Look at me, I'm all beat up anyhow. I can't do nothin' to you," Kyle begged.

Shane stood, contemplating the idea. He looked over and saw Ella staring back at him with sad eyes. Shane leaned over and whispered into Kyle's ear, "Okay, but if you cause us any problems I will bleed you out."

CHAPTER 20

The deck of the small riverboat was empty. David was pacing nervously, shouting instructions to the rest of the crew as lines were being pulled up and engines started. Brad moved along the plank wood deck and a crewman indicated for him to drop his gear against a rail. The boat was nearly fifty feet long and twenty feet wide, more of a floating barge than boat—probably used to transport crates of goods up and down the river in better days. A white planked pilothouse divided the barge into two halves. Parts of the white shack and some of the deck looked to have been recently repaired. Scorched and splintered bits of wood still remained.

David moved toward Gunner and spoke loudly so they all could hear. "I'll be bringing the rest of the crew on shortly; you are all to remain on the aft deck. Nobody goes inside, nobody goes up to the bow. Any questions?"

Gunner nodded and pointed to the fresh pine planks and burnt decking near the corner of the pilothouse. "You doing some remodeling?"

"It's dangerous out there; we had some trouble on our last cruise," David said, pointing to the distant shoreline.

Gunner walked closer to the repaired bits of the pilothouse and pointed at the unpainted bits of plank. "Burn marks and frag bits. So the Primals are throwing grenades now?"

David looked away toward a pair of incoming small boats. "Like I said, it's dangerous out there. Here comes your crew, stick to the aft of the barge and I'll have you at your destination by morning."

David turned and walked into the pilothouse, leaving a pair of crewman to help guide in the small boats. Brad saw Doctor Howard standing alone holding his pack, so he guided him to the rail and told him to drop his bag. Howard sat on the deck with his back to the rail as Brad stood over him with his rifle in his hands. Gunner and Meyers were standing near an opening in the aft deck, coordinating the transfer of gear and personnel from the other ship. The small boats pushed off unceremoniously and motored back into the harbor in the direction of the Coast Guard boat.

Once the crowd cleared from the opening in the rail, Brad could see bags of gear stacked in the center of the barges deck. Men crowded around them and then dispersed to find places of their own along the rail. Meyers shot a thumbs-up to David who was observing the transfer through a window in the pilothouse. The engines gurgled and the riverboat picked up speed in the water.

Brad looked across the deck, seeing Vilegas, Parker, Brooks and Sean—all of the shooters from the group. He smiled and moved forward to greet them when Chelsea passed between Brooks and Sean, carrying a pack in one hand and her rifle in the other. Brad stepped forward, trying to hide the shock at seeing her onboard. He moved closer and took the bag from her and tossed it next to the rail close to his own.

"What are you doing here? I thought you would stay with Kelli at the fort."

"I'm needed here," she said, taking her rifle and slinging it over her shoulder. She was dressed in her USMC camouflage uniform, but was now also wearing a British military chest rig filled with NATO magazines in detachable pouches. "Besides, if we find her, what do you all know about taking care of a little girl?"

Sean walked up from behind and slapped Brad on the back. "She's right, and I ain't turning down any extra rifles in the fight. Everyone here volunteered."

Sean pointed to the piles of gear bags with British Navy decals. "Get geared up. We figure we will be deep in Indian country for at least three to four days. The Limeys parted with some of their rations, but you know they only gave us the shit they didn't want."

Meyers laughed at the comment. "It's the Queen's finest boiled sweets, Yank; so no whining."

Brad shook his head and moved to the pile of olive drab bags. He found his own multi cam rucksack and separated it from the mix. He opened the compartments and began to dump personal items on the deck next to it. He started the task of preparing his kit for patrol. Chelsea walked up next to him and knelt down, unzipping a large vinyl bag. She pulled out a stack of filled magazines, three at a time, and placed them next to Brad's gear. Brad looked over at her as she continued pulling items from the bags.

"I don't think this will end well," he said.

"Probably not, but when it does… I want to be out there with you all."

She reached into a bag, pulled out a 24-hour pack of rations, and pushed it in Brad's direction. He reached for it and grabbed her hand. "You shouldn't have come."

"Well, I did, and that's the last I want to hear about it," she said as she got to her feet and moved back to the group of men talking at the far side of the deck. She took a seat at the corner of the rails where Gunner and Meyers had placed their packs. Brad broke down the rations and loaded his rucksack. As he worked, he took notice of the armed crew members patrolling the tops of the pilothouse. Traveling down the river, he expected them to be on watch and alert, but they all appeared to be looking down at his team instead of at the shoreline. Brad finished with his pack and secured the straps. He moved to a corner of the rail where Sean and Brooks were laid out on the deck.

Brad dropped next to them and leaned against the rail. He looked to the shoreline, which was now closer as they headed out of the harbor and into the mouth of the river. The sun was setting and he could just make out shadowy figures moving on the far off boardwalks and beaches. He could hear howling but was unable to determine if it was the wind or the creatures over the rumbling of the engines. A close-by crew member noticed Brad staring far off and pointed out a distant structure, a high walled building on a narrow island.

"That's the Castle. People made it there early, came by boat or anything that could float. They hid out there pretty well for a bit too."

Brad stared at the walled structure without looking up at the crewman. He could see distant forms moving along the beach in front of the castle's walls. As the barge moved past, he could see more and more of them standing shoulder to shoulder watching the slowly moving vessel. Some of them walked knee deep into the water and reached out at them.

"What happened?" Brad asked.

"They lost control. Same as most places do. Somebody gets in, infects the rest. They kill each other off. I was out here on the water watching when the place fell. We could hear their screams, the gunshots. They fired flares; some even tried to swim out to us."

Brad turned and looked up at the crewman. "You didn't help them?"

The man shook his head and dug through a shirt pocket. He took in a deep breath as he placed a bent hand-rolled cigarette between chapped lips and lit it with a disposable lighter. "No, it's Captain's rule – if they *running* we don't help. If they *walking?* Now, *walking* we will barter with 'em, see what they want. But in cases like that," he paused and pointed the glowing cigarette at the quickly fading island castle. "Yeah, like that, we don't get involved."

"You mean you leave them to die," Brad said looking at him disgusted.

"Shit, you say what you want, but that's how we stay alive. Not getting involved." The man leaned out and spit over the rail, then turned to walk back to the pilothouse.

Brad watched the man leave. The sun had fully set now and the surface of the boat was bathed in darkness. The pilothouse held dim lights that cast a soft glow. The distant shore was nothing but a silhouette of blackened outlines. Brad pushed back against the rail and pulled his knees up into his chest. He watched the men on the roof of the pilothouse pace back and forth, patrolling. One turned and stared down at the pile of olive drab bags of gear. He seemed to focus on them a bit too long, long enough to make Brad feel uncomfortable.

"What are you thinking?" Brooks whispered.

Brad looked over and saw Brooks lying against his pack with his boonie cap pulled low over his eyes. His hands were crossed in his lap over the grip of his Heckler & Koch Mark 23 pistol.

"Something isn't right about this crew and this captain," Brad whispered.

"No shit, Sherlock. These guys have been out here working the river since day one. I'm sure they have seen some dark stuff."

"It's more than that. Those two on the roof seem to be more interested in us than the Primals. And the one keeps checking out the gear."

Brooks yawned and crossed his legs. "His special attention to our goodies hasn't gone unnoticed. Just sleep with one eye open tonight. And keep your weapons close," he said, patting his pistol.

Brad brought his right hand down to his hip, felt his pistol, then shrugged his shoulders and cradled his M4 in his arms as he pushed back against the rail. He closed his eyes tightly and then opened them; looking up at the roof, he saw that the patrolling guard had moved. He let his eyes drift now and saw David, the captain, looking out of the window back at the soldiers sleeping on his aft deck. Brad stared at the man in the darkness until the captain turned and disappeared back into the shadows of the pilothouse.

He lay back, trying to push the dark thoughts from his mind. He couldn't leave the suspicions of the crew. He knew the captain was hiding something and wondered why he agreed to help them without even bartering for compensation. Who were these men that left the innocent to die? Brad reached back down to his holstered pistol and drew it out. He held it with his right hand and covered the slide with his left. He wouldn't be sleeping tonight.

CHAPTER 21

Bacon sizzled on a well-seasoned cast iron skillet. It didn't take much to restart the fire in the center of the garage because the coals were still hot; some stirring, a few handfuls of kindling, and it was soon burning bright. Shane found piles of split wood just outside of one of the bay doors. He discovered the plastic barrels were rain catches. All over the building, and even outside, he saw boxes of canned goods and packaged containers of smoked meats.

Shane cut another generous slice from the hunk of bacon and was rewarded with the splash of grease as it hit the pan. Using the same knife, he pried open a can of diced peaches. "So where'd all this stuff come from, Kyle?" he asked without looking up from the skillet.

"Uhh, what stuff?" Kyle answered, dazed like he had just woken up. Kyle was slowly sipping from a Mason jar, sweat beading on his forehead. Shane had finally softened his attitude toward the prisoner. He had cut his bindings, splinted the man's broken leg, and even allowed him some shine for the pain. Kyle's belly had swollen and his breathing had become labored. Shane was sure he'd suffered internal injuries in the attack—probably a broken rib, maybe worse.

Even though he wanted to, he didn't enjoy seeing the kid suffer.

"The food... the whiskey... everything – where'd you get it?"

Kyle straightened his arm and pushed himself up into a seated position. Grunting through the pain, he twisted until he was resting against an old seat cushion. "Farmers' market in town, we hit it early. They had a butcher shop; made their own meats and such. Most of the market was sacked, but nobody thought to crack open the delivery trucks. A lot of the meat was spoiled; you push through all of that and the canned, dried, and smoked stuff was good."

"This is a pretty big take. You could have helped a lot of people."

"Yeah... there was more folks here for a bit," Kyle said before taking a long drink, then pausing to cough; he looked down at the blood on his hand before wiping it on his shirt.

"Take it easy with that stuff. It'll help with the pain, but if you have internal bleeding, it's just going to make it worse." Shane used a fork to lift slices of bacon onto a plastic plate, added hunks of canned peaches, and placed the plate on Ella's lap. "You know, this is the best we have eaten in a while; even at the fort we rarely had fruit. So where'd they go? The others?"

"They just gone," Kyle said uneasily.

"Gone? Without all of their belongings, huh?" Shane said, pointing to the piles of clothing and luggage. "So what, you got them buried in the back somewhere?"

Kyle looked away and put his head down. "I'm not even supposed to be here. I should have been at college... never shoulda come back to this place," he sobbed, pausing again to cough. "When it all started, I was about to go to school. I'd already got an apartment and a job up in Hampton. Momma begged me to come home when things started getting really bad.

"Hell, classes wouldn't ever start again anyway... so I left and came home. It was nice and quiet out here—far from the city and all—like nothing was going on, but folks knew it would get here eventually. Me and Earl, we tried to get the house ready for Momma. We did what we could with what we had but needed supplies, so we made a run into town. We hit up every shop we could think of, buying stuff till the truck couldn't hold no more. Paid with a credit card too," Kyle said with a soft laugh.

"People weren't panicking yet, not then, not this far out from the city. But we all saw it on the news. You know the way people were acting? Even around here, folks were starting to get scared. Everyone was nervous, being on edge, keeping their distance. We loaded up the truck and drove back home. When we got there, we found Momma… dead," Kyle said.

"Infected?" Shane asked.

"No. Robbers we suspect. She'd been shot. Probably angry when they realized she had nothing worth taking. We called the sheriff, but they was too busy. The dispatcher told us we should just call the funeral home. Shit, they wouldn't answer their phone. We drove Momma down there, but the place was empty, all closed up. We buried her ourselves, next to Daddy, over at Oak Creek Cemetery.

"We didn't feel like staying at the house no more. So we came here, to the scrap yard. Earl'd gone to high school with Gary's son, Jasper, and we all knew their cousin Andrew from spending time out here at the yard. We knocked on the gate and Gary took us right in. It was good here, safe, ya know? Even when shit got really bad on the outside; even after the power went out. They have enough solar cells to keep a few lights on. And Hell, there was nothing that got through them fences."

"So when did it all go bad?"

Kyle shrugged his shoulders and took another long sip from the Mason jar, drinking it dry. He coughed and spit red onto his shirt sleeve, then lay back on the mattress, and stared up at the ceiling. "I don't know man, but… I guess you was right killing us all. We ain't good people… not no more, we ain't," Kyle said, beginning to slur his words. "We took in a family for a bit, but it didn't last. The husband was always getting angry about the way Gary talked to his wife. The way he stared at her."

Kyle coughed hard. "You want to know what we was doing out there on that road?"

"It doesn't make any difference now," Shane said, looking at the boy. He was growing paler by the hour and sweating profusely. Shane got up and grabbed another sealed jar from a shelf and switched it with one in the boy's hand. The boy pushed the jar away and pointed to a wooden box on the shelf. Shane retrieved the box and found it full of hand rolled cigarettes. Shane shook his head, "I don't think you should be smoking with that cough."

Kyle forced a small laugh. "Don't worry, I have a prescription. This is Jasper's personal stash. Ha, I don't think he'll mind though." Kyle reached into the box for a small cigarette and Shane helped him light it. After another long coughing fit, he breathed in deeply and lay back again.

"You was right; they was out looking for people, Earl and Gary. Not to attack, though, like you was thinking. We didn't have enough guns for that. You know to fight folks fair. Shit, that pistol I was carrying? It ain't been loaded since I got it. Jasper had lots of bullets for his SKS, and Andrew, his rifle only had a few rounds left. Andrew was the one you kilt trying to sneak up on you. I liked Andrew; he was always a good friend to me." Kyle paused, staring up at the ceiling.

"You have 7.62?"

"What?" Kyle asked as if waking from a dream.

"The SKS; you have ammo for it?"

"Oh, yeah… on the shelf, by the shine – buncha' boxes of it. Jasper was a prepper; or he thought he was. He's the one that set all of this stuff up. The lights, water… all of it."

Shane walked back to the sedan and retrieved the empty SKS he'd pulled off the dead man in the field. He dropped the magazine, then pushed aside jars on the shelves. He found an open Spam can of ammo. He pulled the can closer and located several already-loaded magazines. Shane grabbed one. Loading and charging the SKS, he left the empty on the shelf and returned to the couch.

"Why you interested in that hunk-a-junk? You already have a real nice carbine."

"What would you think if I told you I had less than ten rounds left when you ambushed me?"

Kyle laughed hard, and then coughed until he was spitting more blood. He took a deep breath followed by a long drag of the cigarette. "Ha! Guess we did fuck with the wrong soldier, didn't we?"

"Why would your brother and the old man go so far out on the road with just that shotgun?"

Kyle sighed. "They called it hunting. They'd go a mile or two up the road and set up in the woods. If they got a deer that was great; if not, maybe they'd find a group on the road. Travelers; if they was weak—you know, only one or in a pair—sure they'd jump 'em and just take they things, maybe turn 'em around, maybe worse. But if they was well armed and looked friendly enough, or like they had stuff we'd be wanting, Gary would talk to 'em and tell 'em what we got back here. That we had a nice place for 'em. Usually they agreed and he'd drive them right into our ambush. Boy, was we surprised when you come running through them logs like a bat outta hell." Kyle laughed and coughed up more blood.

"That's not how it was supposed to work. Gary would usually ride in the back with 'em and Earl would drive through the logs and stop. He'd act all shocked and scared while we moved in. Then, when the time was right, we'd take care of 'em. Jasper, enjoyed it, I think. Guess you all musta' got lucky."

"They were after the girl," Shane said.

Kyle coughed again and nodded. "That sounds like Gary; he was always trying to find women."

"She's a kid!"

"I know, mister," Kyle said apologetically, then let the cigarette hang from his lips as he laid his head back.

Kyle stopped talking and took in deep, labored breaths. The sun had dropped and there was only a low glow coming from the hallway light bulb. Shane thought he heard the kid cry. He looked in his direction and saw the orange tip of the cigarette. Shane let the fire go out as night fell. Kyle told him it was safe inside the walls, but it wasn't cold enough to take the risk. He pushed back into an overstuffed couch and felt Ella move up next to him with the wool blanket from his pack. He allowed her to sit on his lap as she curled up against him.

Night came, and so did the moaning sounds of the infected. They sounded distant and random, but it still put him on edge. Shane pulled the pistol from his waistband and held it in his hand as it rested on the arm of the couch. He considered tying the kid back up, but then he heard a gurgling snore come from Kyle's direction. In the distance, Shane thought he heard the low *whoomp, whoomp, whoomp* of a helicopter. He listened intently but the sound quickly faded.

He lifted Ella and laid her on the couch with her head resting near him. He tucked the green blanket in around her, then eased back into the cushion, prepared to stay awake and determined to guard her through the night.

Another string of wet coughs and painful grunting came from Kyle's direction, followed by the wheezing snore.

"I'll let you sleep Kyle, it's more than you deserve," Shane whispered even though he knew the boy wouldn't hear him.

CHAPTER 22

Bright flashes and explosive gunfire jerked Brad's body awake. He rolled to the left, knocking over his rifle while trying to bring up his pistol, but not finding a target. His ears were ringing and bright flashes bled away his night vision. Brad looked up, squinting, and saw a crewman take a burst of gunfire to his chest, then stumble backwards, firing a shotgun blast into the sky. Another man ran for a rail but was cut down by a long, unsuppressed burst from Brooks' MP5.

Sean and Meyers were already on their feet, pressed against the sides of the pilothouse. Meyers brought back the butt stock of the SA80 and slammed it through a window, effectively smashing the glass out. Nearly simultaneously, Sean pulled the pin of a flash bang and tossed it into the compartment. Both men looked away as the crack of an explosion and a bright flash shocked the air. The door was blown outwards and Meyers swung around it and stepped through. Moments later, Brad saw Sean on the roof of the structure and heard Meyers shouting, "All clear," from below.

"Dammit! I think I'm hit," Parker yelled, pulling up his T-shirt and exposing a long, red gash across his right hip. Joey quickly moved to his side, opened a gauze bandage, and slapped it to the wound. "It's just a scratch, stop pouting. Doc Howard, can you have a look at this?" he shouted while keeping pressure on the bandage.

Gunner walked through the mess. "Anyone want to tell me what the hell just happened?" he yelled.

Meyers came through the door, dragging a crew man out by flex-cuffed hands. He dropped him heavily to the deck and turned to watch Sean drag out the captain.

"Their skipper's bleeding out. Ain't much left of him," Sean shouted.

Brooks walked over, stepped around the captured men as he switched out magazines in his MP5, and looked to Gunner. "They tried moving on us. Those two over there," he said, pointing at two crumpled forms by the deck. "They come out of the pilothouse with weapons up, then more lined up on the roof. Looks like they were looking to kill us off and keep our gear. I fired before they could coordinate. That sound about right?" Brooks said, giving the captain a gentle kick to the ribs.

David jerked and turned his head, looking away. Meyers stepped in and gave him another tap with the toe of his boot. "Come on now, mate; don't get shy on us," Meyers said as he knelt to the deck and looked the captain in the eye.

"Your equipment was the only way we're gonna get paid for this trip. Fuel ain't free, you know. It's nothing personal," David said. "We weren't gonna kill you, just tie you up and leave you on shore."

Brooks grunted. "Damn, now this is awkward, I sure do apologize for the misunderstanding."

Brad stood back, watching the scene and spotted Chelsea near Howard and Parker. He moved to her side and he could see she was okay. Parker's wound had already been cleaned and Howard was taping a thick dressing to it. Brad clipped his rifle back to his vest as Sean and Meyers were forcing the captain and the other sailor into back-to-back sitting positions.

"What are they going to do?" Chelsea whispered to Brad.

"Not sure," Brad replied. He turned and looked over the rail. They were in the center of the river and at anchor, even though he could still hear the engines at a low idle. The not so distant shorelines were full of moving shadows—the gunfight had obviously attracted them. Beyond the rows of Primals, Brad spotted a short aluminum dock and a small two story house set back from the river. A loud scream caused him to turn back in the direction of the wounded men. Brooks had his hand on the captain's abdomen and was peeling away layers of clothing. The captain yelped in protest.

"He's in bad shape, nothing I can do for him." Brooks shook his head. "Nope, he won't make it without some high level surgery," Brooks said, probing the wound. "This other one is fine… unless you don't want him to be?"

Gunner squatted and looked the captain in the eyes. "So you were planning to dump us? Like you did the girl and her soldier?"

David lifted his head defiantly. "I got you to your destination. That's the closest structure to where we lost sight of 'em. Did you think this was a free ride?"

"I'm sure we could've worked something out; 'fraid you just put yourself out of business." Gunner stood and looked at Sean. "Toss 'em," he ordered.

Sean looked at Gunner. "Toss him?"

"Chief, throw his pirate ass over the side," Gunner shouted as he moved to the second man.

Sean reached down and grabbed David under an arm as Brooks did the same on the opposite side. They forced him to his feet while David screamed in agony. "You can't do this! *This is my boat*."

The two men ignored his argument and brought him to the rail. Sean adjusted his grip and grabbed a fist full of clothing on the man's back. Then, as he held him out over the edge and dangling above the dark river, he paused and looked back at Gunner. "You sure?"

"I have no sympathy for people like him," Gunner said.

Sean nodded and shoved hard, then jerked back; the captain yelped as he dangled over the rail.

"Stop, dammit! You can't do this!" David screamed.

Gunner stomped across the deck and Sean held tight to the fabric of the man's jacket.

"Look around, David; I'm in charge now. I can do what I want! Now tell me, where did you drop the soldier and the girl?"

David hung over the rail mumbling but not answering the question. Gunner drew his holstered 1911, then turned back to face the second man who was still sitting on the deck, wide-eyed with fear.

"Get him on his feet!" Gunner yelled.

Meyers quickly dropped down and grabbed a shoulder as Brad jumped forward to grab the other. They dragged him kicking and screaming to the rail next to the captain. Sean pulled back on David's jacket so that he was now shoulder-to-shoulder with the sailor.

"Okay, this is speed poker in the worst way it can be played," Gunner whispered, leaning forward so that he was speaking between the two men's heads. "I want to know where the girl is; where you put them ashore," he said just above a whisper.

Gunner took the barrel of his pistol and pressed it against the back of David's thigh. "You're up, Captain."

David growled and spit over the rail into the water. Gunner pulled the trigger, launching a 45 caliber round through the captain's leg and ripping out the front of his quad. David howled and nearly fell over the rail, but Sean caught him and pulled him back in, allowing the man's weight to lie on the railing. The second man squirmed and went weak in the knees. He tried to pull away from Brad, who—although shocked at the events—maintained his grip and helped steady the man on his feet.

"Now you see how this played," Gunner yelled. He took the pistol and placed it against the sailor's leg. "Your turn; where are they?"

"No, no, we didn't put them ashore. The captain, made 'em jump," the sailor pleaded.

"Ding, ding, ding. Gentleman, we have a winner," Gunner shouted. "Bonus round! Where did they jump? I'm asking you, Captain."

David grunted and vomited into the water. He inhaled deeply. "Just up the river… from here, they jumped over… and the damn grunt tossed… grenade that blew up the pilothouse," he said between gasps. "I know they was good in the water… I watched them go around the bend."

"What's between here and the last location you saw them?" Gunner asked.

"Nothing, just fields... we floated to here trying to find them. We anchored for most of the day off this dock. The soldier was smart. If he made it, this is where he would have gone."

"But, you didn't see him?"

David shook his head. "No."

"Very well," Gunner said. He walked closer and relieved Sean of his position, grabbing David by the jacket. "David, nothing personal, but you went against me." He pushed hard and David spilled headfirst into the water. His body dropped below the surface, and then his head came up gasping for air. He kicked his good leg and swam with the current. He swam surprisingly well, considering his condition. He managed to reach the aluminum dock, where he stuck his arms out and grasped the corner of the decking with his fingertips. He pulled himself in and looked back at the barge with a menacing glare.

From behind and above, dark hands reached down and dragged the captain from the water. The Primals howled and screamed in a state of frenzy as they swarmed his body. The mass pulled him away, toward the field, before disappearing into the darkness with the still screaming man.

Brad stood, entranced by the sight on the dock. He felt the sailor in his grip shiver and, suddenly, Brad felt pity for the man. Not wanting to see the sailor's face, he gripped the man tight under the arms and looked away. He heard Gunner walk behind them. "Okay, set him back down."

Brad exhaled a sigh of relief as he walked in step with Meyers to drag the sailor back to the center of the deck. After dropping him, they pushed him back into a seated position. Brad took a stumbling step back and retook his place next to Chelsea; she moved in behind him and pushed against his back. Gunner was still at the far rail, quietly exchanging words with Sean. He nodded, then turned and walked back to the sailor.

Gunner stepped until he was right in front of the prisoner. He squared his feet and looked down at him. "You've got one chance and one chance only. Take us up the river to the last place you saw the pair… or join your captain."

CHAPTER 23

Shane watched the sun slowly rise through a dirty glass window. He'd stayed awake all night keeping the watch and as Shane adjusted himself, he reached beside him to check Ella. She was sleeping soundly under the blanket. He tucked the edges in around her and slowly pushed to his feet, feeling the grinding and burning in his back. He looked across the room at the still figure on the mattress.

Sometime in the middle of the night, Kyle's gurgling snore had gotten raspier, then shrill, and then the time between breaths lengthened. Shane listened intently as the kid finally took his last breath and went silent. Now standing over the body, he felt no emotion for him. Shane pulled the sheet over the corpse and twisted an end shut before he dragged it off the mattress, toward a wall of the building. He would have to dispose of it later.

Shane walked to a window set in the cinderblock wall. He looked outside and into the rear yard. Rows of junked cars and other piled bits of scrap metal stretched for over a hundred yards before ending at the tall, metal-skinned fence. Shane watched silently, looking for any movement; any sign that the compound may not be safe. Somehow, this unlikely place appeared to be a secure sanctuary, a place where they could stay for a while and rest. The only downside was that it was set right on the road, and unlike the bandits, he wouldn't have the manpower to maintain a guard.

He turned and looked around the room at the stacked piles of boxes and crates of food. Shane walked to the hallway and back to the small bathroom he'd spotted the night before. He reached in, flicked a light switch, and was surprised to see a small light turn on. Hoses with clamped ends hung from the ceiling; one stopped above the sink, another about the toilet's tank. Shane walked to the small sink, unclamped the red rubber hose, and a stream of water poured from its end.

Shane smiled and let the water pour over his head and hands as he washed himself. *The hoses must stretch to more rain catches on the roof,* he thought. Shane used the toilet then refilled the tank before he turned and moved back to the large garage space. Digging through a box, he found a can of fruit, then sat heavily in a chair and opened the can. He drank the juice and ate the fruit while he watched Ella sleep.

Ella began to stir; she pulled the blanket off then scrambled to an upright position and looked at Shane. He smiled at her and asked if she was hungry. She yawned and nodded. He got back up and dug through the box for another can, then poured the contents into a bowl. She smiled as he handed it to her. "Are we going to stay here, Shane?" she asked as she brought a spoonful of fruit cocktail to her lips.

Shane looked around. "I think we can stay for a couple days, until we are rested."

Ella took another bite; juice went down her chin and left dirty streaks as she said, "Where is Kyle?"

"He had to go, Ella. You know what? I think it's time we got you a bath," he said changing the subject.

Ella shook her head and put down the bowl. "Where did he go? Is he coming back?"

"No, he won't be coming back," Shane said, getting to his feet. He walked around the interior of the garage and stopped when he found a large pail of clean rags. He sorted through them to find suitable ones that could be used as washrags and towels. A bit more searching and he found a partially used bottle of hand soap. "Okay, Ella, enough stalling; let's get you into some water."

Ella shook her head again, sat back, and pulled the wool blanket over her head. Shane laughed and scooped her up from the couch, blanket and all. He walked her through an open door and into the yard. There were a number of troughs and barrels positioned around the property, filled to varying levels with rain water. Shane walked toward a large plastic basin. He sat Ella down and looked at the tub. Plastic had been stretched over it, with a small hole cut in the center of the thin film. As water hit the film, gravity pulled it toward the center and into the tub. It seemed wrong to waste fresh water, but there were weeks' worth of water all around him.

Shane pulled back the plastic and put his hand in the clear water. It was warm, the solar effect of the plastic having heated the water. He turned toward the girl and removed the wool blanket. He carefully folded it and set it on the ground, then helped the girl undress. He lifted her up and gently lowered her into the tub. She smiled when she felt the warm water and quickly began to play. Shane squeezed hand soap into his palm and began to clean the dirt from her hair and back. She protested but stood still while he scrubbed.

"Do you have a little girl, Shane?" she asked as Shane used the clean rag to wipe the soap from her face.

"I never had any kids," he answered as he put the wet rag over her shoulder.

"Then how come you know how to take care of girls? My Dad isn't good at girls."

Shane let out a deep laugh. "Oh, I don't think I know too much about girls. It's good you're so tiny, or you'd figure it out."

Shane reached into the tub and lifted her out, setting her on the center of the wool blanket. He dried her with a second rag, then hung it over her shoulders as he went to work washing her clothing in the barrel. After pulling the makeshift towel around her, Ella dropped to sit on the blanket and watch him wash the clothing.

"Do you have a wife?"

"Why so many questions? No, I never had a wife."

"Do you have a girlfriend?" she asked, watching as Shane wrung out her now clean T-shirt then began squirting soap onto her soiled jeans.

"No. I did once though; she was pretty like you but she didn't like my job. I left one day and when I came back, she was gone." He scrubbed the fabric, pulled the jeans from the water, and started ringing them out. When he was done, he hung them over the side of the barrel. He pulled the folded edges of the blanket up and around Ella then lifted her into his right arm as he grabbed the wet clothing with his left.

"I like your job, Shane," she whispered as he carried her back to the open garage door. He pulled her in and she rested her head on his shoulder. Shane stopped as he heard the thumping, same as from the night before. Unmistakably a helicopter, but not the large military types he was used to. He stopped, standing motionless just feet from the door. As he listened, the sound got louder then faded away. *Searching maybe?* Shane thought. *Searching for what?* As the sounds of the rotors faded, they were replaced by the infected that were prematurely woken early in the day.

Shane moved through the door and bolted it behind him. He brought Ella to the couch and placed her on the cushions. He left the rags and blankets wrapped around her while he laid her clothing out to dry. Shane used dry wood to build a small nearly smokeless fire. His eyes wandered to the high ceiling of the garage where he watched the light gray wisps of smoke climb and be pulled through a high open skylight. He followed the corner of the ceiling and saw a small metal ladder that led to a roof access.

He saw that it was a pull down ladder currently in its up position. He looked to check on Ella and saw that she had manage to turn pieces of firewood into dolls and was deep in conversation with them.

"Stay on the couch, Ella, I'll be back in a minute," he said.

Shane got to his feet and walked across the garage to the access ladder. He pulled on the control rope and slowly allowed his weight to drop the ladder to its down position. He looked back at Ella; she was still on the couch and occupied in play.

Shane put a boot on the ladder. Finding it solid, he climbed the top and discovered a square metal access hatch that was left open. Shane poked his head through and stepped onto the roof. As he suspected, two large rain barrels and coils of rubber hose sat above where he figured the bathroom would be below. There were large banks of solar panels and a number of homemade wind turbines connected to automobile alternators. Everything was tied into covered banks of 12-volt car batteries.

He walked across the roof to the road side of the building where he could see the gate and the highway beyond it. From his high vantage point, he could see over some of the tree tops and farther to the south. He saw tall electrical towers and noted that there were several homes leading away in the direction he hadn't yet traveled. Shane turned and searched the direction the helicopter sounds had come from. He could see the perimeter fence circling the compound; beyond the fence was a narrow stretch of high grass, then thick forest.

He walked the entire outline of the roof while scanning the perimeter fence. The area appeared secure but he would have to get down and check it closer to also look for an emergency escape route. He saw no signs of the infected, not even on the roads. The houses within his line of sight were too far away to get a good look at, though. If he decided to stay here, they would have to be checked out. He liked the security of the building but worried it would become a target for other wandering groups.

Shane walked back to the hatch and prepared to step down when the loud blast of a distant explosion caught his attention. He moved back to the roof and looked in the direction of the sound. He heard the rattle of small arms fire, followed by more explosions. Smoke billowed far in the distance—it was toward the river, the direction he'd come from. Another loud explosion, rapid gunfire, and the sound of the distant helicopter made Shane scramble for the hatch and drop into the building below.

CHAPTER 24

The sailor guided them back to the bend in the river where the crew had lost sight of the soldier. The barge was brought in close to the shore and the engines were shut down. They waited, watching the shoreline as dawn approached. They found this portion of the river void of life—most of the infected having traveled farther down river, attracted by the noise of previous gunfire and the feeding frenzy of the Primals.

Brad prepped the remainder of his gear, then assisted Chelsea and Parker to go through checklists of gear that Meyers had laid out on the deck. Mostly satellite base systems, GPS, mobile phones, a large antenna array, and, of course, sets of heavy batteries. Meyers was documenting every item as it was distributed: what it was, to which person it was given, and where in each pack it was located.

Parker cussed as another heavy battery pack was tossed in his direction. "What's with all of this stuff?" he asked.

Meyers held up a sat phone. "Mate, if we get into trouble, this handy little item can call in a Tomahawk. I don't think you will be whining about the weight of the battery if it comes to that."

Joey reached down and pulled the battery form Parker's grip. "I got you," he said, dropping the battering into a pocket on the front of his own rucksack.

Gunner stomped out of the pilothouse, breaking up the conversation as he pushed the captured sailor ahead of him. Gunner forcibly turned the man and directed him against the wall.

"I was able to contact the fort on the High Frequency; I let Kelli and Cordell in on current events," Gunner said, looking at Meyers but speaking so that everyone could hear. He turned and looked at the sailor. "I'm tempted to put a bullet in you, but Cordell tells me that this barge and your work are essential to the survival of the fort. So... looks like you will be getting a second chance. I'm counting on you to deliver this barge back to the fort; do it and you're off the hook, cross me again and I'll track you down and feed you to the Primals—"

"Bullshit, man; let's kill this dude. We can get the boat on the return trip!" Joey countered.

Gunner grinned. Looking back at the sailor, he said, "My friend makes a hell of a point. If I thought we would be returning back to this point, I'd probably take him up on it."

"Then how we getting back if the boat leaves?" Joey asked.

"We have Kelli on comms; she will send someone for us. If that fails, Meyers has the sub on satcom and they can relay the message for us," Gunner answered. "Unless you want to volunteer to take ride with our new friend back to Sumter."

"Nah, screw that. I'm a killer, not a stow-away."

"Then I guess we have nothing to talk about," Gunner said.

Joey conceded by shrugging his shoulders. "I don't know, man. Seems like a wasted opportunity to off a scum bag, but you're the boss, Pops."

Sean and Brooks walked away from the rail where they were inspecting the shoreline with a set of binoculars. They joined the rest of the party in the center of the deck. "Most of the riverbank walls are high, but there are a few spots right over there where a person could come out of the water. Makes sense for us to go ashore there as well."

Gunner reached down for his own pack and hoisted it with his strong arm. "Sounds good, Chief. Ready the small boat, we'll head out in five."

The small dingy could only hold three, so the first group went across, dragging a rope behind them that they tied off to a tree on the riverbank. Parker stayed in the small dingy as Brooks and Sean slipped over the side and into the muddy bank of the river. They quickly pulled themselves up and onto the grass-covered ground above. They disappeared for a moment before Sean came back into view, holding up a finger for two more.

Parker pulled on the rope and guided the small boat back to the dingy as Gunner pointed at Brad and Joey. Brad nodded and walked to the rail. Leaning over, he handed his bag to Parker and then did the same with Joey's. Brad put a hand on the rail, climbed over and down into the dingy as Parker held the craft steady against the current as best he could. Joey climbed aboard and Parker wasted no time pulling them back to the bank.

The boat squished against the muddy edge and Brad stepped out, sinking above his ankle in the sticky mud. He took the closest pack and heaved it over the edge, then tossed the second bag behind him. Joey got out next and together, they pushed the small boat off and back at the barge. Brad reached up and grabbed tight handfuls of the thick grass. Using his feet against the bank, he pulled himself up and over the edge before reaching down to take Joey's wrist to pull him up next.

Brad rested silently on one knee until he spotted Sean to the far north on the opposite side of a muddy trail. He turned his head without moving the rest of his body; Brooks was to the south as he had predicted he would be. Brad tapped Joey on the shoulder and indicated for him to pick up near security by pointing to a location between them and Sean. Joey nodded and stepped off quietly with his rifle at the low ready. Brad stood crouching and moved to the south.

In less than ten minutes, the crew had all filed off the boat and lined up evenly spaced on the field side of the trail. Parker was the last one out of the dingy. He tied the rope to a cleat; the sailor reeled in the rope and secured the dingy to the barge. Then the sailor returned to the pilothouse. Gunner ordered him not to move until nightfall. He didn't want him doing anything during daylight hours to disturb the sleeping Primals.

After staying motionless for several minutes to make sure they came ashore unnoticed, Sean turned and walked slowly until he stopped just behind Brad. Gunner was already there and Sean pointed out sets of old footprints in the muddy trail. He located breaks where a human foot had broken into the high grass and possibly moved to the road. Sean used his hand to point to swaths of bent and flattened grass where someone had waded across the field. He explained the trail was hard to identify as the soldier or an infected because of the recent action of the infected moving south to the dock. He suggested they patrol to the house.

Gunner dipped his chin in agreement. Sean walked the line, moving to the rear while signaling for the others to stand as he passed them. When he had everyone up, he slapped the man in front of him and the eight-man team began moving forward in a column formation, staying out of the high grass to remain quiet and avoid detection. Brad was third from the back, Parker just ahead of him; Brooks had taken point and was leading far ahead. Whenever Brooks would pause to examine the trail, the rest of them would kneel down, looking in opposite directions to provide a bubble of security.

Morning dew still held heavy to the grass and the muddy trail, their boots sticking with every step. Brad scanned off into the high grass and to the road beyond it. The sun was breaking through the trees to the east on the far side of the river and casting an eerie golden glow across the field. Brad imagined the Primals retreated there to avoid the daylight. He found it strange that even continents away, the Primal behavior seemed the same. In the deserts, the Primals were less active, so they blamed it on the heat of the day. In the sub temperatures of Newfoundland, they were slower but still became scarce in the daytime hours, so temperature didn't seem to make a difference. The Primals had become nocturnal hunters, pack hunting under the cover of darkness.

Brad recalled the time they watched Primals emerge from the dunes of sand, rising into the night and howling at the stars. He looked at the tall grass and felt his heartbeat quicken as he imagined hundreds of them lying silently in it. He stepped forward and almost walked into Parker who'd stopped on the trail. Brad woke from his dark thoughts and took a knee, pointing outward to cover the field; he scanned to the left and saw the farmhouse offset from the trail.

Sean walked up the inside of the path tapping his shoulder, indicating for Brad to follow as he passed. Brad climbed to his feet and speed walked to catch up. Brooks was on a knee at the head of the column; Sean quickly moved in beside him and Brad stopped just behind to form a backward pointing triangle. Brooks waved a hand at the blood-streaked dock and bits of yellow slicker and canvas clothing that littered the trail and the field.

Sean looked at the house. "Let's clear it," he whispered.

Brooks got to his feet and led off with Sean directly behind him and Brad taking up the rear. They moved past the bloody dock and onto the stone path leading up to the house. Brooks moved hastily onto the porch and pressed against the wall on the knob side of the door. Sean fell in directly behind him while Brad took the opposite wall. When all men were in position, Brooks checked the knob—the door was secured. Sean removed his hawk and stepped in front of the door but Brooks held up a gloved hand to stop him. He lifted a welcome mat and shook his head, then reached and swiped his hand over the wooden trim above the door. His hand stopped and he smiled as he lowered his arm, revealing a small bronze key between his fingertips.

Sean furled his brow. He again took his position behind Brooks who inserted the key and heard the click of the lock. He again turned the doorknob and heard a clunk before it easily swung inward. Before it was all the way open, Brooks swept through the opening quickly with his submachine gun at the ready; Brad filed in after him, with Sean moving in last. They were hit with the fading smell of death; it was distant and musty, not like the rotting meat they'd become accustomed to. Without commands, the trio fanned out into the farmhouse kitchen. To the left was a stairway. Looking through the kitchen, they saw a countertop and stove, beyond that, a darkened living room.

Sean made a clicking sound with his cheek, causing the other two to look over at him. He was pointing at a drawing made on the table top, scribbled in grease pencil. It was a rough sketch of a stick figure holding a rifle. Next to him was a smaller stick figure with a ponytail. Brooks put his hand on the table and swept up crumbs and sticky drops. "This was recent," he whispered. "There's dust on all the chairs but this one, and the table is clean." They inspected the kitchen and found a pot with drops of water still in the bottom. Brad waited by the back door while Brooks and Sean cleared the rest of the home; room by room, floor by floor. When Sean walked down the stairs, he stopped at the bottom briefly, then he moved back to the kitchen door, stuck his head out, and waved his arm to motion the others to come forward. He moved back in and stared at the drawing on the table before walking to the counter and taking a seat on top of it.

Howard was pushed through the door with Meyers, Chelsea, and Gunner close behind. Parker and Joey were picked to hold sentry on the back porch. Brad sat in a chair at the kitchen table and pointed at the drawing. Meyers smiled as he walked closer to examine it. "Did you find anything else?"

"We got two dead in the living room; Grandma and Grandpa been there a while, a young man chained to a wall upstairs – some crazy shit, the blood is still sticky, someone did some slicing and dicing on it. Master bedroom has been slept in recently and from the dusty footprints on the floor I'd say with certainty our soldier was here. And unless he is an idiot savant, the girl drew these pictures.

"How long ago?" Meyers asked.

Sean shrugged looking at Brooks who was leaning against the stair rail. "Two days, maybe a bit longer. Front door is unlocked and open; I'd guess they headed up and stuck to the road moving southwest."

Meyers took a drink from a canteen. "Okay, we ain't staying; let's move –."

Joey poked his head in the door interrupting, "Chief, I hear a helicopter!"

Sean jumped off the counter and briskly walked to the covered porch with the others close behind him. Just as Brad made it through the doorway, a small, fast moving, powder black AH-6 Little Bird helicopter flew by just above the water's surface. Parker prepared to step off the porch and wave when Howard yelled, "No! Don't."

The others turned to look at Howard with surprise just as they heard the *swoosh* of a rocket, immediately followed by a loud explosion. The pitch of the helicopter's rotor changed as it turned and climbed for elevation. Sean pushed everyone back inside, closed the door, and stood watching by the window. The helicopter made another low pass, then hovered as men on the skids fired rifles up river. The helicopter pivoted on its axis and let loose a second salvo of rockets. Black smoke plumed from where they knew the barge was anchored. The Kiowa hovered in position then cut a larger arc before flying off.

Sean turned and stomped to Howard. He grabbed him by the collar and spun him around, slamming his head onto the countertop. "What the fuck is going on?"

Howard struggled against Sean's weight, trying to stand. Meyers moved closer and waved Sean aside. Sean stepped back, releasing Howard's collar. Meyers pulled out a kitchen chair then manually moved Howard until he was sitting in it. "Now, Doctor, would you fancy an explanation?"

Howard looked up at them with sunken eyes. "They shouldn't be here."

"Who shouldn't be here?" Meyers asked.

Howard shook his head. "They are the CNRT."

"Who?" Meyers asked again.

"The Coordinated National Response Team, but this makes no sense; they already have the Aziz specimen, they don't need the girl!"

Brooks dropped his arms as Sean stepped forward, looking at Howard. Brad's jaw dropped with shock. "Back the fucking train up, what did you just say?" Sean said, looking flustered.

"The CNRT, that's what they call themselves. They are looking for a cure, but they want it for themselves. No, this isn't right; they already have patient zero, the source."

"Aziz is the source?" Brad mumbled.

"Not exactly. Like the girl, we believe he shares a rare genetic mutation that makes him immune. He used his own blood to make the serum, the basis for the *Primalis Rabia*. Like a key to a lock, his blood is also the cure. We were onto him early at the CDC and Public Health Service. Aziz is a narcissist. He published his findings on known terror websites days into the global attack; he boasted and taunted us. We tried to unlock the virus' code, but without a source patient, decoding the virus was nearly impossible under the time constraints. The CIA tracked Aziz to a few remote locations and training sites. We were close, so close, but we always got to him too late. He was eventually pulled from the mountains of Afghanistan by the CNRT before a team could be scrambled to recover him."

Brooks picked up a kitchen chair and threw it down the hallway into the living room. "Are you fucking kidding me?" he shouted as he walked away into the other room.

Howard paused uncomfortably, watching Brooks leave the room. Meyers pulled out a second chair and sat across from Howard. "Why didn't you tell us this before, mate?"

Howard looked down at his lap, fidgeting with his hands. "I'm sorry, I didn't know if I could trust you. Every effort we have made to find a sample has been thwarted by the CNRT; they are everywhere."

"Who are they?" Meyers asked.

"They're us. Before the split, you know, after the Meat Grinder."

Sean grunted, "Doc, what the hell are you talking about?"

Howard looked at Sean confused. "After DC; you know… the failed defense of the city, the Battle of the Meat Grinder? The government split, the executive branch refused to give up the city. Most of the house and senate had already retreated to their home districts.

Finally, after days of losses and entire military units deserting, the joint chiefs made a call. They ordered the evacuation of the city against the orders of the president. Not everyone listened, but much of the military and a good deal of the federal government went far west."

"And they became the CNRT?" Sean asked.

Howard nodded. "It was like they went into a mountain bunker as the US Government and came out the Coordinated National Response Team. I was working in Virginia when it all fell apart. It's only by chance that I'm not with them now. We were given the evac order and they brought caravans of helicopters to evacuate us back west. Several of us were separated, but we managed to link up with some National Guard units and local law enforcement. They moved us north, all the way across the Ohio River to a hospital at an air force base near Dayton."

"You said you were with the Public Health Service?" Sean asked.

"I am, but with the Midwest Alliance."

Gunner shook his head and slammed a fist onto the table's surface. "Okay, all bullshit aside; what are the facts we need *now*?"

"Bottom line, if we ever want a chance at a future… a cure, we need that girl. If the CNRC gets to her first, they will kill her and burn the body."

"How did they find us?" Gunner asked.

"Probably didn't, they're thorough and probably have the same info we did about Fort Collins. They're good with electronics—."

"They probably hit on the HF radio call this morning," Meyers said.

The helicopter flew closer before making another wide arc and disappearing. Joey ran through the living room and looked out of the front door while Sean took back his position at the kitchen window. "Chopper's gone but by the looks of that smoke, so is the barge. I'm sure the Primals will be up early."

Gunner stomped across the room, grabbing his rucksack and throwing it up onto his shoulders. "Okay, we need to get moving before this place is overrun. Suppressors if you got 'em; we roll two by two on the road," he said as he reached into a side pouch on his hip, pulled out a screw on can, and attached it to the end of his SA80. "Let's go, ladies!" Gunner stepped off through the home, nearly kicking the front door off its hinges as he burst out onto the front porch.

CHAPTER 25

Shane dropped into the space of the garage and looked to the couch were he'd left Ella. She was curled into a ball, hiding under the green blanket. He moved to her side and pulled it away from her head. She looked at him and whispered, "I heard bad people, Shane."

"It's okay. I heard it too, but it's far way. Nobody knows we're here," Shane said, trying to hide the concern in his voice.

"Can we leave now, Shane?"

Shane put his hand on her back and laid back against the couch searching for an answer. She climbed out of the blanket and lay in his lap. In the distance, he heard the helicopter again. He debated building a fire to signal them.

But the gunfire… who or what was that? Maybe just battling the infected. Maybe not… No, can't risk it, don't know who they were. Stick to the plan, Shane; get the girl to Savannah.

"Okay, Ella, we can leave. We'll get the car ready to go and leave in the morning, okay?"

Ella lifted her head and smiled. She climbed from his lap and, standing on the cushion next to him, gave Shane a hug. He squeezed her back. Shane didn't have any experience with children. In the past, he always thought of them as annoying tiny people that required a lot of attention. The girl's need for affection used to make him uncomfortable. It'd been awhile since he'd allowed anyone to get close to him. At first he faked it, but now the feeling for her was real; he wondered if this was what it was like to be a father. To know you would protect someone with your life. To have something to fight for.

Shane kissed her on the forehead and got back to his feet. He grabbed the car keys from the table in front of him and pushed a button to pop the trunk. He'd have to prioritize the food and get as much as possible into the sedan. With the vehicle, and sticking to rural roads, Shane thought they could make Savannah in a few hours' time – leaving just before noon and arriving at the hottest part of the day. He would have to have a contingency plan, just in case Savannah was gone, or they didn't make it there.

Shane walked to the trunk of the car; there was plenty of space and would be more if he pushed the seats forward. He noticed a board on a wall with more sets of keys. There were vehicles all over the property and he debated selecting something different; one of the wreckers out front perhaps, or a rusted van he'd spotted from the roof. In the end, he stuck with the sedan because it was a known and the bandits had selected it for a reason.

He found two large canvas duffel bags filled with junk; Shane dumped the contents on the floor and returned to the food stores. He began selecting things that could be considered entire meals or that were high in protein. He stuffed the spaces in between with the plastic-wrapped dried meats, small packages of crackers, and other dry goods. He found four large jugs of water that he stored behind the backseats. Shane loaded the rest of the empty SKS magazine and poured the remaining rounds from the Spam can into a pouch on his rucksack.

Once the car was fully packed and loaded, he pulled it out of the garage and parked it just in front of the sliding gate. *Tactically parked,* he called it. If anything happened and they needed to bug out quick, he could slide the gate and go. Last thing he wanted was to be surrounded and stuck in the garage with the things pressed against the sliding door. This way he could cause a distraction near the overhead doors and sneak out a different exit. He left the keys in the ignition and walked back through the front door of the building. He found Ella with the tiny backpack. She was sorting through other cans of food and had apparently discovered a secret stash of candy.

"Hey, where'd you find the goodies?" he asked, watching her sort through a large freezer bag of individually wrapped chocolates.

"There," she answered, pointing to a wooden foot locker.

Shane walked across the room and opened the lid. It was stuffed with personal items—socks, faded T-shirts, periodicals. Shane found a small leather bag; inside it were bottles of prescription drugs. He stared at one labeled *Vicodin* with a woman's name. Shane removed the cap and shook the bottle; it was at least half full. He had stopped taking his own pills the morning he left his apartment, fully intending not to see another day. His pain was still real—a constant reminder of his injuries—but his thoughts were clearer now. Shane poured the contents of the bottle into the palm of his hand. He looked at them, moving them around with his index finger.

"Did you find candy, Shane?" Ella asked.

Suddenly feeling guilty, Shane closed his palm on the pills then poured them back into the bottle. He placed the bottle back into the small leather bag, zipped it shut and held it, trying to decide what to do with it. He reached across and slammed the wooden locker shut before returning to the task of packing for the trip. As he walked by his rucksack, he stuffed the leather bag into an outside pocket. It was still medicine and might be needed, he justified to himself.

He built a small fire and prepared cans of chicken soup for lunch. He made coffee and strained juice from the cans of fruit to mix with water for Ella. He kept the fire small and made up of dry sticks so that the smell of wood smoke would be harder to detect. He was still unsure about the sounds of combat he'd heard earlier in the day and he didn't want to attract unwanted guests. He ate as much as he could hold and encouraged Ella to overeat as well. It was important to pick up as many calories as possible when they had the opportunity.

Shane let the fire burn itself out, not wanting to smother it and cause extra smoke. Ella was asleep again. She didn't like to let him know, but he was aware how hard the traveling was on her. Shane poured the rest of the fruit drink mix into a glass on the table and then went to clean up their dinner mess. He checked the back doors to make sure everything was bolted tight, then went by himself to search the front offices he'd bypassed earlier.

He walked the hallway and stopped at the wooden office door. The bottom of it was kicked and broken, the glass cracked and chipped. Shane turned the knob and let the door swing in. The office was dark and stunk of cigarette smoke. A clay ashtray filled with butts sat on a desk covered with yellow receipt paper and other forms. An old beige computer was on the floor in the corner with a dusty tube monitor sitting on top. Shane moved around the desk and sat in a torn vinyl roller chair. He opened the top drawer; it was filled with junk, rusty car parts, and bolts. The next drawer held files and a box of envelopes. Shane leaned back in the chair and looked at the walls. There were photos of old men on the covers of calendars – previous owners he imagined.

Shane got up and left the office, closing the door behind him. He walked into the storefront and looked around. An antique register was on the counter. Shane hit a button and a drawer rolled open to reveal the tray still filled with cash, small bills, nothing larger than a ten. Paper currency no longer held value, but he still grabbed a fistful of the dry bills to use as fire starter. He folded the stack in half and stuffed it in his pocket. Shane turned to leave, then paused as he heard the sound of the helicopter.

He walked to the front door and cracked it open. There was little cloud cover, the skies were blue, and he could see the treetops blowing in a soft breeze high above the fence. The helicopter was high-pitched and getting louder; it seemed to be moving in his direction. Shane stayed in the cover of the doorway searching the sky as it flew past him, traveling just above the treetops and flying fast. It was a small scout helicopter. They'd called them Little Birds when he was in the army. He could see two men clad in black holding rifles, hanging from the sides and riding the skids of the helicopter.

The Little Bird moved fast then climbed at a sharp angle before seeming to float in the sky. The nose turned around, it quickly dropped altitude, and then shot back up the road in the opposite direction headed for the river. As it moved out of sight, Shane recognized the sound of 70 millimeter rockets being launched and the sharp explosions. Deep in the trees, less than a few miles away, dark plumes of gray smoke filled the air. Automatic weapons fire joined in the mix; he could tell from the sounds that it was ground based and 5.56. More explosions and more gunfire sounded before the Little Bird sped past him again, made the same turning motion, and dropped low to the road. Shane watched as the men on the skids fired down the street while the Little Bird shot past, just above the treetops, and straight down the road.

He felt a thump against his leg and saw Ella had found him; her head was buried in the fabric of his pants. Shane dropped his right arm to her shoulder as he backed into the storefront. He pushed the door three-quarters of the way shut and looked at the sky through the narrow crack. The helicopter changed pitch and made a whining sound. As it drew closer, he watched it cut up out of the tree line at an odd angle; it spun around to the side, gaining altitude as it spun. Its nose dipped, then it dropped and increased speed before it completely vanished out of his line of sight. A large explosion shook the trees. Shane pulled inside and closed the door behind him. He then turned the bolt lock, latching the door.

Ella was sobbing. He reached down and picked her up. She buried her head in his shoulder and cried. "Can we go, Shane?"

Shane leaned back, pressing against the door, trying to decide what to do. Keeping Ella cradled in his arms, he hurried to the living space. He grabbed his nearly empty M4 and placed it on top of his rucksack, clipping the D-ring to one of the straps. He slung the SKS over his shoulder, reached for his bag, and then paused, second guessing himself. Shane paced around the room, fighting the acid bile of panic building in his stomach. He took a deep breath and stood in front of his rucksack.

It started; the wailing of the infected. The helicopter and gunfight stirred up everything in the area – and they were on the hunt. They were loud and seemed to surround him. Even inside the fences and enclosed in the block building he could hear the howls as they woke. Shane, still carrying Ella, moved to a back window and pulled back a roll down blind.

The yard was still empty but the moans of the infected filled the air, then slowly turned to a roar. They were no longer hunting… they'd found their prey.

CHAPTER 26

Sean, Brooks, and Meyers were setting a quick pace in the front of the formation. The rest of the team made up the rest of the column, staggered on the left and right sides of the road. Howard was next to Gunner who was still grilling him for information.

During the Battle of the Meat Grinder, the military switched from a defensive operation to a full withdrawal. The Pentagon was evacuated along with every high-ranking government official who was willing to go. The President held firm though; most of his staff, and even some of the elite military units, stood by his side to the end. There were rumors he was alive in a bunker or on some remote island. People even claimed to have seen a video broadcast from Bermuda.

After the Meat Grinder, states retracted from the federal government. Territorial lines were drawn and new alliances were made. Howard and his group landed in the southern portion of the Midwest Alliance. Texas was the second stronghold, and then there was Colorado. By circumstance, the CNRT was located in bunker complexes deep in the Rocky Mountains.

Early on, the Coordinated National Response Team was just what the name said it was; they shared national resources to help provide stability to what was left of the nation. As state governments became more isolated, the CNRT began losing control of federal assets located within state borders – reserve units, federal agencies, major airports, and oil pipelines. The CNRT grew more aggressive. It was then that the leaders of the Midwest Alliance discovered the CNRT's efforts to prevent the nation from finding a cure. Defectors claimed the CNRT leadership believed the only way to unite the country would be with a cure, and the party holding the cure would come out on top.

The group didn't make it far before they picked up on the sounds of the searching helicopter. When they heard the thump of the Little Bird, Sean waved them into the wood line. They quickly scrambled into the trees moments before the helicopter cut perpendicular to the road, just behind and north of their location. It flew fast, making itself visible for less than a second.

Sean called them back up and took off again, this time at a near run. The sounds of the helicopter faded, then slowly increased as it looped back for another run.

"How the hell do they know we're here?" Gunner yelled as he pushed Howard ahead of him.

"I don't know!" Howard said wheezing. "Maybe the boat crew said something... told someone we were looking for the girl."

The helicopter sounded like it was right on top of them and Sean, again, signaled for them to get off the road. Brad ran for thick cover just as the helicopter, this time coming from behind, flew down the center, following the road just above the trees and continued past them.

Sean yelled all clear and called them back to their feet. As Brad moved to the road, he saw the bloated body of a fat man with gunshot wounds to the head and face. He pointed it out to Gunner, who only nodded in response. When they resumed running, Brad saw a spot where the gravel on the shoulder of the road was chewed up and black tire marks covered the pavement. Primal bodies were in the grass and lying on the blacktop near the spot. As they ran by, Brooks paused to grab the loose gravel and tumble it through a gloved hand. Brad ran up and stopped beside him.

Brooks looked at him. "Something happened here. We're getting closer."

"Did you see the dead fat man?"

Brooks looked up the road as the last of the team ran past. "I did, and those were .22

shell casings on the ground, same as at the farmhouse. I think the soldier was our shooter."

Brooks stretched out an arm and pushed Brad into the tree line as the Little Bird came back into view directly ahead of them. The Little Bird lined up and angled down. Brad saw a flash as rockets smoked in their direction. He ran farther into the trees and buried his head. The rockets overshot and landed more than fifty feet behind them before the explosions shook the ground. As the bird flew out of range again, everyone was back up and running—this time without being told. The helicopter's pitch changed as it turned and lined back up with the road. Again, they dove for the tree line as it flew by; Brad and the others rolled to their backs, now firing on the helicopter. The bird juked and rose in elevation but continued its track down the road.

Sean ordered everyone on their feet, and then pointed to logs crisscrossing the road far in the distance, "Go, go! When you hear it, get to cover."

Sean stood on the side of the road and had removed the long rifle from his pack. "Let's finish this shit, Brooks!" he yelled when Brooks and Brad hit his position.

Brooks stopped, understanding the suggestion. He removed his own rifle from his back and dropped to the grass on the side of the road next to Sean. "You better catch up with the team, Brad," Brooks said in a calm voice as he removed the lens caps from his rifle's scope.

Brad turned and sprinted, trying to catch up with the others. The Little Bird cut back into view far to the south. It looked blurry cutting through the heat waves of its own exhaust as it dropped lower and angled forward. Brad watched the rest of the team dive for cover. Men in black uniforms leaned out from the sides of the Little Bird. Suspended from safety lanyards, they stood and raised their rifles, firing at Brad's men crawling for cover.

The world slowed down. Brad felt rage seeing the men hanging and firing on his people. He stopped in the center of the street and planted his feet. He raised his rifle and aimed high, just above the quickly approaching helicopter. He used his thumb to rotate the selector switch to full auto and pumped the trigger, releasing three to four round bursts and adjusting his point of aim after every trigger squeeze. In slow motion, he watched the road all around him become pockmarked as incoming rounds impacted the pavement and kicked up tiny clouds of white dust.

Brad was focused on the windscreen of the Little Bird. It was close enough now that he could see the helmeted men wearing dark goggles at the controls. Brad pulled the trigger again, feeling the bolt lock to the rear. Keeping his eyes on target, he used his firing hand to push the magazine release button. His left hand dropped, found a new magazine in his chest rig, and fed the rifle. Slapping the magazine in place, he brought up his left thumb and pressed the bolt release as he watched the Little Bird's windscreen split and spider web.

The helicopter dipped, losing altitude, then screamed as it turned abruptly, climbing at a steep angle directly into the sky and nearly clipping nearby trees. It cut up and out of sight to the right, then shot past them; nearly inverted as it crossed over the road diving at a deep angle.

Brad felt the concussion in the trees as the helicopter impacted with the ground.

"Hey, dumb ass! What was that?" Sean yelled from behind him.

Brad let his rifle hang in his right hand. He turned, looking back as he reacquired his senses.

Sean was still on the ground, changing magazines in the rifle. He got to a knee and climbed to his feet just as Brooks did the same thing to the right and a few feet behind him. "Maybe make this the last time you play chicken with a helicopter," Sean said, stepping back onto the surface of the road.

"I think we can discuss Sergeant Thompson's extreme acts of dumbassery at another time. That helo crash is gonna piss off the Primals; you know how ornery they get when they wake up early," Brooks said, walking past at a quick pace.

Fulfilling Brooks' prediction, they began to hear the sounds of the screaming Primals. Brooks picked up his pace and Brad joined him on the road at nearly a full sprint. The team was ahead, setting up a hasty fortification in the log barriers. Gunner was pointing and yelling instructions as the others closed off the logs to build a square logged-in perimeter. Parker and Joey were dragging in more trees from the edge of the woods. Brad ran to assist them and helped Joey toss a log into the barrier as the first of the Primals came into view.

Meyers raised his rifle and dropped the first creature with two well-placed shots. Brad quickly climbed over the logs and took a position facing the tree line. The others spread out, providing cover in all directions. Howard was standing in the middle of the circle, not knowing what to do, while Gunner slapped Brad on the back and pointed him to a section of the perimeter. Brad dropped his pack on the ground in front of him, pulled his extra magazines from pouches and laid them on top, then unsnapped his tomahawk and stuck it into the log to his front. He readied his rifle and looked ahead. He was watching the twelve o'clock portion of the perimeter and was responsible for anything from nine to three. Sean and Brooks to his left at the nine would overlap their sectors, covering from twelve to six. This repeated around the circle of security.

He could hear the sounds of the Primals crashing through the brush, the moans eerily echoing through the dark trees. Chelsea moved in beside him and looked over at him uncomfortably. Brad reached out his left hand and squeezed her shoulder. "We got this, breathe and shoot," he told her over the roar of the Primals.

Chelsea forced a nervous grin and brought the rifle into the pocket of her shoulder, her voice cracked when she spoke. "We got this."

Joey was to Brad's right on the three beating his chest and screaming profanities back into the woods. "Come get some, you Primal pricks! I'm going to shoot you in the fucking face!" Joey's yelling motivated the rest. Parker joined in screaming back at the Primals and they were all yelling as the first mass broke the tree line behind Brad. He heard Gunner and Meyers open up at the six o'clock position, then Joey and Parker at the three.

When Chelsea turned to assist them, Brad held up his hand and pointed back to their front. "Watch our sector; they will call out if they need us." As he spoke, he saw a male in jeans and a blood-stained T-shirt, his face overgrown with a matted beard and a head of gnarled hair, running full speed and screaming. Brad hesitated, captivated by the crazy's fierce eyes as he ran, crashing through brush unconcerned by the limbs pulling and scratching at his face. Chelsea fired to his left. Brad brought up his rifle and pulled the trigger, dropping the bearded Primal. He then shifted to the next one and pulled the trigger.

He shifted fire; they were coming in twos and threes, closing on them quickly. Chelsea called out that she was reloading. Brad pivoted so that he could see farther and cover her position. She went back online as he fired a last round. He hastily reloaded as one of them broke into the front of the barrier. Brad turned hard, grabbed the hawk, and slapped the Primal hard on the head, knocking it off its feet. He finished reloading and shot the thing in the head just as it began to get back up. To the front, they were stacking up, pushing into each other as they ran out of the trees in a full mob, and tripping over the bodies of those already dropped.

Brad swiveled left and right, taking aimed shots, but as fast as he knocked one down, another would take its place. They were now in against the logs, trying to climb over and get at the shooters inside. Gunner called out over the gunfire and roar of the infected. "Keep it up! Nothing gets through. Every shot counts!"

Joey yelled, "Frag out!"

Brad looked to his right and saw why. The road was packed with them; a parade of infected, pressing against each other, struggling to get to the barricaded men. The grenade exploded, creating a deep void in the mass that was quickly filled in by more. Joey laughed manically, "Is that all you got you pussies!" He reached down and lifted the M249 Squad automatic weapon that Parker had packed in, but they had hesitated to use because of noise discipline. Noise was no longer a concern. Joey climbed up on the first row of logs and let loose with a long burst. "How you like that?!" he screamed as he cut through the advancing wave.

Parker joined in the screaming; firing a 40mm from his M203, the grenade landed deep in the mass. The ABHE round bounced off the road and detonated just above the heads of the advancing mob. The blast was loud, the concussion nearly knocking Brad off his feet. A fifty meter swath of Primals was blown to the ground, tiny bits of fragmentation ripping their bodies apart. Parker reloaded and fired into another mass with the same effect. "Yes!" he screamed as he reloaded to fire again.

"Get some Parker! Get some!" Joey screamed as he swung to the left, firing the rest of the belted ammo until the SAW was dry.

Brad turned back to the front. The mob was thinning out; many were on the ground dying, and the logs were twisted with their shattered and wrecked bodies. He searched, knocking down any still on their feet. The attack was over, the wave destroyed.

"Mount up; we need to move before more show up!" Gunner yelled.

No time for high fives or celebrating, they quickly reloaded their weapons and threw their rucks over their shoulders. They were back on the road and running through the broken, ravaged bodies of the Primals. They had to get out of the area quickly before more packs showed up. Brooks and Sean were at the front of the column. Occasionally, a suppressed burst from their weapons would cut down a stray Primal that intersected with them.

They rounded a corner where a vehicle with a smashed-in front sat, blocking the road. Farther into the field, they saw a truck buried in mud to its floorboards. They posted security around the car as Brooks pried open the front door.

"Keys are in it," he shouted as he slid into the seat. The car cranked hard, then started. The fan belt squeaked loudly as Brooks revved the engine. Sean used his hawk to pry bent and twisted sheet metal away from the front tire. Brad reached in with gloved hands and grabbed portions of the destroyed fender. Together, they managed to pull enough away so that Brooks could turn the wheel.

"Pile on," Gunner ordered.

They pushed Howard into the back seat with Gunner on one side and Chelsea on the other. Sean and Meyers crammed in the front with Brooks. The rest climbed in or onto the vehicle, searching for a spot to attach themselves. Brooks put the car in gear and eased it onto the roadway. It pulled to the left and made an awful sound as it rolled, but it still beat walking.

CHAPTER 27

"Stay ahead of it," Shane mumbled, standing on the roof looking far down the road.

Ella was next to him; she'd refused to leave his side since the first sounds of whatever battle was raging. He'd seen the helicopter crash and had climbed to the roof for a better vantage point as the roars of the infected built. They were all congregating at a point somewhere north on the road. He could hear them moaning and howling as they closed in on their prey.

Gunfire erupted; slowly at first, then all at once, there was a heavy barrage of concentrated fire. He heard the familiar sounds of a SAW and the thump of a forty mike-mike. Smoke billowed up in the trees; it was close, just near the position where he met the bandits. The shooting stopped after the moaning, indicating that, whoever they were, they survived the onslaught. They were well-armed and well-trained.

Are they friendly?

Shane looked at Ella—he couldn't risk it. He lifted her up and she wrapped her arms around his neck in a tight hug. He moved back to the ladder and had her hold on tight as he dropped back into the garage below. The moaning was gone. The gunfire stopped. He knew the battle would attract others and they would be heavily concentrated in this area by sundown. Large packs all over the countryside were probably already on the move, trying to get here to join the hunt.

Now was the time to go.

He put Ella down and had her hold his belt, wanting to keep her within arm's reach. He lifted his heavy rucksack with his left hand and pulled it over both shoulders. He took the SKS in his right hand and checked the action, verifying it was ready.

"Are we leaving now?" Ella asked. Her face was pale against the dark purple rings under her eyes. She was frightened and sensed the lurking dangers. The stress was taking a heavy toll on her. Shane reached for her hand and felt her cold fingers. He stopped and dropped to his knees, facing her.

"We're leaving now," Shane whispered to her.

She moved forward and clung to him in a tight hug, burying her head in his chest. He put his hand on the back of her head. "It's okay, Ella, I'll take care of you," he whispered.

"I love you, Shane," she said.

He let his hand drop to her back. As he hugged her tight, he felt tears forming in his eyes. Shane hadn't heard those words spoken to him since he was a boy her age – from his mother, maybe. His Grandfather wasn't the type to be slowed up by emotions.

"I… love you too, Ella," his voice breaking as he whispered the words.

He slung the rifle and lifted Ella, cradling her in his arms. He stood easily, not feeling the weight of the pack. Shane walked through the building to the front for the last time and opened the store's front door; a quick look left and right verified the yard was still clear. He moved to the sedan and strapped Ella into the front seat. He removed his pack and stuffed it into the trunk with the rest of their stuff, then closed the doors and climbed onto the hood of the car so he could see over the fence. He listened intently. It'd been some time since he'd heard a gunshot or infected moan. He needed to move while he could. Shane jumped off the hood of the car and faced the cipher lock. He drew a blank trying to remember the code.

"Oh no, it was some NASCAR shit. What was it, dammit?" He stepped back looking at the fence.

Shane punched numbers and turned the knob. It refused to move. "Oh, what the hell!" he said frustration growing. "Where's Kyle when you need him?"

"880…" he said to himself.

He punched in the three numbers, not remembering the last. *8800,* nothing; *8801,* nothing; *8802,* nothing; *8803,* the knob turned and the latch clunked open. Shane reached for a pull handle and slid the door open, then returned to the car. The engine started easily and he pulled through until he'd just cleared the gate. He looked at the opening for a moment, then jumped from the car. He grabbed the gate and slid it shut, not wanting to give up the refuge to the infected. Shane ran back to the open door of the car and heard a loud squeal coming from up the road.

"What now?" he said just above a whisper.

He was standing in the open doorway with his rifle still slung over his shoulder. He looked north as a vehicle slowly came into view. It was smoking from a smashed in front end. He recognized it as the car he'd plowed into with the old pickup truck. Uniformed men were riding on the hood and roof of the vehicle; they were armed with military rifles and wearing web gear. Shane considered getting in the car and racing away.

He could see the men clearly; they looked back at him with their weapons down. Shane felt the weight of the SKS on his shoulder. He removed it and held it loosely in his grip as the car approached. He froze, watching them. Ella undid her seat belt and climbed across; she sat up on her knees next to him.

"Look, Shane! Soldiers like you," she said.

He let go of the SKS and put his hand on her shoulder. "Okay, Ella, let's see."

The car pulled up close, then parked diagonally on the road. The driver cut the engine and the vehicle coughed and sputtered. Soldiers on the roof leapt off and took up security on both sides. Shane immediately noticed that no one had pointed a rifle at him. Doors opened and more soldiers got out; a man in a flight suit approached speaking quickly, too fast for Shane to understand. He said he was a doctor and that he was looking for them. He moved at Shane; Ella was scared and cowered behind him.

Shane shielded her with his arm. "Okay, that's close enough!"

"Is it her?" the doctor asked.

Shane looked at him confused. "Who are you?"

"Her arm, was she bitten?"

Shane looked down at Ella then at the doctor, understanding what he was asking. He took his arm off of Ella so she could lean out. She held up her wrist and carefully rolled up her sleeve, showing the nearly healed wound. The doctor suddenly laughed and stepped closer. Shane again held up his hand, cautioning the doctor to stay back, this time putting the other on the grip of the pistol in his waist band.

An older man with a 1911 in a shoulder holster stepped forward, putting a hand on the doctor and directing him away. "It's okay, soldier. We've been looking for you; looking for the girl to be honest with ya. We know you were at Fort Collins."

"You know about Collins?" Shane asked.

Shane looked at them all. They were military; he could tell by their posture. A young woman smiled at him. She noticed his stare. "You did good. We're here to help you."

The old soldier spoke again, "Why don't you take the girl into the back seat with you, we really need to put some distance on this place. We can talk on the way."

Shane looked at all of them again and nodded. He turned, allowing Ella to climb into his arms, and stepped away from the open door. The young woman came forward and opened the back for him and he dropped into the back seat, the female moving in beside him. The doctor ran around the car and got in the other side, cramming him into the middle between them. The old soldier got in the driver's seat while another got in front.

Shane sat back in the seat while Ella curled into his lap and hid her face from the others. He looked straight ahead. The second vehicle cranked back to life. Soldiers jumped into it, slamming doors. The old soldier in front put the sedan in gear and they pulled away. The doctor next to him reached for Ella's arm. Shane's hand shot up and snatched the doctor's wrist. "Not now!" he said calmly.

The old soldier looked in the rear view mirror at him and the rank on his uniform. "It's okay, Sergeant. The Doc just wants to make sure she's okay."

Shane let go of the doctor's wrist and looked down at the rank tab on his jacket. "She's fine. Just tired is all; and I'm not a sergeant anymore. I was medically retired years ago. You can call me Shane."

"Well, Shane, you've done a hell of a job. You could call me retired as well, although it'd be hard to tell these days."

"Who are you? Where did you come from?"

Gunner made introductions, then explained to Shane what their mission was and how the British were involved. The doctor told him about Ella, how important she was, and how she may be immune to the virus. Shane stayed quiet while listening to their story.

"Where were you going?" Chelsea asked. When she spoke, Ella lifted her head and looked at her.

Shane looked down at Ella, moving the hair out of her eyes. "Savannah. I thought it might still be there. Heard stories about them back at Collins."

Gunner looked back at him. "Makes sense, it's not far from here. What do you think, Doc; you know anything about Hunter Air Field, near Savannah?"

Howard shook his head. "Never heard of it."

Gunner nodded. "Hunter it is then!"

CHAPTER 28

"We need to find a place to hold up," Brooks said, looking wearily at the gauges.

They'd been driving a couple hours, following the Sedan in front of them and not knowing where they were going. The car was overheating and they could barely make thirty miles an hour before the wheel would begin shaking so bad, Brooks couldn't control it. Brooks was growing frustrated trying to keep up with the sedan. He would speed up and listen to the engine squeal as the belts rubbed and blue smoke shot from the exhaust.

"I'm serious, man; this thing is barely holding together," Brooks said.

"Flash your lights and see if you can get their attention," Sean answered.

Brad was riding in the back of the car behind Brooks, his rucksack on his lap. He wasn't paying attention to the conversation in the front. He had his head turned, looking at the dilapidated and abandoned homes on the side of the road. He'd seen this all before, but that was far from home. Now things were setting in. The US was affected; things really had fallen apart here and his family may *not* be okay. Parker's head dropped and hit Brad's arm. He shrugged, waking Parker who jumped up, looking in both directions before laying his head back and drifting off again.

It was frustrating not knowing where they were headed. He thought they would race back to Charleston or back to the river and take the quickest route back to Sumter.

Why south?

After they located the girl, they loaded up in the cars and drove south. At the time, it seemed logical; they'd just fought off the horde on the road to the north. But still, he thought sooner or later, they would loop back around toward the river, contact Kelli, and wait for evac. They took several turns when roads became blocked or a bridge was out; always moving south-west away from the river. They kept an eye open for other vehicles, something they could upgrade to, but most things with wheels were already cannibalized, pushed off the road into ditches, or deadlocked in massive pileups.

Brooks cautiously sped up and drove close to the sedan in front of them. He tapped his horn and flashed his lights. The lead vehicle pulled slightly to the side and Gunner lowered his window. Brooks pulled up alongside as Sean leaned out an open window.

"This thing is about to shit the bed. We need to find someplace solid to hold up before we get stranded on the road."

Gunner nodded in agreement. "Meyers' map shows a town ahead. We can hold up there."

Gunner put the sedan back in gear and pulled back ahead. Before long, they were passing signs pointing to a town a few miles ahead. Brooks slapped the dash. "Come on, baby, we're almost there."

The country road grew more congested as they approached the town. Cars blocked the center of the road and barriers were set up at intersections. Long since abandoned police roadblocks were marked with decomposed bodies and deserted police cruisers. Brooks eased the car onto the shoulder, following the sedan, and drove through the tall grass, avoiding roadblocks and disabled cars. The sedan approached a rolled over, burnt out bus blocking the road and turned onto a residential street, searching for a way around it. The area they entered was devastated. The entire block had burned to the ground; only charred skeletons of homes remained.

The sedan in front slowed as they spotted an old brick school building at the end of the street. One story and shaped like a shoe box, the building was fenced in and its heavy, wooden double doors still remained closed at the entrance. The rest of the doors appeared closed, as well, and the windows unbroken. The sedan pulled along the fence and followed it around, to an access road that ran to a blacktop parking lot and back entrance. The sedan stopped, then backed up slightly before the engine shut off. Brooks parked farther away, turned off the key, and listened to the motor sputter to death.

Brad and the others exited the broken car and gathered at a small sidewalk that led to a chained fire door. Brad turned in a slow 360, surveying the area. They were in the center of a small neighborhood that was clearly abandoned—presumably because of the fire that had swept the area and consumed every home within eyesight. A row of destroyed storefronts sat on a far street, windows shattered, doors removed. Looking closer, the school sat alone surrounded by tall grass. The brick-faced elementary building filled an entire block and was set back from the road on all sides—probably the only reason it was spared as the fire leapt from home to home. Brad could see the sky was beginning to darken; a wind had picked up and black clouds were on the horizon

Gunner and the others approached from the sedan. Brad saw the soldier carrying the girl and walking between the doctor and Chelsea. "Let's get inside," Gunner said.

Sean grunted and looked at Brad and Brooks. "We're up. Joey, you and Parker have rear security. Once we clear the entrance, get everyone inside while we clear the building."

"Aye, Chief," Joey answered.

They moved to the chained door with a large combination lock attached. Brooks pulled out his tomahawk and placed the spike into the hasp attached to the building rather than the chain. He pulled down using his weight, causing the hasp to bend, twist, creak away, and then pull out of the door frame with its long screws still attached. With the chain removed, Sean stepped forward and, using a lock pick, quickly opened the door. It clunked; an old rusty spring protested as it was used for the first time in months. Brooks shrugged his shoulders, stretched his back, then brought his MP5 up to his eye and stepped into the hallway. Brad followed him through next, then Sean.

Brooks stepped, looking to the right while Brad took the left. The hallway was still dimly lit by the fading light, but they would have to move quickly. Soon it would be too dark inside for the unaided eye. The hallway was spotless; no sign that anyone had walked the halls in months. Classroom doors on both sides of the hallway were closed. A tall window sat dark with blinds covering the glass. Brad moved to a wall and kept his rifle up, looking down the long hallway while the rest of the team filed in. Joey moved up next to Brad, then took a knee next to a wall filled with lockers. "I got ya, Bro," Joey whispered.

Brad slapped him on the shoulder before turning to meet up with Brooks and Sean. They moved down the hallway to one end, checking rooms as they passed. The classroom doors were all locked so they looked through the glass and spotted empty classrooms with chairs up on the desks. They checked every classroom on one end then turned and walked back in the other direction, doing the same. They met a dark intersecting hallway where Sean ordered them to turn on their lights. They moved down at a slight angle. Near the midpoint of the hallway was another tall double fire door. Brooks quietly moved to it and pushed on the operating bar; the door clunked and swung in, revealing a large, open gymnasium with a cafeteria window on the back wall.

Brooks turned to look at Sean who gave him a thumbs up. They continued down the hall to where the front entrance was. The tall double doors were also secured and, looking through the window, Brad could see there were chains on the outside. They turned and walked back up the hallway, passing the long glass window of what was the front office. A large banner was hung in the window, encouraging passersby to *enjoy your summer!* The office door was locked and they didn't bother attempting to gain entry.

They returned to the back entrance where the rest of the group was waiting. Sean moved up alongside Gunner and spoke to him quietly. "Okay," Gunner said, "there's a gymnasium and a cafeteria up front, let's get settled in there."

Brad stood by the wall as the others picked up their weapons and moved past him. He checked the back entrance and found it locked. "What are you doing?" Chelsea said.

Brad turned around to look at her in the dark. "I just wanted to make sure the door was locked before we left the hallway… and to grab some quiet time." Brad walked to the opposite wall and sat on the floor, his back pushing against the lockers. Chelsea removed her rucksack and sat next to him.

"What happens now?" she asked.

"I don't know. Did Gunner say where we're going?"

"Savannah," she said.

"The Ranger base? We aren't going back to Sumter?"

"Shane—the soldier—said he was headed there; he thought there may be something left."

"What did you think of him—Shane?"

"He's a mess, same as the girl. She didn't speak the entire way here. He mumbled a bit and has that look like he's lost inside."

A rumble of thunder sounded from far in the distance. They sat and listened as the wind picked up and a hard rain started to fall. Gusts rattled the door, causing Chelsea to jump. Brad put his hand on her knee and she slid closer.

"Did you see Joey during the fight," Chelsea asked.

"Yeah. He turned things around for us."

"Is it always like that?"

"It's never the same."

Brad got back to his feet and pulled Chelsea up. "Let's join to the others before rumors starts," he joked.

"I've missed you, Brad."

"I know; I missed you too."

CHAPTER 29

The school was dark and from where they were gathered in the gymnasium, only the sounds of the howling wind and rain beating on the flat roof above them could be heard. The small school cafeteria was searched but found empty. They weren't really surprised; the school was closed up for the summer session so the pantries and storage rooms were bare. Once settled in, they broke into the office and set up an observation post behind the pane glass windows. Sean posted them in separate teams of two with a roving guard making rounds every fifteen minutes. Brooks and Joey were in the front office, with Parker and Brad holding position in a back classroom that overlooked the parking lot and their vehicles.

Sean moved between the posts, switching off with Gunner and Meyers when needed. The observation teams would hold in position until dawn, one of them being allowed to sleep while the other would stay on the IR scope, making sure nothing snuck up on them. Using a GPS and Meyers' map, they were able to pinpoint their location; still a good hour's drive from Savannah by car. They checked in with the submarine using an encrypted satellite phone that Meyers guaranteed couldn't be tracked. The sub, in turn, would relay a message to Kelli at the fort and warn her of the CNRT.

Shane stood guard in a corner of the gymnasium. It took some convincing, but he finally agreed to allow the doctor to give Ella a thorough examination – as long as the female marine stayed close by and kept an eye on things. He had his back to them as they undressed her and went over every inch of her body. The sun had completely dropped now. The only light coming into the room was from the sharp bolts of lightning and a low battery-powered light they allowed the doctor to use.

He began to meet some of the team; they were an odd and mixed group. Sailors, soldiers, Marines, even some sort of British Special Forces guy, then the doctor, and who knew what the crusty old soldier was. Shane figured him for a black water type, one of the seasoned contractors he'd seen doing special project work for the government in Iraq. Regardless, they all seemed friendly and took a special interest in keeping the girl safe.

The day he found her, he thought he would turn her over to the first trustworthy group he found. That he'd be happy to be rid of her and back on his own to continue his *death wish,* as others would see it. Shane touched his hand to his shirt pocket and pulled out the photo. Carefully, he unfolded it; the image had faded but he could still see their faces, He knew all of their names. He didn't consider himself suicidal; he just didn't give a shit anymore. Or, he used to feel that way. Since Ella, he had a new purpose, he felt energized again… needed. She saved him.

Shane knew she was special, but was having a hard time digesting the story that the doctor told him. That she could be used as a cure. The healed bite marks and the fact that she never turned was undeniable. Shane couldn't explain it, why she didn't turn. He was never a big picture kind of guy; he didn't concern himself with such issues, and he never tried to. In Shane's mind, he counted the girl as blessed, lucky, maybe it wasn't a Primal bite. Maybe they were wrong and maybe something else happened to her. He asked her about the wound before, but she didn't remember or refused to talk about it. Shane didn't press her; in the end he didn't care. It didn't matter to him.

Shane heard Ella whine and he spun around. The doctor held a syringe in his hand and was trying to restrain Ella's arm. She was crying and pulling away. The female was kneeling, holding Ella's other hand, stroking her back, and speaking to her calmly. The doctor was startled by Shane's quick movement and pulled back the hand holding the syringe.

"What are you doing?" Shane asked, stepping forward.

"It's okay, Shane. The doctor just needs a blood sample," Chelsea answered in a low voice.

"I'll decide what's okay. Why does he need a sample? I don't see a lab here."

The doctor stopped and looked at Shane. Speaking clinically, he said, "We need a complete medical record on her in the event we fail to deliver her to the facility in Ohio."

"You what?!" Shane said, stepping forward. He snatched the syringe from the doctor's hand and dropped it to the floor, then crushed it with his boot. "You need me to smash anything else, or can we end this conversation?" Shane put up a closed fist as if he was ready to hit the doctor. He slowly lowered his hand and walked to Ella who jumped from the chair and climbed into his arms. Shane turned to walk away and find their spot near the table with the others.

Howard chased off after him. "Are you mad? Don't you understand that this girl's blood could save the world?" Howard said, becoming enraged.

Shane spun around and pushed forward, looking the doctor in the eye. "Do you understand that this little girl *is* my world, that she's all I care about? If you need a sample, you better help me get her to Ohio."

Hearing the discussion, Meyers woke from where he was resting on a cafeteria table. He yawned intentionally loud to catch the others' attention. "Problem, mates?" he said, providing the break Shane needed to walk away. He moved across the room and sat Ella on his pack, then pulled the rolled green blanket from the side carrier and wrapped it around her shoulders.

Howard stepped away from the examination area, glaring at Shane and walked quickly to Meyers. "Your friend here is refusing to allow me to take a contingency sample!" he gasped.

Meyers stretched and prepared to answer, but before he had the chance, the gymnasium doors opened; Brad and the Navy chief poured in. Shane looked up, watching the men close and secure the door behind them.

"We have a problem," the Seal Team chief exclaimed.

Gunner yawned and pushed himself up to his feet. "I knew I should have slept with my boots on, what is it?"

"We are being watched. Brooks and the others are keeping eyes on them," Sean announced. "They must have found us, or followed us… who the hell knows how."

"Drones," Howard answered, not being asked.

Gunner chuckled and looked at Howard patronizingly. "Doc, if they had drones, they would have parked a Hellfire up our asses hours ago."

"No, I assure you they have drones; they are limited, and not many left, but I promise you they have them. If they called in the recovery teams, it would make sense they would have a drone watching. I've seen the imagery. What they *are* short of is munitions. Most of it was expended weeks ago, but as long as there is fuel and spare parts, they can keep the drones in the air. They've probably seen everything since the bird went down."

Gunner put his hand up, silencing Howard. "Chief, what did you see?"

"We spotted one, but if there is one, there will certainly be two. He's in the rubble of a home across the street. And before you ask, it's not a Primal, and he's definitely not a random survivor. He's dug in and packing good equipment, but he's no pro. He used an IR flashlight. It gave away his position and lit up his hide. He only did it for a second and must have been aware of the error because he hasn't done it again since.

"He knows we're in the school, but I don't think he's aware that we're onto him. If he did, he would have improved his position, but this guy is staying put. Recon element I figure, scouting for a larger team holding back someplace, waiting for the opportunity to move on us. My guess is they will babysit us through the night then hit at dawn while the Primals sleep. That's what I would do."

"Suggestions?" Gunner asked.

"Hoping the *drone* was pulled off its surveillance," Sean said skeptically looking at Howard, "I'd like to go out there and snatch his ass, then cut on him until he tells me everything about his unit and what they have planned for us. But the fucker picked his position well, he's sitting tight on the cross streets. If we move on him, he would see us crossing the danger areas. If I took the stealthy route, it would be daylight before I reached him. Plan B, I'll go up to the roof and put a suppressed round through his skull. Wait for someone to check on him, and kill that one – mix, stir, and repeat."

"Won't that force their hand?" Gunner asked. "They'll know we're on to them when their scouts don't check in – "

"I'm putting my money on them rolling in hard once they realize we're on to them, but by then… you'll all be far away from here."

CHAPTER 30

"Chief, you can't expect them to go cross country in the dark and on foot," Brooks whispered.

The trio had gathered in a far corner of the gymnasium. Brad watched as Chelsea and the others repacked their gear and prepared to move out. There was a lot of fuss about the girl. Parker used a k-bar and a roll of duct tape to cut down his rain parka so that it would fit her. She was giggling as he tried to get it over her head. Rain pounded the metal roof over their heads; it would help them to evade the Primals. One thing they learned was that Primals shared the irrational fear of water with the symptoms of rabies. It wasn't a fool-proof theory, but they were less likely to show themselves in rain.

"They only need to go a few miles; then you can hold up someplace or secure another vehicle," Sean answered.

"You? Oh hell no, I'm staying here," Brooks said.

"Sorry Brooks, if they have any chance of making it, they're going to need you; but don't worry bro—I'll have the good sergeant here with me," Sean said, winking at Brad.

"Bullshit, Chief!" Brooks protested. "Brad needs to go with the group. I'd do better back here with you, and you're going to need me on the rifle beside you."

Brad cleared his throat. "Do I get a say in all of this?"

Sean paused and looked Brad up and down. "Sure… what would you prefer: stay here with me, or have me stay back here with you?"

Brooks shook his head and grabbed Brad by both shoulders and looked him in the eye. "Trust me; this is the last place you will want to be when they move up that road. Chief plans to run a delaying action with one rifle. That's no way to fight. Let me stay behind and do this and you stick with the group, help get them to Savannah. They have Gunner and Meyers and the grunts; they don't need me."

Brad dropped his eyes. He looked at the corner of the room where Chelsea was doting over the little girl, while the soldier hovered over them. He looked back at Brooks and forced a smile. "No, Chief's right. They need you."

"Brad, he isn't going to tell you this is a suicide mission… but I will!"

Sean put his hands up. "We'll make contact with their rear element. Put some fire on them, slow their roll, and bug out. I don't plan on dying here, Brooks."

"What if they bring in more helicopters?" Brooks countered.

"I think they are used up… if they had more birds, we'd have been hit again. I'm guessing they're low on resources. That Little Bird we took out was flying solo, without an escort. Why would they go like that without a wingman? I think they're spent, no wingman because they didn't have one. If Howard is right, and the CNRT is based in Colorado, this is a long way from home. I'm betting my life on them only having a small ground element out there. Something small enough that they won't risk a night attack in Primal country."

Sean paused and looked across the room. Gunner was suited up, standing by the door and the others were gathering behind him. Gunner looked back at Sean and tapped his wrist. Sean turned to Brooks. "Get them out of here. I'm tired and I don't want to argue about this."

"Very well, Chief, I'll get them settled and circle back for you," Brooks said, abruptly walking away before he could be told no.

Brad followed him; he wanted to say goodbye to Chelsea and the others. None of them were happy to hear he was staying behind. Parker and Joey eagerly volunteered to stay as well, or take his place. Chelsea was quiet. He knew he once again disappointed her; she would never understand why he seminally always chose the Chief over her. He had to explain the importance of getting the girl to safety. He promised them he would catch up after daybreak. Chelsea stared at him while he spoke. He knew that she wanted more of an answer or a private conversation. Brad was thankful that there wasn't time for long goodbyes. He needed to get his head in the game, and thinking about her would only be a distraction.

He walked with them to the rear entrance where they stacked up on the door, waiting for Sean's command before they moved out. In the dark of the hallway, he hugged Chelsea goodbye and shook the hands of his men before walking to a boiler room, where he met Sean by a roof access ladder. Sean was waiting in the entrance of the door. "How are your comms?"

Brad plugged in the ear piece of the device and powered it on. Sean gave him a quick squelch of the mic and Brad responded with a double click.

"Okay, good. Take the spotting scope and set up back from the window behind the reception counter. I'll be focused on the shooter out there so I need you to keep an eye on my flanks."

Brad nodded and took the scope in his hands. He powered it on and scanned down the hall; the green and black speckled image came back grainy in the interior space. He heard Sean beginning to clank up the ladder and felt the rain on his shoulders when the hatch above swung open. He turned the scope off and walked across the hallway into the office. He moved to the end of a long counter and crept around it. He got to his hands and knees so he was below the window, then crawled to the back of the room where a row of flattop desks sat. He found one covered with family photos and fake plants.

He ducked in behind the desk and slid the chair out of the way. The scope had a small set of adjustable tripod legs that Brad deployed. He positioned the scope on the desk so that he was looking between the sets of potted plants. Brad checked his rifle and laid it flat on the floor in front of his knees. He reached up and powered up the scope; the soft green glow lit the cup of the eye piece. He pushed his eye against it and began to scan.

"I'm up, but I don't see anything," he spoke into the mic.

"Start at the left corner; count off four structures."

Brad did as instructed and then scanned the structure. A small ranch house, or what was left of some of the framed walls, was still standing but stripped of its sheathing. The roof had fallen to the side and was lying in a mass of rubble.

"The stone chimney – target is to the left of it."

Brad found the chimney and carefully turned the scope to the left, then dialed up the resolution. The man was hidden well but wasn't on the rifle like Brad expected. Instead, he was sitting back against the chimney wearing a parka, the hood pulled over his head. He was drinking from a thermos and looking down, rarely looking in the direction of the school.

"I see him," Brad said.

"Good, start scanning."

Brad continued passing to the right, letting the scope hang on anything that could provide concealment. He moved beyond the structure and off to the next. Another destroyed home. As the scope smoothly moved to the left; he thought he saw a splash of motion. He paused and dialed out the resolution. There was a small aluminum garden shed still standing. Brad looked to the left and right of it and spotted more movement, then the silhouette of a man at the corner of the shed. He moved again and disappeared.

"Second target, fifty meters to the right, between the buildings. See the garden shed."

"I see the shed, no target."

Brad watched the small building and saw the man step back to the side, exposing himself for just a second before dropping back. Then the man walked completely around and opened a door on the shed before slipping inside.

"He's inside the shed."

"Roger, stay on him… firing… target down."

Brad watched the man walk back out of the door and stand there looking in the direction of the school. His rifle was slung and his hands were in his pockets. He looked left and right as if he'd heard a sound, then turned and looked off into the distance away from the school.

"I got him... firing... target down."

Before Brad could respond, he watched the man take a direct hit to the high center of his back. His body jerked forward, then collapsed. Brad scanned back to the stone chimney and saw the first man slumped forward. "Confirmed two targets down."

"Get them out the door."

Brad flipped off the scope, scooped up his rifle, and crawled to the door. Even though he knew the scouts were down, he didn't want to take any chances. He reached the hallway and ran down it at a jog. He passed the tail of the group leaning against the hallway walls, and ran to the door where Gunner and Brooks were standing.

"Both are scouts are down. Sean's up top."

Brooks nodded. He reached down, put on his pack, and rolled out the door. Gunner stayed in position, pushing the others out behind him in a close line formation. Brad watched as each of them filed past, not being able to see their faces in the dark of the hallway. The last of them filed by and then Gunner leaned over to Brad. "Good luck, son. Don't stay longer than you have to. Get your ass to Savannah; we'll be waiting for you there." He slapped Brad hard on the shoulder then rolled out after the others.

Brad pulled his night vision over his eyes, stepped into the doorway, and crouched down. He watched the team moving away—three in the front, then the soldier carrying the girl, Chelsea and two more bringing up the rear. A bright flash of tightening washed out his night vision. He powered them off and lifted them off his head. Brad blinked hard, readjusting to the darkness. Looking left and right, he backed into the doorway.

"Grab your shit; time to find some new real estate."

CHAPTER 31

He carried her close to his chest. The SKS slung over his shoulder and the ammo-replenished M4 strapped to the top of his back. The other men had offered to help carry the girl, but when Shane refused they finally convinced him to let them carry his gear. His ruck was now nearly empty, only some blankets and a day's rations left in it. He felt refreshed moving with this new group, some of the responsibility having been removed from his shoulders.

It was dark. The rain poured down and gusts of wind blew his hood back from his head. Ella curled tight against his chest causing him to perspire. Even though it made him uncomfortable, he knew it would keep the girl warm. The group had given him fresh batteries for his PVS-7, but with the rain and lightning, he chose to trust his natural eyesight and not rely on the night vision device. They moved quickly, sometimes at a near run, through alleys and over backyard fences. At one point, they paused and Shane heard several suppressed gun shots, then they were back up at a near run.

The pace continued for what seemed like hours. When they finally stopped under the overhang of a tall building, Shane checked the iridium dial on his watch and saw they'd been on the trail for forty minutes. A bit after midnight, it was prime feeding hour for the infected, or *Primals* as the group called them. This unit was smart; they had experience moving among them. Shane spent the majority of the outbreak behind the walls of Fort Collins. Rarely did he move outside the wire after the early days of the outbreak, especially at night. He found from listening to their stories that these men were well traveled and experienced in this new form of warfare.

The signal was given to move out again. After traveling two blocks, they were met with ankle deep water that gradually rose. Months without maintenance, the gutters and street drains were becoming clogged with refuse. Rainwater filled the streets and with no place to go, it backed up into yards and low lying areas. They crossed diagonally through a vacant lot littered with floating garbage. A man held down a strand of a wire fence so the rest could climb over it, and then they climbed a steep embankment that topped out at a set of railroad tracks. When everyone was back online, they knelt down and used the high ground to get their bearings.

Lightening streaked across the sky, reflecting light off the sheets of water. The flooding made everything look as if it was encased in ice. The thought sent chills through Shane's body; the wind whipped and blew cold rain against his neck that slowly worked its way into every crevice of his person. His legs were already soaked to the bone. His arms throbbed from holding Ella; even though she barely weighed fifty pounds, the awkwardness was starting to drain the blood from his limbs. He relaxed his grip and let her rest on his knee as the men ahead of him worked out their next move.

Chelsea moved up beside him. He felt her touch and she whispered in his ear, asking if it was okay if she checked on the girl. Shane adjusted his grip and allowed Ella to sit up on his knee. Chelsea pulled back the girl's hood and touched a hand to her forehead. She whispered to her, and offered her a bottle of water to sip from. Ella held the bottle in her fingers and sipped thirstily before passing it back. She pushed into him and he grimaced feeling the back injury begin to tighten up.

Chelsea saw his expression and the look of pain. "I can take her for a while," she whispered.

Shane looked at her and shook his head slowly. "I got her."

Chelsea stood, moving back to her position. Shane gently touched her wrist. "Thank you," he whispered.

The word was passed to move out. Shane adjusted his grip on Ella so that she was higher on his shoulder and taking the weight off his arms. He climbed to his feet and followed the man in front of him. The ground was uneven on the railroad tracks. Without maintenance, the ties had lifted out of the ground and become trip hazards. He could hear the men in front of him step and slip on the limestone boulders that filled the rail space.

Sounds of moaning and Primals on the hunt began to fill the air. Subtle at first, but as they moved, the sounds increased and mixed with the noise of splashing water. The winds continued to pick up, and soon the rain was nearly vertical. Something was happening; Shane didn't know what, he couldn't see far ahead in the blowing rain, but could feel it. Brooks increased the pace. Shane was nearly at a jog when the soldier in front of him tripped on an uneven railroad tie. Shane stopped and went to help him up but Chelsea was there pulling the soldier from the ground before he could assist.

Gunfire erupted from the front; he could hear the clacking of the suppressed weapons as the muzzle flashes mixed with the lightening. Shane stopped and prepared to turn back. Gunner ran down the line speaking to them in a loud voice. "We just hit a mob head on; stay as quiet as possible, no loud rounds! We have to fight through it, don't let up." Gunner slapped him on the back and moved to the next man down the line.

Shane began to panic. He turned and saw Chelsea move in close beside him. "My rifle isn't suppressed," she said through the noise of the raging infected.

Shane stood close to her. He pulled Ella from his shoulder and kissed her on the cheek. "Ella, I'm right beside you. Miss Chelsea is going to carry you now," Shane said to her.

Ella nodded and Shane handed her to Chelsea. He removed the M4 from his back and attached the bayonet. He stepped in front of them and prepared to step off. Parker and Joey, who'd been near the back, came ahead with their tomahawks in hand. They saw what Shane did and took flanking positions on Chelsea and Ella. Shane looked at them and dipped his head. "Nobody touches her!" Shane said.

"Roger that, Sergeant; they gotta come through me first!" Joey replied.

Gunner stayed in the back, holding the six position. "Let's go heroes, we ain't got all night."

Shane started off at a jog in the direction of the muzzle flashes. He nearly tripped when his toe caught a mangled body, then side stepped and leapt over a Primal with a shattered head. More bodies stacked up; the muzzle flashes were just ahead. He heard a moan and thrashing of grass. Shane pivoted, spotting one on all fours scrambling up the embankment. To his left, Joey lifted a leg and stomped down with the heel of his boot. Two more came out of the shadows between him and the muzzle flashes. Shane put his weight on his rear foot, shuffle-stepped forward, and plunged the bayonet through the first creature's head. He then stepped to the side while twisting out the bayonet and bashing the next in the head with the butt stock.

He paused only long enough to make sure Chelsea was still behind him. He picked up the pace to close the gap with the muzzle flashes. He heard the *thwack* of Parker's hawk impact the body of a creature. Another crawled up the embankment at an angle; not slowing, Shane veered to the side and soccer kicked it under the jaw, flipping it backwards and down the slope. Ahead, he saw Brooks and Meyers standing side by side. They were canted at opposite forty five degree angles. He couldn't tell why until he was right on top of them; they were pressed up against a stalled railroad freight car, covering the left and right corners. Brooks heard the group approach and pointed to a ladder on the side of the car without taking his eyes from the field of fire.

Shane ran to the car. He turned back, grabbing Ella from Chelsea, then climbed the rungs, spilling onto the top of the train car. He sat Ella on the center of the roof, then looked back and grabbed Chelsea by the wrist and dragged her to the top. He pulled her over the lip of the car and pointed her to Ella, before reaching down and grabbing the next soldier on the ladder. Straining, he pulled Joey nearly all the way up before he grabbed the top edge. Joey rolled over the lip and pushed Shane forward to make room. Shane struggled to his feet and found the roof of the train car slick in the downpour. Dropping back to his knees, he crawled forward to the far end of the car and held his position, waiting for Chelsea and Ella to move up behind him.

Chelsea moved slowly, guiding the girl ahead of her then stopped when she was less than five feet away. Chelsea had her rifle up and was looking off to the side of the car, searching the terrain below. Others climbed the ladder and crowded on the roof of the railroad car. Shane could hear Howard complaining and arguing with Gunner who was threatening to slap the shit out of him if he didn't keep his voice down. Brooks was on his feet and walked down the center of the car. Stepping over the others, he moved up to where Shane was sitting. He turned looking in all directions, and then crouched down next to Shane.

Brooks looked left and right, and then lifted his night vision off his head before dropping it into an assault pack. Meyers moved up the edge of the freight car, inches from spilling onto the railroad bed below. He pushed around Chelsea and Ella and dropped to his rear, sitting with his legs dangling over the edge.

He spit over the side then pulled his own goggles off. Shane looked over the edge; it was high, at least fourteen feet off the ground below. When the lightning flashed, it reflected back the cold stares of the Primals below. Shane looked away, unable to handle their gaze.

"That all turned to rat shit!" Meyers cursed under his breath.

Myer dropped his pack and placed it in his lap. He dug for a small canvas satchel and removed a small leather case. He fidgeted with it in the dark. "What is your estimate on sunrise today, Mister Brooks?"

Brooks looked at Meyers confused, he glanced at his watch. "With the overcast and cloud cover; maybe oh-seven-thirty?"

"Very well," Meyers responded pulling the satellite phone and GPS from the leather pouch.

"What are you doing?" Brooks asked.

"Trying the mobile; ordering take-away from the greasy spoon. How do you like your eggs, mate? I prefer mine with a side of cruise missile."

CHAPTER 32

He felt the weight of the pack cutting into his shoulders as he took long steps, running against the wind and rain. Brad struggled to keep up with Sean who was sprinting ahead as if he already knew where he was going. They cut across the school's front lawn and pushed through a break in the chain-link fence. Sean was leading them to the storefront positioned on a far street across from the unkempt playground.

They ran, weaving through swings and playground equipment. Brad was worried that while he was running, he couldn't see to defend himself at the same time. They were being stupid, taking risks; it wasn't their way. Sean continued the fast pace then quickly stopped to a halt behind a large oak tree near a sidewalk that skirted the street. He crouched and dropped his goggles over his eyes. Brad came up behind him, slowing to a walk and trying to control his heavy breathing as he dropped to a knee behind his partner.

Sean was scanning the small storefronts across the street. Without speaking, he tapped Brad's elbow and pointed to a small building almost directly across from them. It looked like an insurance office. It had one narrow glass door to the left and a wide tall window to the right.

Brad nodded and again they were on their feet running. They crossed the street and moved to the building's front wall. Sean slid across the surface and tested the door; it moved in his hand and swung out easily. Brad quickly dropped his night vision into place. Sean looked back at Brad, held up three fingers, and ticked them down. On the last finger, he moved to the other side of the door and pulled it out.

The door jangled from a large set of chimes hanging from a hook set in the ceiling above it. Sean ignored the noise and swept into the room with Brad close behind him. Sean reached back and latched the door. Instantly, they were hit in the face with the stench of Primals. They froze, listening intently, while the chimes still bumped into each other causing what seemed like a decibel-bursting *ting, ting, ting*. Sean reached up a hand without looking back and grabbed the set of bells. Yanking down, he ripped them from the ceiling and tossed them to a corner in another loud clatter of bangs as they slapped against the tile floor.

"Bit harsh wasn't it?" Brad whispered.

Sean held up a hand in response. A slight rattle sounded from down the hallway in a back room. Sean sidestepped, ducking behind a desk to his right. Brad did the same moving to his left. Brad scanned the space; it was clean, a typical office with plants, calendars hanging from the walls, and a water cooler in the corner. Looking down the narrow, litter-covered hallway, he could see a number of office openings to the left and right as the hall led straight to the back of the building and ended at a heavy, windowless door.

Sean reached forward on his weapon and powered up the IR laser, then looked at Brad and flashed a thumbs up. Brad nodded his head and returned a one finger salute. Sean returned the nod and grabbed a coffee cup resting next to him. He lifted it with his right hand and fired it down the hallway before he crashed against and knocked over a file cabinet, causing a loud slam of metal and porcelain. In an immediate response, a Primal jumped from a space in the back and leapt into the hallway. Sean lined up the laser and a spit of the MP5 knocked the Primal over and to the ground. Two more barreled out behind it and Sean fired, hitting the lead in the shoulder and the second in the throat, yet they both continued on. Brad waited for Sean to fire again. He looked to the right; the MP5 was jammed. Sean had already let it hang from its sling and was drawing his sidearm. Brad squeezed the trigger, his own suppressed round cutting down the hallway. His fire not accurate, he let loose a barrage of rounds that tore through the chest of the leader and continuing to the tail runner. Sean's side arm was up. He level out and after a loud *pop, pop, pop*; the creatures lay on the floor bleeding and dying.

"Damn, Chief. You ever clean that thing?" Brad asked, referring to the MP5's malfunction.

"It's that shitty ammo we picked up," Sean retorted.

"Sure, buddy. I'll check out the rest of the office while you clean your weapon," Brad said, getting to his feet. He stepped lightly to the hallway; the view in front of him played out in a speckled green and black of the night vision. He kept his barrel forward in the direction he was walking to compensate for the lack of depth perception. He moved to the first office door which was already unlatched. He pushed the door and let it swing in. The room held a small table surrounded by chairs. The room directly across had an identical setup.

Brad continued down the hall. Approaching the first of the dead Primals, he probed the body with his barrel, then stepped on the base of its skull to be certain before moving past it. Another was on the ground in a twisted pose. It was an elderly woman in a pantsuit, her sleeves torn and bloodied. Brad started at it and watched as its back vibrated with a rattled breath. A swift blow from the spike of his tomahawk stilled it. Protruding from the entrance to the last room was the one Sean had taken down first. Its head was pockmarked with impact holes and the back of its skull missing where the hollow points ripped out of the back.

He carefully stepped over the destroyed Primal body and stood in the doorframe of the last room – a small break area. He could tell by the heavy stench of human waste that this was where the Primals nested. Set up as a lunch area, smashed coffee pots, an overturned refrigerator, and broken tables covered the floor space. He scanned from left to right without entering the space, then backed away after finding nothing. Turning to the right, he faced the tail of the long hallway where an empty restroom closed out the building. The back door was slightly ajar, the cool moist air still blowing in. Brad kicked bits of leaves and refuse out of the way and attempted to press the door shut. It wouldn't latch; the months of being open and exposed to the elements caused the doorframe to swell. Brad removed a fire extinguisher from the wall and placed it next to the door to hold it shut.

When he returned to the front of the room, he saw Sean had built a mini bunker. He had dragged furniture away from the center of the room and positioned it against the walls, then moved two long book cases and positioned them below the windows. He had his rifle up and on the bipod. Sean's rucksack was on the floor; he was leaning over it, removing gear and tossing it into a corner.

"What's up?" Brad asked.

"You're going to want to lighten your load. When we move, it will be at Mach 3 and you won't want a heavy pack slowing you down. Ammo and water, I wouldn't hold onto much else," Sean huffed.

"What about food?"

"You can't eat it if you're dead. Set up on the window, get that scope back out, and see if you can get a fix on that hide site. I figure they will know by now that their eyes have been shut. When I finish, you can lighten up your pack."

Brad nodded and moved to the window. He removed his goggles and placed them into the top of his assault pack. He pulled the spotting scope and rested it on top of the bookcase. He powered it up, looked across the playground and back to the school. Panning to the left, he was able to find the neighborhood of destroyed houses and after a short search, he spotted the dead scout's body resting against the stone fireplace. He scanned farther to the right but the other ruins blocked his view of the garden shed. He panned back, put the scope on the stone fireplace, and dialed back the resolution so he could see a wider area.

The image went fuzzy; he pulled his face away, closed his eyes tight and then opened them slowly to relieve the eye strain. He looked through the window and nearly screamed when he saw the naked, bloodied belly of a Primal directly in front of him. Brad froze, too terrified to move; the creature was looking into the window. It leaned forward, tapping its forehead against the glass. Its scarred and greasy scalp squeaked as it squeegeed its head from left to right across the surface of the window.

Brad stood as still as a statue. The creature backed away from the window pane and turned to the left before it continued to stumble down the street. Brad leaned back off the scope as he watched more move past. A large pack of thirteen or more filed down the sidewalk, moving past the school and deeper into the neighborhood. Brad continued to slide back away from the window as Sean looked over at him and arched his eyebrow, acknowledging that he saw them too.

More and more filed past in an ever growing procession of Primals. Women and men in all layers of dress—some in shoes, other plodding along in torn, bare feet. Brad could hear their shoulders scrape and bump against the door as they moved past. "Where are they all going?" Brad whispered.

"Something pushed them this way, we've never seen so many."

"The storm maybe?" Brad asked.

Without warning, the sky suddenly flashed full of light. Sean moved across the room, crouching low next to Brad. Suspended below a parachute high in the sky, they saw a flare shining brightly. Soon afterward, a red firework exploded high above the school and then another as the first dimmed.

"Mystery solved," Sean whispered.

The Primals arched their backs and moaned before lurching forward as they gradually picked up speed. They wailed and howled at the dropping ball of light. The once recognizable packs quickly formed into a single massive raging mob as they raced toward the school.

"Drop your shit and cover that window. It won't be long now," Sean said speaking plainly, no longer needing to whisper above the screams emanating through the building's walls.

Brad crawled across the floor, allowing Sean to take his place behind the scope. He reached his pack and quickly began dumping extra items from the main cargo compartment. With the bag nearly empty, Brad found that the difference in the bag's bulk and weight made moving it along the back wall much easier. He moved to the window on the left wall, as Sean instructed, and pushed in against the corner, gazing out at a forty-five degree angle and trying to stay concealed from the raging Primals outside.

"You think the CNRT, or whoever the hell they are, brought them in?"

Sean was on the wall a few feet from him, his shoulder pressed against the book case and ducking so only the top of his head and eyes were exposed to the window. "Still a few hours from dawn. Using the Primals to soften up the school, then hit after daybreak to pick up the pieces. Smart… hoping to force us into a fight… expend our ammo… weaken our defenses. Might have worked too, but they fucked up."

"Because the team got out?" Brad gasped, feeling overwhelmed.

"No… because as soon as they show their heads, I'll start poking holes into them."

CHAPTER 33

"Get some rest people. The strike is at dawn and we need to be moving before the smoke clears," Meyers said as he walked the train car from the front to the back. "We have two packages being delivered. The captain didn't part with his missiles lightly, so we need to make this count, gents.

"These are dispenser variant Tomahawk cruise missiles, the only two on the boat. She'll be dropping over 300 BLU-97 sub-munitions, providing us a wide avenue to haul ass."

"Cluster bombs?" someone asked.

"Exactly, mate." Meyers continued walking the railcar and stopping next to Shane. He dropped to his rear and let his legs dangle over the sides of the railcar. He looked down at the Primals below then at Shane. "Something I will never get used to," Meyers whispered.

"I don't know that we ever should. Get used to them, I mean," Shane answered.

"Aye, I'd put every last one of them down if I could."

Shane thought back to the night in the tower and how the one stared at him. How it seemed to direct the others to focus on his position. "Have you ever seen anything? I mean signs of intelligence, like there is something more to them."

Meyers shot Shane a cross expression. "You'd be bloody barmy to believe that—look at them."

Shane pushed himself up so that he could see over the edge of the car and down at the railroad bed. The rain had let up and the moon was just beginning to break through the dark, fast moving clouds. Shane looked down the grassy slope to the streets packed with Primals; the mottled heads and glowing eyes below stared back up at him. They moved slowly, as if one big organism, in a twisting and swirling rotation. Not standing still but in constant motion.

"There was a time that I thought that but… I've seen things," Shane whispered.

Meyers drained a small plastic bottle of water, then tossed it over the side and watched it bounce off the head of what was once a bald old man. The thing didn't react to the impact, didn't look away, and didn't flinch. "Would you consider that an intelligent reaction?"

Shane shrugged. "Have you ever watched them move? Seen them hunt? Not now in this mass, but when they are in small packs. The way they communicate through their howls; the way they always seem to have a dominate leader. Even now, look at the man with the red shirt at the corner of the far building," Shane said; his voice raising. He lifted a hand and pointed to a small structure at the bottom of a slope.

All along the road, the creatures pressed and swarmed, massing around the train car, pushing their way to get closer as the weaker ones were pulled out of the way and pushed to the back. Across the street a large male, hunched with its arms at its sides, stood alone next to a building. He looked back at the train car, but differently than the others; he was enraged but also appeared to be studying them.

"That's your Grey Wolf right there," Shane whispered. "You might not think so, but he is in charge; he coordinates the hunt."

"Impossible. It's probably injured, just sticking to the fringes," Meyers replied.

"I've witnessed it myself. Watched them change the tide of battle… watched them point out prey. I think something is still ticking in some of them, some basic animalistic instinct to hunt."

"Well, I'm not sold on the idea." Meyers stared at the man with the red shirt a bit longer. He lifted the SA80 that he was cradling in his lap and aimed across the street. A single trigger pull and the man's head snapped back, its brains coating the wall behind it. "No reason to take any chances though."

Shane nodded and looked back to check on Ella. Far in the distance, he saw a glowing light floating high in the sky. "Meyers," Shane whispered, reaching out a hand to tap the man on the shoulder just as a *pop* echoing sound of a starburst flare found its way to them.

Meyers focused his eyes on the flare and the sparkling red lights. "Starburst grenades… it's begun then. Damn, we should have been farther away by now."

Gunner moved to the front of the car, kneeling with the others. He pointed down the railroad tracks. "See those concrete structures ahead? That should be US-17. If we can get there, it will take us right into Savannah."

"How far out?" Shane asked.

"On a normal day under 30 minutes by car; today... let's just get to the highway."

The mass below became agitated as some of them picked up on the distant fireworks. The horde broke up and began to shift. Small groups on the edge of the mass separated into packs and took off at a full run toward the floating lights. The sounds of battle joined the chaos of the moans echoing off the buildings. Thumping sounds of a light machine gun, a distant explosion, and bright flash of light lit the horizon accompanied the steady *pop, pop, pop* of the illumination rounds.

Brooks sat upright and looked into the distance with his binoculars before he glanced at Meyers. "How long till the strike?"

"Short of twenty five minutes, just waiting on the sun," Meyers answered glancing at a countdown running on his wristwatch.

"Can you move it up?" Brooks asked. "If we don't stop this migration to the school, Sean and Brad won't have a chance."

"We all have our role, mate; it's not likely to be a bloody snap for us either. Our success is dependent upon a daylight strike—"

A large explosion cracked in the distance. A bloom of smoke climbed into the sky and an orange glow lit the horizon. The rate of small arms fire increased while another boom echoed against the building walls. The Primals started to move away from the train car, suddenly more interested in the stimulation of sounds coming from the battle.

Brooks stood upright. "We all have our role," he muttered. Brooks turned around and took a deep breath. "Fuck that, get on the horn and get those Tommys in the air now. The sun won't make much of a difference if Chief's position is overrun."

Gunner looked at Meyers. "Get them in the air."

"Okay, mate, I'll make the call. But have these people ready to move."

***

Shane's head was buried atop the train car, the heels of his boots facing the direction of the blast zone. Ella was beneath his chest,

Chelsea just beside them. He lifted his head and looked to the east; the flares over the school had stopped, but the sounds of battle still raged. The mass of Primals had thinned out some but were still heavily congested around the train car. Shane's eyes swept the eastern horizon – he could just begin to make out the first rays of daybreak.

"They're on the way, keep your heads down," Meyers yelled, clicking off the sat phone. "First salvo will be just off the car, dispensing bomblets from east to west; the second will be right behind it. They're moving at eight hundred kilometers per hour, so it won't be long."

Shane curled his head down and pulled Ella in tight. He felt her squirm beneath him. He heard the blast of the missile's engine milliseconds before the detonation of the sub-munitions. Deafening explosions shook the car, causing it to rattle on the track; it vibrated with impacts from shrapnel and upturned earth. Shane curled to his side, pulling Ella in even tighter. The second missile screamed overhead and the roar of explosions continued, seeming to steal the air from his lungs. The car seemed to levitate and Shane swore it was tipping, the motion taking away his sense. The explosive ripping of the air suddenly stopped. He rolled to his back and attempted to sit.

Shane looked in all directions. His vision was choked with smoke and falling debris.

Meyers was already at the ladder firing into Primal bodies lying on the ground and others that were trying to get up. Shane leaned forward, righting himself, and pulled Ella to his lap. She was sobbing, her hands gripping his shirt so tight, he could feel the pinching. He used the pack as balance to climb to his feet. Chelsea was next to him. She took the girl and tried to comfort her as Shane grabbed his bag with the SKS tied to the top and tossed it over the side of the car. He grabbed the M4 and clipped it to his harness, then took Ella. She was still sobbing uncontrollably and he wanted to comfort her, but there was no time. He moved to the ladder and crowded behind the other soldiers scrambling to the ground.

Brooks reached out and took Shane by the back of the pack, helping to steady him as his feet found the rungs of the ladder. He slid to the ground quickly, only catching every other rung as he dropped. Gunfire was on all sides as the men moved west, firing into any body that moved. He caught his bearings and aligned himself into the formation of soldiers while Ella clung tightly to his shoulder. A wall of Primals was rising at them from their flank. Shane spun and let loose several shots. Some dropped, others broke though; a skinny man dove at him and Shane narrowly dodged it, deflecting the man with the stock of his rifle. The Primal's body hit the iron railroad track and thudded to a stop a moment before Chelsea fired her rifle into it.

"Move," she screamed at Shane, pushing him forward.

Shane nodded and rushed ahead. He saw Doctor Howard in the middle of the group chasing after Meyers with a small pistol in his hand. A Primal lunged at Shane, who juked and jumped out of the way, barely avoiding the Primal's attack. The crazy changed course and tackled Parker from behind. Parker hit the ground hard; he rolled and wrestled with the beast, nearly sliding down the embankment. Joey jumped in and the Primal turned its attention toward him; clawing, scratching, and knocking the Marine to the ground. Joey was pushing the thing away while stabbing it in the ribs with his K-bar. Gunner was quickly at his side and shot the creature with his sidearm. He kicked it away, then yanked Joey to his feet as another broke through the cloud of dust. Nearly flying, it caught Gunner across the body, tearing a long strip of flesh from his face. Gunner fell to the side, rolling on the tracks. He popped to his hip and pushed his pistol under the thing's chest, firing wildly.

Parker was on the ground, unconscious, with a large gash across his neck, blood pooling around his shoulders. Chelsea was quickly by his side and reached down to help.

"Leave him! He's done. Get the girl out of here," Gunner ordered before climbing to a knee then firing more shots, knocking down a screaming woman. Cussing and screaming, Gunner swapped out magazines. "Go, go," he yelled, pushing the others ahead of him. He removed a bandage from his belt and lashed it to his face with his left hand while still firing at the charging beasts with his right.

A large mob charged the flank. Shane turned into the screaming beasts, raised his M4, and fired. Gunner moved up beside and again unloaded his pistol. He tucked the sidearm into his belt and grabbed the SKS from the back of Shane's pack. He leveled the heavy rifle and fired, point-blank, into another cluster, knocking them off their feet with hits to the chest. "You have a reload for this piece of shit?" he yelled as he covered their position.

Shane paused to look at Gunner. He could see the field bandage soaked with blood. Shane knew Gunner was finished, he'd been infected, and from the look on Gunner's face, he knew it too. Shane reached into his cargo pocket and handed Gunner a stack of three magazines. The old soldier accepted and tucked them into the straps on his belt. "Now get the fuck out of here! Get the girl to the highway, I'll catch up."

Joey turned to the tail of the group. Brooks and Meyers were ahead with Howard, clearing the way with suppressed weapons.

"Come on, we have to move! What are you waiting for?"

Shane looked at Gunner; Joey saw the blood running down his jaw and neck. Gunner raised his rifle and fired at two more running directly down the tracks.

"Go, I'll cover the rear. Keep moving to the highway, don't wait for me," Gunner ordered.

Joey went to speak, but Gunner turned and again fired into the darkness, walking backwards. He would fire to the left and shift fire to the right, one to two round volleys, taking out targets as fast as they became visible. Shane turned and, with Chelsea at his side, they ran ahead to catch up with the others. Joey fell in on the right side, looking into the darkness. As they approached the impact area of the cluster bombs, the earth became churned and cratered. Observing noise discipline and now relying on suppressed weapons, they saw less and less of the Primals as they traveled.

Shane didn't want to look back. As he ran, the sounds of the SKS became more and more distant. He knew that Gunner wasn't behind them, that he broke away and was running into the city while drawing off the horde with the sounds of the 7.62 rifle. They heard the loud crack of a frag grenade and saw a building ignited in flame. Shane dropped his head, thinking Gunner was finished, when he heard more firing from the SKS. Brooks stopped the group at a cross street near a turned over school bus. Just ahead was a high embankment that led to the highway.

The sun slowly moved above the horizon. The ground was blanketed in a heavy layer of mist and smoke that helped conceal the team as they knelt beside the burnt remains of the bus.

"Up the hill and to the highway. I'll go first to secure it and then the rest of you keep moving," Brooks whispered.

Several blocks to the north of the railroad bed, two shots of the SKS sounded off.

"We should wait for Gunner," Chelsea whispered.

Joey shook his head. "Gunner's dead and he knows it," he said looking down to hide his emotions. "He saved me. I watched the Primal take his face… right after one killed Parker."

"But we can't just leave him out there!" Chelsea argued looking around the group at the solemn faces of the team.

Joey forced a smile as the SKS fired another salvo. "He's right where he wants to be. Let's go, Pops will be pissed if he sees us standing around."

CHAPTER 34

The Primal horde charged the school. Enraged by the flares and starburst grenades, they rushed the fences and crashed their bodies against them. All too soon, they were at the walls. The chained doors held, but they broke windows surrounding the perimeter. Brad watched as he saw several collide with the glass office doors and pour inside the building where he'd previously stood.

Brad pressed his back against the wall and raised his scoped rifle to the window. He scanned the area of the stone chimney and spotted a row of four blacked-out SUVs parked online behind the ruins of the home.

"There's a—"

"I see them," Sean said. "Figuring to let the Primals do their dirty work, huh? Yeah… let them wipe us all out and then withdraw in the afternoon sun without firing a shot."

Brad watched the SUVs. A man clad in black stood between two of them, shielded from the charging Primals. The man raised an older style M79 thumper into the air and launched another flare. He cleared the round and loaded another before he moved beside the SUV and prepared to fire again.

"They know we killed their scouts; won't they guess we moved?" Brad asked.

The man raised the M79 and fired a red starburst round that exploded high above the school, streaking streams of red back to the ground.

"Probably; that's why I'm going to put a round through our little fireworks coordinator over there. Don't return fire unless they pinpoint our location."

"Wait, but won't that—"

"Firing," Sean whispered as he pulled the trigger. The first suppressed round exploded the glass of the insurance office.

Brad watched as the man aimed the M79 at a point high above the school, then stepped back as Sean's high caliber round impacted his chest. His arms dropped and he fired the round, point-blank, into the ground. A bright flash illuminated as the parachute flare exploded at his feet between the SUVs. The man rolled to the side and went to stand.

"Fucker's wearing a plate," Sean whispered. "Firing," he said again.

Brad watched as the man's head snapped back and his torso rotated and smacked into the SUV next to him. A rear door opened and another man ran forward, kicking the bright burning flare into the street. It was too late; the Primals had taken notice and were moving in the SUVs' direction. The man turned and ran for the SUV door when Sean fired again, low this time, taking out the man's unarmored leg. He fell just feet in front of the SUV and crawled forward. Another man left the passenger side and ran to the injured man's aid. He grabbed the back of his shirt and dragged him to the vehicle. Just as Brad thought he might make it, Sean fired again, hitting the assisting man low in the torso. The assisting man staggered to the left and bent over at the waist. Dropping to the ground, the assisting man fell on top of the first wounded man just as the horde hit the SUVs.

The SUVs' doors slammed shut, locking the wounded men out. The vehicles slowly backed up away from the horde that was now swarming the downed men. "I'm going to try and disable a vehicle," Sean whispered.

Brad watched the blacked-out vehicles slowly reverse, staying in line.

"Aiming for the engine block, fir—"

The window above Brad's head exploded. A round smacked through the drywall above Sean's head. Sean pulled back from the window and rolled across the floor. Brad ducked and dropped below the bookshelf as more rounds exploded into the room.

"Well shit, son! Looks like they have a sniper on their side too. If not for that plate glass, that round would've been in my head."

"No shit, Sean!" Brad yelled.

Rounds snapped over his head and exploded into the walls around him as the men outside opened up with a light machine gun. Brad pressed his face against the dirty tile floor, pushing his body away from the assault, desperately searching for cover. The interior space thundered with the sounds of return fire. He rolled to his side and saw Sean with his weapon at the ready. His shoulder was pressed against the wall; not bothering to look, Sean lifted the MP5's barrel over the edge of the shattered window and let loose an extended burst of suppressing fire.

When the magazine was empty, he pulled the weapon back to his chest just as a barrage of counter fire again ripped through the room. "You've got to move and you got to move now!" Sean yelled over the intense fire.

Brad looked at him and struggled to nod, fear and adrenaline causing his muscles to tighten. Sean pointed a gloved finger toward the back of the room. "You need to move. I'll be right behind you," he said as he used his other hand to switch out magazines in the submachine gun. "I'll cover you. On my fire, go!"

Brad rolled back to his stomach and readied himself for the dash. Before Sean's first shot, he was blinded by a bright flash and thundering explosion coming from the rear of the building. A cloud of smoke rolled up the hallway, pushing debris and a toxic ash that burnt his lungs and caused him to choke. He heard Sean's weapon fire. Brad willed himself up and took a long step trying to steady himself. He stepped out fast; surprised that he was able to stay in motion, taking step after step, he rushed down the long hallway that was now quickly filling with smoke.

His ears were ringing, his senses deprived by the thick cloud of dust and acrid gas. Brad took another lunging step and hooked the toe of his boot on rubble. Already unsteady, he lost his balance, fell hard to the floor, and slid headfirst into the hallway. He caught himself with his left elbow, wincing in pain. He rolled to his right side and pushed his rifle forward as he saw the first of them. Emerging out of the smoke, they moved in; dark silhouettes standing out from the gray haze of the smoke. Two by two they came, wearing all black and protective masks, rifles at the low ready. Their lasers cut the space, but they were looking over and beyond him – not at his lifeless form prone in the rubble and blanketed in dense smoke.

Brad twisted hard and leaned into his rifle. He leveled it at the chest of the lead man and pulled the trigger. Three rounds tore into the point man; dust and smoke popped from two hits to the center of his tactical vest, the third striking the chin cup of the man's protective mask. Brad shifted the barrel to the left and with quick pulls of the trigger took down another. The remainder of the opposing team fired blindly through the haze in his direction. Bits of sheetrock and shattered glass pelted his face and exposed skin. Brad rolled hard and reached out. Grabbing the edge of a nearby doorway, he pulled himself into a room that intersected with the hall. Brad low-crawled forward, away from the doorway and deeper into the room, ducking under a round conference table. While rounds were cutting the walls and zipping over his head, he dragged himself to a sitting position against a chair. He leveled his rifle and aimed into the open space of the door.

He watched as a barrel cautiously broke the cover of the door frame. Brad raised his own rifle and aimed just to the right of the barrel, firing rapidly through the wall where he knew the shooter would be standing. He paused as a masked figure dropped forward, still clutching the weapon. Brad launched himself back to his feet. He hugged the door frame, then spun into the entrance, firing blindly as he flew across the open space to the opposite wall. He saw another man fall victim to his fire. Brad paused against the wall, holding the rifle to his eye and focused down the long hallway toward the rear entrance. The firing behind him had ceased; he could hear Sean reloading his rifle and the clinking of spent brass as he crawled across the floor.

"You alive back there?" Sean yelled.

Brad kept his chin on the stock of the rifle and stayed focused on the far exit. "I'm still standing, if that's what you're asking. I have four down back here."

"Something's got them pulling back," Sean said.

"That's a good thing right?" Brad acknowledged, relaxing his grip on the rifle while trying to control his breathing and fighting the urge to vomit.

Sean moved up the hall and shoved Brad's assault pack into his arms. "Yeah… it would be great if it weren't for the hundred plus Primals pouring down the street in our direction," Sean said.

A man lying face-down moved an arm and went to lift himself up. Sean rushed ahead as he walked past Brad and turned over the dying man. He was wearing a black utility uniform without name tape. A subdued American flag patch was on his shoulder. Sean grabbed the sides of the tactical vest and pulled off the Velcro to release it. He tore open the vest and pushed it aside, then ripped the buttons on the man's blouse.

Seeing a white cotton T-shirt, Sean pulled at the collar to reveal a blood-spilling entry wound just below the collar bone. Sean rolled up the man's sleeves then looked him in the eye.

"Who are you with?" Sean asked.

The man coughed phlegm and blood, foam coming from his nose; he smiled at Sean with red stained teeth. "You know who we are. We're trying to save the girl before you and that hack doctor can kill her."

Sean looked up at Brad, trying to hide the shock. "Bullshit, what are you doing here?"

The man continued coughing, his face quickly becoming pale as blood spilt from the entry wound with every beat of his heart. "We had her at Collins; the fort was over-run before we could extract her by air, lost her after that, then picked up her signal again on the road… we tried to get a bird in the air… she disappeared from the scanners before we could triangulate."

Brad leaned forward and put pressure on the injured man's wound, no longer able to ignore it. "Wait! If you're trying to help the girl, why did you attack her?"

The wounded man looked up at Brad, his eyes growing faint. "You stupid bastard. We attacked *you* not the girl, she is implanted with a low level tracking device. She needs to be outside for us to get a signal from the UAV. We know she isn't in the school; she is south-west of here. We've been trying to stop Doctor Howard from getting to her and we know he's traveling with you." The man coughed hard; turning to the side and spitting blood, he struggled to take another wheezing breath in. "We'd be with her now, could have followed her away, if you assholes didn't kill our recon team."

The man coughed hard again and gagged as he struggled to take another breath. He kicked his leg and choked before his eyes rolled back in his head. Brad let go of the wound and looked down at his blood soaked gloves. Sean reached in, turned the man to the side, removed his wallet, and then got to his feet. He pulled open the wallet, dumping items as he walked towards the exit.

"What the hell are we going to do?" Brad asked as he struggled to keep up.

Sean tossed the wallet over his shoulder and stood in the doorframe. "I don't know; he wasn't military. White undershirt, no tags, no tattoos, no military ID. Who the hell are these guys? And who the hell is Howard? Why the *fuck* is everyone lying to us?"

CHAPTER 35

Shane pulled himself up the highway embankment while holding Ella tight in his left arm. His feet slipped in the mud. He gripped long blades of uncut grass with his gloved right hand, pulling himself up. He looked above and saw Howard standing over him with Brooks and Meyers. Howard reached down as Shane pushed Ella up ahead. Howard took her hand and pulled her up, freeing Shane's left arm to climb the muddy slope. At the top he turned back and pulled up Chelsea, then assisted the others.

Brooks and Meyers positioned themselves on opposite ends, pointing up and down the highway respectively, providing security and allowing the men to catch their breath before they moved on. The rain had stopped with the daylight but heavy cloud cover still remained, casting a gloomy gray over the terrain. Both directions of US-17 were congested with broken and twisted vehicles; a fire had at one time raged up the highway, destroying everything and leaving black molten hulks of vehicles. Shane walked quietly and retrieved Ella from Howard who glared at him suspiciously.

He set his bag next to the shell of an older model station wagon and put Ella on top of the pack. He poked a hole in the top of a can of fruit and encouraged the girl to drink the juice. Ella took the can and sipped while Shane used a rag to wipe the dirt and grime from her face and cheeks. Chelsea moved in behind him and took a seat next to the bag. Leaning against it, she removed a bottle from her pack and took a long drink of water. Chelsea lifted her hand and pulled the girl's bangs from her eyes. Ella smiled at her and took another sip from the fruit juice. Shane took the can back, completely opened it, and then used an MRE spoon to feed her the fruit cocktail.

"You're good with her. Do you have kids of your own?" Chelsea asked him.

Shane grinned as he gave Ella the last of the fruit and set the can under the car. He wiped her face and put the rag back in his shirt pocket. "I'd say she's good with me. No, never been married, never had any kids."

"You don't talk much do you, hun?" Chelsea said as she stroked Ella's hair.

"She will; when she has something to say," Shane said, winking at Ella.

Brooks gave the signal to move out. Shane tucked their belongings back into the pack and got Ella to her feet. He loosened the improvised parka's front and allowed her to walk beside him. Chelsea moved next to Shane, keeping Ella between them. The highway was quiet and void of life as it rolled on straight ahead. According to Meyers' map, they were less than thirty miles from the base. It would be possible to cover thirty miles in a day if they weren't carrying the pack and escorting the girl. Even then, that pace would make it impossible to stay alert and still able to fend off attacks. Twenty miles was more likely but still would mean setting a grueling pace.

Shane could tell by the way Brooks set off that he had no plans of reaching the base in a single hike. He moved slowly and methodically, keeping the team spread out. He walked point far ahead and kept Joey staggered to the left behind him. Howard walked alone in the middle while Meyers was some distance to the rear, ensuring they were not being followed. They walked on the inside shoulder near the median where they would have the greatest warning to oncoming threats. The farther they traveled, the less damage they saw to the vehicles; the fire hadn't spread beyond the city limits.

Brooks put up a hand and motioned them into the tall grass of the median and down to the ground. Shane held Ella close and crouched behind the tires of a large cargo van. He tucked her in beside him as he pulled up his rifle. He turned his head to the side and watched under the vehicle as the pack of Primals passed by on the opposite side of the road. A small group of five, they staggered ahead in a straight line toward the city; probably attracted by the activity of the previous night.

Brooks waited for the Primals to pass then quickly got the group back on their feet and moving again. Chelsea moved closer to Shane and spoke just above a whisper. "How long has it been since we heard Gunner's rifle?"

Shane looked at her then down at his watch. "Three hours... if he hasn't turned yet, it'll be soon." Shane saw her expression change and he immediately regretted his words. "I'm sorry. I didn't mean it like that. I know what he did for us, what you all have done," he said turning back to the road.

"Do you really think the Rangers will be there after all this time?" Chelsea asked.

Shane looked ahead, pondering the answer. "If not, then we'll just find something else. Keep going till we find a safe place."

"It seems like that's all there is anymore: moving, finding places. I don't think we will ever rest again." She stopped and pointed ahead; Brooks had moved to the median and called the others in. Howard was standing in the center of the group waiting for them, holding his leather satchel. Shane and the others increased the pace as they walked to meet up with Brooks. Joey stayed on the flanks, providing security.

Brooks pointed far ahead at a small red vehicle on the shoulder. He signaled for them to join him. A small import hatchback, two bucket seats in the front and a bench in the back. Brooks had the rear hatch and a back door opened.

Meyers approached from the rear, letting his SA80 hang limp in his right arm. "Ayup?" he asked.

"I found one that runs and it's small enough to get around the traffic jams to get you to Savannah," Brooks said walking around the car. He reached into the hatchback and removed two suitcases, setting them on the ground to make room for the team's packs.

"It's too small, we won't fit," Chelsea said.

"We're not all going. I'm taking Joey and going back to look for Sean and Brad," Brooks said as Meyers walked up.

"No... no way. We all stay together," Chelsea argued looking at the small car.

Brooks nodded at Meyers and said, "Don't worry, you'll be in good hands and you all will make better time in the car."

Shane walked to the vehicle, looking down the highway. "Maybe we could hold off until we find something larger."

"Doesn't matter, you could find a tour bus, I won't be continuing on. I'm going back for Chief," Brooks said, lifting Howard's bag and dropping it into the back.

Howard walked around to the driver's door. "We need to continue on; the girl is what's important."

Meyers shrugged. "He's right, lass; load your gear, we should get going."

"We can't just leave! How will we find you again?" Chelsea argued.

Shane walked to the hatch and dropped in his pack. He removed the rifle and walked Ella to the back seat. "Come on, they'll meet us at Savannah. If not, once the girl is safe, I'll help you find them."

Chelsea walked to Brooks and grabbed the front of his shirt. "Make sure you bring them back!" He nodded a silent response before taking her pack and loading it in the car. He escorted her around to a passenger door and reached down to open it. Shane slid in on the other side with Ella ahead of him and closed the door, waiting. Howard entered the driver's side and started the engine. Before Shane knew what happened, the car was in gear and racing ahead.

"What the hell are you doing?" Shane yelled.

Howard looked at Shane in the rearview mirror. "It's okay, I have it from here," Howard said before reaching over the back seat as the car whipped away. He aimed a small Browning pistol at Shane and fired, hitting him in the chest. Shane bucked hard, slumping back in the seat. Struggling to move, he fell against the door, and then toppled to the bench as the car veered around obstacles. Shane sighed deeply, gasping for air. Ella screamed. Shane tried to sit up, but couldn't feel his body. He fought the darkness closing in on him as he struggled for breath. He felt his warm blood running down his side. Ella leaned over him pulling at his hair, her tears falling on his cheeks; he knew she was calling his name but it sounded far away and muffled.

Shane struggled to move, to speak. "Relax, soldier, enjoy the time you have left," Howard said, keeping his eyes on the road as he drove down the shoulder of the highway.

"Damn, you all made it awful easy for me. I thought we would have a harder time getting away from the CNRT. Hell, when they captured Aziz I thought we were finished, but this girl… yeah, she's important to the cause. Well… not all of her, just her blood. But don't you worry, soldier, I know how important she is to you. Once I get my sample, I'll make sure you two stay together. I'll find you a nice spot in a ditch to spend eternity."

Shane lay on his back staring at the ceiling of the car struggling to keep his eyes open, barely comprehending Howard's words. Ella was leaning over him, screaming. He rolled his head to the side, staring into the sun. He saw his team gathered around the Humvee; he wanted to walk to them, to be finished with the pain. Ella's cries clouded his thoughts and brought him back. Shane forced everything to his right arm and let it drift to his belt, his thumb glanced the .22 pistol in his belt clumsily. His hand grasped the grip of the Walther pistol. He struggled to remove it but didn't have the strength. Ella grabbed his wrist and tugged, helping him remove the weapon. Without straightening his arm, he aimed up at the back of the driver's seat. Ella guided and steadied his aim as he pumped the trigger.

CHAPTER 36

A loud explosion ripped through the night air far to the south. Sean threw up a fist, halting Brad. They ducked into the cover of an overhanging roof as they heard the sounds of small arms fire.

"That's got to be the team; let's go," Sean whispered.

He stepped off quickly, crouching low through the alleyways, the residential neighborhood quickly turning commercial. The gunfire became random and the location scattered; the sounds echoing off the buildings made them hard to track. Sean set course for the sounds of the initial explosion. They veered into a warehouse district filled with sheet metal buildings and concrete loading docks. The farther they moved, the more the water began to rise. They slogged through until it hit their knees then climbed to their waist.

Sean continued, pressing forward, holding his rifle above his shoulders and pushing through the water down the center of the street. The gunfire stopped and the sounds of the Primals' moans faded. They rounded a corner and saw an elevated railroad bed. Sean pointed and then moved quickly in that direction. The water almost reached their necks before it began to recede near the embankment of the railroad tracks. The duo climbed to the top and knelt down beside the rail.

Brad looked up and down the tracks in both directions. Ahead, the ground was churned with twisted rails and upturned railroad ties. Behind them was a lone rusted freight car. The embankment area where they rested was covered with spent shell casings and Primal bodies.

"They definitely came this way," Brad whispered.

Sean rolled his eyes. "Nice tracking skills, Tonto." Sean looked up and down the tracks picking up the spent brass and rolling it in his fingers.

"Do you think the men in black will be following?" Brad asked as they climbed back to their feet.

Sean looked behind him, scanning both sides of the railroad embankment. "By air maybe, but the SUVs won't make it through that flood water. They'd have to cut all the way around to the highway. Our guys would do the same. Okay, let's go. Stay close to me."

In a bend, they spotted a uniformed body. The two men held up and looked at it from a distance, not wanting to approach. Not speaking, they slowly stepped forward together. They spotted the M249 strapped across the soldier's back and the M203 on the crushed limestone just in front of him. Brad froze and took a step back. Sean moved forward and knelt next to the man's body. Carefully he removed the machine gun and leaned it against the railroad track. Sean looked back at Brad who was standing quietly, he shook his head slowly.

"It's Parker, isn't it?" Brad mumbled.

Sean nodded. "'fraid so."

Brad turned around, not looking at the body. "Do we have time to bury him?" he asked.

"Not properly, but if we hurry, we can at least wrap him in his bedding and cover the body with limestone."

Brad took in a deep breath and exhaled loudly. He turned and walked to the body, grabbed the man's rucksack, and removed a blanket. "I'll carry the SAW if you take the 203," Brad said, lifting the M249 and leaning it against his own pack. He then reached in the man's shirt and removed his dog tags. Brad laid out the blanket so it was flat. Not speaking, Sean helped Brad move the body to the center of the blanket where they tightly wrapped it.

"Let's get this done," Brad said grabbing handfuls of the loose stone from the railroad bed.

***

They traveled slowly now, staying in cover, sinking into the high grass of the embankments when they sensed movement. A small group of Primals sloshed through the water next to them as Sean chose to hide rather than fight them. They encountered more small packs scattered about the city that were not following their normal pattern of disappearing during the day.

"The action last night seems to have stirred them up... dragged them far from home," Sean whispered, pointing to a small cluster standing on a loading dock trapped by the flood waters. A tall female stood by the steps leading to the loading dock, looking out. Her clothing was soaked to the chest and the others gathered behind her, some sitting, but most standing in the shade of an overhang.

"They look lost, like they got turned around in the storm," Brad observed.

"Let's go," Sean whispered getting back to his feet, walking crouched while trying to hide his silhouette from the stranded Primals.

As they approached the highway, Sean picked up the pace. They saw less and less shell casings and Sean was concerned they'd lost the trial. When they approached a cross street with a rolled over bus, there was an empty water bottle with a label from the submarine. He pointed it out without speaking then followed the bus around to the muddy slope leading up the highway. There were obvious signs of boot prints and drag marks where the team climbed the muddy rise.

"I'll go first," Sean whispered clipping his weapon to a harness and grabbing clumps of grass as he made his way up the hill. Once reaching the highway, he assumed a lookout position and signaled for Brad to follow him. At the top, Sean pointed to an empty fruit can and muddy boot prints. They turned and headed off, not wanting to waste any time knowing the trail was hot. Sean moved them at a quick pace, only stopping to duck below or under vehicles to let wandering Primals pass by.

They patrolled beyond the destroyed hulks of vehicles and out of the city limits. Sean climbed on the hood of truck to see farther over the horizon. They heard it at the same time, a loud engine noise coming from behind. Sean spun on his heels while Brad climbed the truck and saw it—a column of four black SUVs racing down the median of the highway; sometimes having to weave between vehicles or using their winches to make a path.

"They'll be on us soon. What do we do?" Brad asked.

"We can't let them pass," Sean answered, taking the rifle from his pack.

"But the man, he said— "

"Doesn't matter, we can't trust anyone. We need to get the girl to Savannah. How do we know they won't kill us on sight?"

"So… that's it then?" Brad asked.

"Trust no man but God," Sean said setting up his rifle. "Don't worry. I'm not killing anyone; I just want to delay them."

Brad jumped off the truck and ran to the front where he set up the SAW on the bipod, aiming across the hood of the truck. He attached a plastic box holding 200 rounds. He yelled up at Sean, "I'm set, just suppressing right? Not killing anyone."

"That should work for now. Be ready to haul ass when I say," Sean answered.

Brad watched as the vehicles moved onto the highway and squeezed between the stopped vehicles. Sean waited for them to drive around a blue van then into a narrow lane—a solid bottle neck. Sean rapidly fired into the lead vehicles engine block, steam and spray exploding into the air. The lead vehicle stopped dead; the vehicles behind, trapped in the column, attempted to back up. They bumped into each other and tires squealed as they attempted to push free. The second vehicle slammed forward, trying to push the first disabled SUV ahead and out of the way. Brad aimed low and let out a twelve-round burst, skipping rounds across the road and into the surrounding vehicles.

The trail SUV stopped pushing and reversed, looking for a way out. Sean switched his angle as the last vehicle in line attempted to maneuver around the blue van. Sean took more well placed shots and exploded a front tire to prevent the SUV from turning. It cut at a sharp angle and collided with the van as the third vehicle spun back and pinched it in, effectively blocking the entire convoy. Sean held his fire. Brad stayed on the SAW observing. A man opened a truck door and dove out to cover.

"They're on the move!" Brad yelled.

"Tracking," Sean called out firing another round into a fender to keep the man's head down. More doors opened and they started taking return fire. A round hit the windshield over Brad's head; he spun, let off another burst of machine gun fire, and hit the vehicles around the SUVs, trying to back the men off.

"Okay," Sean yelled, "let's haul ass before I kill someone".

Brad pulled the SAW off of the truck and turned to run down the highway. He stopped dead in his tracks and leapt back into the cover of the panel truck. "Oh shit!" he yelled.

Sean dropped off the top of the truck landing next to Brad, "Wha – "

Ahead in the road was a swarm of charging Primals. More were coming out of the woods on all sides. Rounds impacted the panel truck, trapping them. Brad leveled the SAW and cut down the first line of Primals, but more filled the void as they poured in and over the abandoned cars. Another salvo of rounds pinged off the body of the panel truck.

"Wow, are we screwed or what?" Sean laughed raising his rifle and firing, knocking down a fast runner before shifting and hitting another.

"You're fucking nuts, man!" Brad replied as he fired an extended burst into the charging crazies watching them get closer. Brad pulled a grenade and tossed it ahead; they didn't duck for cover, firing through the blast instead. Quickly tossing another, Brad turned to look around the corner and fired at the SUVs. "You got to be joking, they are moving up on us," he said as he watched the men in black bounding forward, firing at the panel truck as they moved. Brad leaned around the corner to fire again as a round cut into the truck and hitting the M249's hand guard. Brad tossed it away as plastic bits and metal exploded, hitting him in the face.

Brad spun back behind the cover of the truck. Sean had the M203 out, pumping 40mm grenades and firing the rifle at the approaching Primals. A round skipped off the pavement, clipping Sean's boot and knocking him to the ground. Another round tore through the corner of the truck hitting Sean in the shoulder, spinning him around and forcing him to drop the rifle. Brad dropped beside him, firing his M4 in an attempt to slow the advancing mob. The world exploded with the sounds of heavy machine gun fire. Vehicles on all side of the duo exploded. Brad crawled over Sean to shield his body as more explosive projectiles impacted the ground all around him.

He heard the sounds of an M2 machine gun thumping, rounds ripping overhead, and an MK19 barking as it fired grenades at the masses. Brad crept his head up and saw the Primals being ripped apart as they were turning to face a new enemy. They fell backwards in a wave as a large, olive green eight wheeled Light Armored Vehicle tore through the mob, crushing them under its tires and easily knocking disabled cars aside. Two more LAV-Strykers rolled forward, blasting away with their M2 machine guns, as the third launched projectiles from its MK19. The Strykers rolled past the truck, shielding the men.

The lead vehicle launched a rapid burst from the MK19 and destroyed the parked SUVs. A ramp dropped from one of the vehicles and a troop of men dressed in army combat uniforms rushed out, firing and providing security. They grabbed Brad and Sean and dragged them back to the Stryker. The crew piled back in and the ramp closed. The heavy vehicle rocked and crunched as it backed into cars in and attempt at a three-point-turn. A medic piled over Sean, cutting away his vest and shirt to work on his wound. For the first time, Brad saw that Brooks was on board. He was assisting the medic, sticking an IV needle into Sean's arm. Brad fell back in his seat as the Stryker crunched over a vehicle as it raced down the road. He looked around the cabin into the solemn faces of helmeted and goggled men.

"How?" Brad mumbled.

A soldier wearing captain's bars on his Kevlar helmet sitting in a seat across from Brad leaned forward. "We found your people up the road," he yelled speaking over the noise of the engines. "Are you hurt, Sergeant?" the captain asked pointing at Brad's face.

Brad touched the side of his face feeling the bloody cuts where the bits of SAW cut into him. "Oh, my rifle exploded," he mumbled, causing the other soldiers around him to chuckle. Brad looked at them uneasily. "Where did you come from?"

"We're out of Combat Outpost Savannah. What's left of the 3rd Infantry Division, 75th Rangers, even have some Jarheads we picked up near Paris Island. Sounds like you folks had a hell of a party last night. Scouts heard the ruckus; we decided to send a patrol up the road and ran into your friends—damn, your friends are persistent, we normally don't patrol this far up the highway."

EPILOGUE

He walked alone down the long hallway and past the reception desk. The lights were dim; the base was running solely on diesel generators and some solar cells. Windows were open, allowing a cool breeze to flow though the hallways. Brad made his way to a closed door and compared the number above it to one written on a scrap of yellow paper.

He looked down at his fresh boots and new uniform and knocked at the door. He put his hand to the knob and pressed it open to find a man with a heavily bandaged chest and an arm hooked to machines. Sleeping in a chair by his side was Ella, curled in a ball under a thick blanket. Brad turned when he saw Chelsea jump to her feet and rush across the room to hug him.

"I heard you were back. How is Chief?" she asked, letting go and backing away. "Please have a seat," she said motioning to a set of chairs. Brad walked across the room and sat by a window, Chelsea sitting next to him.

"He's good, Chelsea. The Doc said he should be back up in no time. How are they?" Brad said indicating Shane.

"Doing good, considering… she was only bruised up in the car accident. Good food and water and she's finally putting on some weight.

Shane was hurt bad, lost a lot of blood; he will lose mobility in the arm, but he's tough. He'll pull through," she said looking at Shane. "We gave the doctors the satchel; they'll make sure the information on Ella gets to the right people."

"That's great," Brad said, staring ahead.

"Who were they, Brad?" Chelsea asked, "Howard, the men in black, all of them?"

Brad shook his head and sighed. "I don't know, but if the people here do, they aren't telling us. Sean is determined to get to the bottom of it; he'll find out. They have no records of a Doctor Howard," Brad said, pausing. "Yeah, and Meyers has been relaying messages to Sumter via the sub. Kelli and the others are doing great. The Army has been able to resupply the fort and bring some of the survivors back here. We should be able to go there soon."

Chelsea looked at Brad and touched his hand. "I'm not leaving, Brad. I'll be staying here."

"Oh... yeah, you should do that. They could use your help here, with the generators and...," Brad paused then got to his feet. "You know, I should go; Sean and Brooks are waiting for me in the lobby, we have things to do." He stepped quickly to the door. Chelsea stood and grabbed his arm, stopping him. Brad turned around facing her.

"You could stay too," she said, looking him in the eye.

Brad shook his head. "You know I can't."

Chelsea clenched her jaw and looked away, not speaking. Brad hugged her tight and then turned to leave the room, closing the door behind him. He couldn't stay; he still had men in the desert.

Thank You for Reading

If you have an opportunity Please leave a review on Amazon

Lundy W. J. (2014-05-01).

Whiskey Tango Foxtrot: Volume V

****

ALL NEW FROM WJ LUNDY

THE DARKNESS

The Darkness is a fast paced story of survival that brings the apocalypse to Main Street USA.

While the world falls apart Jacob Anderson barricades his family behind locked doors. News reports tell of civil unrest in the streets, murders, disappearances, citizens are warned to remain indoors.

When Jacob becomes witness to horrible events and the alarming actions of his neighbors, he and his family realize everything is far worse than being reported.

Every Father's nightmare comes true as Jacob's normal life, and a promise to protect his family is torn apart.

From the Best Selling Author of Whiskey Tango Foxtrot comes a new telling of Armageddon.

March 2015

http://amzn.com/B00QQIF93I

Thank You for Reading

If you have an opportunity Please leave a review on Amazon

Lundy W. J. (2014-05-01).
Whiskey Tango Foxtrot: Volume V

W. J. Lundy is a still serving Veteran of the U.S. Military with service in Afghanistan. He has over 14 years of combined service with the Army and Navy in Europe, the Balkans and Southwest Asia. Visit him on Facebook for more.

OTHER WORKS BY WJ LUNDY

OTHER AUTHORS UNDER THE SHIELD OF

SIXTH CYCLE

Nuclear war has destroyed human civilization.

Captain Jake Phillips wakes into a dangerous new world, where he finds the remaining fragments of the population living in a series of strongholds, connected across the country. Uneasy alliances have maintained their safety, but things are about to change. -- Discovery **leads to danger.** -- Skye Reed, a tracker from the Omega stronghold, uncovers a threat that could spell the end for their fragile society. With friends and enemies revealing truths about the past, she will need to decide who to trust. -- Sixth **Cycle** is a gritty post-apocalyptic story of survival and adventure.

Darren Wearmouth ~ Carl Sinclair

DEAD ISLAND: Operation Zulu

Ten years after the world was nearly brought to its knees by a zombie Armageddon, there is a race for the antidote! On a remote Caribbean island, surrounded by a horde of hungry living dead, a team of American and Australian commandos must rescue the Antidotes' scientist. Filled with zombies, guns, Russian bad guys, shady government types, serial killers and elevator muzak. Dead Island is an action packed blood soaked horror adventure.

Allen Gamboa

INVASION OF THE DEAD SERIES

This is the first book in a series of nine, about an ordinary bunch of friends, and their plight to survive an apocalypse in Australia. -- Deep beneath defense headquarters in the Australian Capital Territory, the last ranking Army chief and a brilliant scientist struggle with answers to the collapse of the world, and the aftermath of an unprecedented virus. Is it a natural mutation, or does the infection contain -- more sinister roots? -- One hundred and fifty miles away, five friends returning from a month-long camping trip slowly discover that death has swept through the country. What greets them in a gradual revelation is an enemy beyond compare. -- Armed with dwindling ammunition, the friends must overcome their disagreements, utilize their individual skills, and face unimaginable horrors as they battle to reach their hometown...

Owen Ballie

SPLINTER

For close to a thousand years they waited, waited for the old knowledge to fade away into the mists of myth. They waited for a re-birth of the time of legend for the time when demons ruled and man was the fodder upon which they fed. They waited for the time when the old gods die and something new was anxious to take their place. **A young couple was all that stood between humanity and annihilation**. Ill equipped and shocked by the horrors thrust upon them they would fight in the only way they knew how, tooth and nail. Would they be enough to prevent the creation of the feasting hordes? Were they alone able to stand against evil banished from hell? **Would the horsemen ride when humanity failed?** The earth would rue the day a splinter group set up shop in Cold Spring.

H. J. Harry

17670351R00195

Printed in Great Britain
by Amazon